David Upton read English Literature at Durham University. After graduation, he worked for 27 years at the National Foundation for Educational Research, where he was the Senior Editor and subsequently Editorial Manager. While at the NFER, he edited reports on all aspects of the UK's educational system. He was also the Assistant Editor of *Educational Research*, an international academic journal, and the founding Editor of *TOPIC*, a looseleaf magazine for teachers drawing out the practical applications of research in education. A keen musician, he is an ex-trumpeter, and has been the rehearsal pianist for Windsor and Eton Operatic Society since 1976. He has travelled widely, and lives in England. This is his second novel.

SHERLOCK HOLMES'S CHRISTMAS

Also by David Upton

The Lost Holmes

SHERLOCK HOLMES'S CHRISTMAS

David Upton

Park Publishing

First published in 2005 by
Park Publishing, Flat 15,
51 Upton Park, Slough
SL1 2GB

© David Upton, 2005

The right of David Upton to be identified as the author
of this work has been asserted by him in accordance with
the Copyright, Designs and Patents Act 1988.

All rights reserved. No part of this publication may be
reproduced, stored in a retrieval system, or transmitted,
in any form or by any means, electronic, mechanical,
photocopying, recording or otherwise, without the prior
written permission of the copyright owner.

1SBN 0-9545067-1-5

Printed in Great Britain by B & B Press, Rotherham

Book design by Mary Hargreaves
Cover illustration by Geraint Derbyshire

IN MEMORIAM

BRIAN CHARLES UPTON (1919–1995)

With grateful thanks to *the real* John Ayto for his helpful comments on the penultimate draft.

"You stand in the way not merely of an individual, but of a mighty organization, the full extent of which you, with all your cleverness, have been unable to realize."

Professor Moriarty

("The Final Problem", *The Memoirs of Sherlock Holmes*)

The characters in this novel are imaginary and bear no relation to actual people whose names have been used.

The map below contains some real places and features as well as some that have been made up.

Eton and Windsor 1894

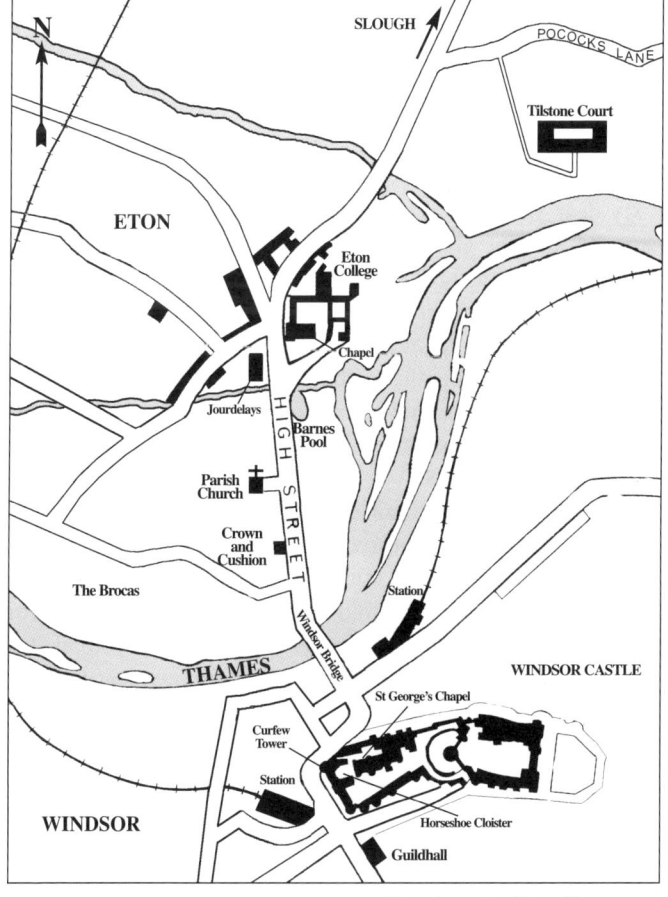

Map drawn by Mary Hargreaves

PREFACE

To Sherlock Holmes it was always a failure. Never mind that he solved completely one of the most complex cases ever to come his way; the fact that he whom Holmes ever regarded as his greatest adversary succeeded at last in evading justice rankled to such an extent with my friend that for years he has absolutely forbidden me to articulate the facts concerning the singular events which took place at Tilstone Court in the winter of 1894.

Then suddenly, a few months ago, I received a letter, despatched from Holmes's little retirement home in Sussex. "My dear Watson," he wrote. "Have you a couple of days to spare? I shall be glad if you will come and stay with me and sample my excellent country fare. As you know, the air and scenery are perfect hereabouts. Moreover, I have decided that the time has come for the world to learn for the first time the true facts surrounding the curious affair of Major Yates and the Eton Horrors of '94. Pray come, my dear fellow, and we will discuss what is to be done about the matter. Yours sincerely, SHERLOCK HOMES."

It was a perfect summer's afternoon when I arrived at Holmes's charming villa, set upon the southern slope of the Downs, and commanding a fine view of the Channel. My friend lived there with only his old housekeeper and his bees for company, and his greeting was characteristically cordial. "A thousand thanks for accepting my invitation, my dear fellow," said he warmly. "My house has been a lonely place since your visits dwindled to the occasional weekend. Take a chair, and try one of my cigars. Will you have some whisky and water?"

I accepted his hospitality, and Holmes sank back in his chair, staring up at the ceiling with dreamy, lack-lustre eyes.

"I understand that you wish me at last to add an account of the Tilstone Court adventure to my annals, Holmes," I observed. "What has led to this change of heart?"

"Well, well, Watson. You know that I have always considered the case to be incomplete. But I have come to accept that the principal culprit, albeit not himself the actual murderer of any of the three unfortunate victims, has escaped my net, and will continue to remain at large – that is, if he is still alive – no doubt hidden in some dark corner of the globe. There have, of late, been some spurious references to the case in the press, and I think it is time for you who have been good enough to chronicle one or two of my little problems to set the record straight and establish the facts in the public domain."

At this, Sherlock Holmes rose to his feet, and selected a small chocolate and silver volume from his amply stacked shelves.

"These are my own notes of the case," he remarked. "No doubt you will feel free to use them as the basis for your usual highly sensational and flowery rendition of the incidents which they address."

I shall leave it to the reader to judge of the accuracy of Holmes's prediction. For myself, I consider that if, in laying the facts before the public, I have added, here and there, a touch of colour to the bare narrative, this will in no way detract from the brilliancy of those faculties of deduction and of logical synthesis which my friend displayed in the course of events which culminated in one of his most meritorious finales.

John H. Watson, M.D.

LONDON
November 1913

CONTENTS

		Page
1	A Visit from Major Yates	1
2	Tilstone Court	16
3	The Horseshoe Cloister	33
4	The Eccentric Soloist	47
5	Christmas Eve	62
6	The Face at the Window	77
7	A Close Shave	91
8	The Two Diaries	110
9	The Spoilt Pillows	125
10	An Impossible Murder	142
11	The Innocuous Intruder	156
12	The Camden Ripper	169
13	The Master Blackmailer	176
14	The Gosling Street Bank Robber	187
15	The Hackney Forger	200
16	The Final Contest	214

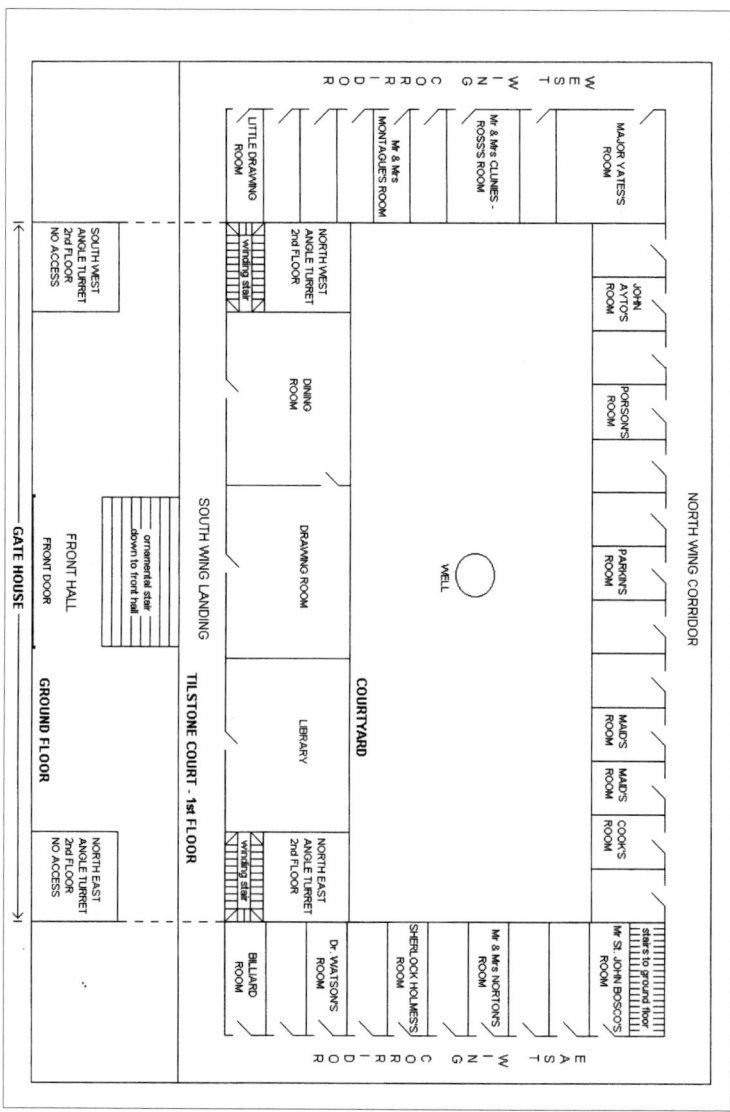

Plan of Tilstone Court drawn by Ian Dukes

1: A Visit from Major Yates

"Very well, Watson. If your mind is quite made up, we will have a goose for Christmas rather than a turkey."

It was a cold evening a few days before Christmas during the Great Freeze of 1894. The snow had been falling steadily for some hours, and Baker Street had been ploughed by the traffic into two deep furrows, flanked on either side by thick white drifts which made walking a hazardous pursuit. Indeed, only a few, dark, bedraggled figures were abroad, struggling gamely through the swirling flakes, which shimmered and flickered in the gaslight against a backdrop of dun-coloured buildings. Sherlock Holmes and I were seated on either side of the fire in the familiar surroundings of No. 221B. It had been some months now since Holmes's sensational return to London following his fateful contest with Professor Moriarty, and I had grown accustomed once more to the idiosyncrasies of his household. Here was the chemical corner and the acid-stained, deal-topped table; there, upon a shelf, the row of ponderous indexes and common-place books which contained the fruits of his many investigations; whilst elsewhere in the room lay his battered violin-case, his pipe-rack and the Persian slipper which accommodated his tobacco. I had been staring intently at the fire when Sherlock Holmes's unexpected remark broke in upon my reverie.

"Yes indeed, Holmes. I would prefer a goose – but how, pray, did you know that my thoughts had turned to the question of our Yule-tide fare? Have you perhaps added mind-reading to your innumerable talents?"

Sherlock Holmes yawned and stretched his long, thin arms above his head. "Tut! Tut!" cried he. "The inference was a simple one. But I am afraid that I rather give myself away when I explain. Results without causes are much more impressive."

"None the less, Holmes, I should be interested to learn how you arrived at your conclusion."

"Your face is a window to your soul, Watson. You were sitting in front of the fire basking in post-prandial contentment, when your glance fell upon the seasonal sprigs of holly with which Mrs. Hudson has seen fit to decorate the mantelpiece. Your features relaxed into a smile, and I could see that you were thinking of Christmas. Almost immediately you transferred your gaze to the table, on which are situated the remains of our excellent supper. At this point you licked your lips and turned your eyes to the hearth, and I could see at once that the association of Christmas with food had established itself in your mind, for I recalled how many times you had eulogized to me on the virtues of a good fat goose, roasting in front of the fire on the 25th of December. And when I further remembered your somewhat lukewarm reaction to the scrawny turkey which was served up to us on Christmas Day last year, I naturally felt compelled to endorse your preference for the former."

"Of course, it is quite obvious now that you explain it, Holmes," said I, a trifle disappointedly.

"Quite so," observed Holmes ruefully. "But hark, could it be that we have a client at this late hour?"

There had come the stamping of a horse's hoofs in the heavy snow and the long grind of a wheel as it rasped against the icy kerb. Moments later the clang of the front door-bell was followed by heavy footfalls clattering on the stair, and a man burst into the room, pushing his way impatiently past the boy in buttons.

Our visitor was an extremely tall and obese individual of about fifty, with a florid face. Dressed in a dusty black frock-coat faced with faded silk, dark waistcoat and grey Harris tweed trousers, with brown gaiters over worn elastic-sided boots, he appeared to be in a state of high agitation. He scanned the room with wild, deep-sunk, fat-encircled eyes, and his hand clawed nervously at his hair in a desperate attempt to restore order to his dishevelled appearance. For all his corpulence, I could see that he had once possessed a fine figure, for his shoulders were broad, and his back rigid and straight.

"Mr. Holmes?" enquired he, addressing my friend in a deep voice which vibrated with emotion. "You do not know me, but I am here to prevent a grave injustice. An innocent man is about to be arrested for murder!"

"It is true that I do not know your name," replied Holmes, "but I do know that you are a military man, a singer and a bachelor, that you are not as rich as you once were, and that you have travelled here from the Thames Valley, in great haste and partly on foot, without having had your dinner."

"Then you are a magician, sir. Either that or someone has been here first and told you all about me."

"On the contrary, what seems inexplicable to you is only so because you do not follow my train of thought or understand the small details upon which larger inferences may depend."

"Well then, how do you deduce that I am a military man and a singer?"

"You have a soldier's bearing, and you share Watson's habit of carrying your handkerchief in your sleeve, indicating that you were once accustomed to wearing a uniform. As to the fact that you are a vocalist, there is a spirituality about your face, betokening an artistic temperament; when I take that in conjunction with the silver watch-charm fashioned in the shape of a treble clef, and the melodious richness of your voice, I consider myself amply justified in concluding that music is your *forte*, and singing your specialism."

"That is all very well, sir. But you also mentioned that I was single, and that there had been a decline in my fortunes."

"Your clothes are dusty and unbrushed. As I have had occasion to mention before when examining the hat of Mr. Henry Baker, a previous client, no wife would allow her husband to leave home in such a slovenly state unless she had ceased to love him. Yet you are a man of full habit: you do not possess the figure of one who has suffered from matrimonial disappointment. That you are now comparatively impecunious is obvious, for had you a sufficient number of servants, the sartorial services of a wife would not in any case have been necessary. That you were once wealthy is shown by the excellence of the silk with which your coat is faced. Yet you are apparently unable to afford to restore it to its former magnificence, or to replace rather than re-sole those frayed boots of yours. As to the further facts that you have come from the Thames Valley, that you left home hurriedly, and walked part of the way, and that you have not eaten this evening, I would refer you to the characteristic Buckinghamshire clay which adheres to your boots and to the bottoms of your trouser-legs; to your failure to don a muffler before leaving despite the cold, and the unsuitability of your footwear, whose damp and soiled condition shows clearly that you have braved the snow on foot even though you were ill-prepared to do so; and to the hungry glances which you have directed not once, but no less than three times, towards the *detritus* of our humble repast."

"Well, I must admit that you are correct on every count, Mr. Holmes. I did leave in haste, for I am much exercised in my mind about Mr. Lestrade's suspicions concerning my paying-guest. It is also true that I walked from Paddington. I find that the cabs go slowly through the snow."

"I beg that you will sample some of my bread and cheese, sir, and then perhaps you would have the great kindness to favour me with some details. This is my friend Dr. Watson, before whom you can speak as freely as before myself."

Our portly client helped himself to the victuals which my friend had offered him, and I poured him a whisky and soda. Sinking into the vacant chair with a heavy sigh, he puffed out his chubby pink cheeks, and commenced his narrative.

"You must know, Mr. Holmes, that my name is Major Reculver Yates, and that I live at Tilstone Court in Eton in the county of Buckinghamshire. As you surmised earlier, pounds have not been so plentiful with me as they once were. Tilstone Court is a large mansion, and very old – much of the building remains substantially unaltered since the sixteenth century – and, whilst I inherited the property, I lack the funds to maintain it. The banks of the Thames at Eton are prone to flooding – there was a sizeable inundation earlier this year – and the costs of repairing the damage exceed the limitations of my purse. Apart from a small annuity, my only income derives from my duties as a lay clerk at St. George's Chapel in the grounds of Windsor Castle. I sing bass in the Chapel choir, for which I receive a trifling remuneration and accommodation in the form of a small grace-and-favour apartment at the Castle. I often stay there over-night, rather than return to Tilstone Court on the other side of the river, when there is an evening concert at the Chapel or when I am required to attend late-night choir practice.

"However, as I say, the wages are slight. I have – or, at least, had, until recently – but six employés – John Ayto, my secretary; a butler named Porson; Sam Parkin, the gardener; a cook and two maids. But with such a limited staff, I am compelled to take in paying-guests and to treat the place as if it were an hotel. Normally I have several such guests in residence at any one time, but it so happens that at the moment there are only two: a Mr. Randal Norton of Coalville and his wife Carolyn. All my other guests at present are either personal friends or acquaintances of one sort or another."

"Then since you have intimated already that murder has been done, I beg that you would enumerate these persons as well, Major Yates."

"Certainly, Mr. Holmes. My other guests number five in all. I met Grafton and Celia Montague last summer when I was touring in the Lake District. We struck up a friendship at a small hotel near Wast Water in a remote part of Cumberland. It is a bleak and lonely place. The evenings were long, and the only entertainment was of a spirituous nature. Montague is an historian who is collecting material for a book about Windsor and its Castle. Over a succession of glasses of the finest malt whisky, we agreed that he and his wife should come and stay at Tilstone Court as my guests, in order that he could further his researches into the Royal Town. They have been staying with me for about a week.

"Also resident at the Court are William and Rosalind Clunies-Ross. I have known Clunies-Ross intimately for many years: indeed we were at Eton together. He is always delighted to come and stay with me at Tilstone because of its proximity to our *alma mater*. I believe the town of Eton is his favourite place in England – and not just because of the College.

"The only other person staying at Tilstone at present is Henry St. John Bosco, the famous writer. As you no doubt know, he is the Editor of the acclaimed periodical *Thomson's Miscellany*, in which connection he reads between sixty and eighty manuscripts a month for possible publication. He is always busy with proof-reading, revising and editing articles, and is responsible for arranging payment for each contribution as well as writing his own piece each month. He is presently engaged in compiling his memoirs, but the reason for his presence at Tilstone Court is that he has been commissioned by Peter Thomson, the publisher of the *Miscellany*, to pen an article about me. My military career was a distinguished one, Mr. Holmes, and it is felt that the public would be interested in some of the details."

"Pray proceed, Major Yates."

"Last night, I was performing in a choral concert at St. George's Chapel. Two of my house-guests, Mr. and Mrs. Clunies-Ross, were in the audience – it was a programme entirely devoted to sacred music. There was an interval at about a quarter to nine, when we performers mixed with the members of the audience and partook of some excellent mulled wine and mince pies. The remainder of the concert, which consisted of Christmas music, and was performed by candle-light, lasted until about ten past ten, by which time it was snowing heavily. However, despite this, I decided to return to Tilstone Court rather than remain at my apartment in Windsor Castle, as I wished to be sociable at this festive time of the year.

"I have mentioned already that I am averse to taking cabs in the snow, so I decided to walk home, and William and Rosalind Clunies-Ross agreed to accompany me. We set off down Castle Hill with some difficulty, as the snow had already formed deep drifts, and the pathways were almost impassable in places. Soon we were crossing the toll bridge which spans the Thames between Windsor and Eton, our crisp footfalls echoing across the frozen river as we traversed the snow-girt flags. Eton High Street was white and empty, with pockets of brightness and noise as we passed the various public houses which line it. I could see, through the lighted windows of the Crown and Cushion, the burly figure of my gardener, Sam Parkin, standing in front of a roaring fire, a large pewter tankard in his hand. Beyond the dark, silent houses of the High Street, we could descry the loom of the College buildings, from the windows of which sprang thin lines of yellow light, which pierced the fleck-filled night air. Then, having left Eton, we turned down the narrow, winding country lane which leads to Tilstone Court, and fought our way to the front door through the drifting snow."

Sherlock Holmes was curled up in his chair, with his knees drawn up to his hawk-like nose. A gleam of irritation had sprung to his languid eyes.

"Might I beg that you would have the goodness to omit the poetry and confine yourself to the facts?" said he with a touch of asperity.

"My apologies, Mr. Holmes. But you have a reputation for thoroughness, and I wished to spare you no detail, however slight. You must know that the chief feature of Tilstone Court is its great gate-house, which has in its centre a big archway through which originally vehicles and horses could pass. A large door in the archway leads to the interior of the gate-house, the ground storey of which is known as the Front Hall. This is a large room with a vaulted ceiling and Flemish tapestries hung upon its walls. You will appreciate, Mr. Holmes, that my friends and I were tired after our walk: our clothes were icy, and our feet heavy with snow. I was sure that by now all our servants would be in bed, so I let myself in, and we passed from the freezing Buckinghamshire air into the warmth of the hall. The last, dying embers of a great wood fire were glowing in the hearth, but the room was otherwise in darkness, and I hastened to turn up the gas. As I did so, Mrs. Clunies-Ross gave a cry which struck cold to my heart, and I could see that every vestige of colour had been driven from her face. For there, in the centre of the room, was the body of my secretary, John Ayto, with his brains beaten out and spread all over the floor."

Holmes sat up in his chair like an old hound who hears the view-halloa. "Was there any trace of the weapon?" enquired he excitedly.

"No, Mr. Holmes, not at this stage. But I will come to that presently. For the moment my only concern was to raise the alarm. Porson, my butler, it transpired, was not asleep, but partaking of a night-cap in his room. The other servants were soon roused, and one of the maids despatched to the police-station in Windsor."

"And where, pray, were your guests?"

"Grafton and Celia Montague were in their bedroom preparing to go to bed, whilst my only paying-guests, Randal and Carolyn Norton of Coalville, had already retired for the night. Henry St. John Bosco, the Editor, was in the Library correcting proofs.

"When everyone had been rounded up, we all – staff and guests alike – congregated in the Front Hall, doing our best to ignore the gruesome sight which lay before us. Porson re-kindled the fire, and the waiting-maid assisted us to brandy, while we awaited the arrival of the local police. By now, Sam

Parkin, the gardener, had returned from the Crown and Cushion, rather the worse for drink. He gave a visible start when he saw the entire household gathered together around the disfigured body of my poor secretary, and endeavoured to pull himself together by gulping down a huge draught from the hip-flask which he carries around in his pocket.

"Eventually, the maid re-appeared, accompanied by Inspector Atkins of the Windsor police and a young constable. From the moment he set eyes upon the unfortunate victim, the inspector appeared to be out of his depth. My secretary had received a frightful blow upon the head, which had smashed in part of his skull. Inspector Atkins proceeded to make a cursory examination of the body, and concluded, from the fact that it was still warm and from the freshness of the blood, that death had occurred recently, perhaps not long before my return to the Court. There appeared to be no sign of forced entry, and the inspector was unable to find any clues in the hall. He then interviewed both staff and guests, in order to establish a rough time-table of events.

"Mr. and Mrs. Clunies-Ross and I had left for the concert at about a quarter past seven, and Parkin the gardener at around 8 p.m. to go to the Crown and Cushion. The paying-guests, Mr. and Mrs. Norton of Coalville, had been upstairs in what we call the Little Drawing Room, reading yellow-backed novels. Mr. and Mrs. Montague, my travelling companions of the summer, had retired to their bedroom: Mrs. Montague had complained of a head-ache, and had gone to bed; Mr. Montague had taken the opportunity to write up his notes on Windsor Castle. Mr. St. John Bosco, the Editor, had begun the proof-reading in which he had still been engaged when we returned from St. George's: as I mentioned before, this was in the Library, which is also on the first floor. Nobody had heard anything suspicious. The servants' quarters are on the far side of the house, and all but the butler had been in bed asleep."

Sherlock Holmes, who had been sitting for some time in silence with his head sunk forward, and his eyes bent upon the red glow of the fire, now gave a small wriggle of impatience.

"Pah!" said he. "The inspector is a dunderhead! He does not appear to have even a rudimentary idea of how to carry out a criminal investigation. You say there were no clues. There are always clues! With so much blood about, it is inconceivable that the murderer did not leave traces of some sort. And why not search the body? Or the rooms of the guests? It was utter incompetence!"

"Nevertheless, Mr. Holmes, the inspector concluded that there was nothing he could do, and that the case would be better placed in the hands of Scotland Yard. Leaving the constable behind to guard the body, he returned to Windsor Police Station, with the avowed intention of contacting his superiors in London immediately.

"After his departure, the hubbub subsided, and we all drifted off to bed, it now being extremely late. The following morning, I had scarcely begun my breakfast when there was a crisp knock at the front door, and Porson was announcing the arrival of Mr. Lestrade of Scotland Yard. I was somewhat surprised to see him, even more so when he revealed that he had come in response to a summons from my late secretary, rather than at the behest of Inspector Atkins. 'Mr. Ayto sent me a telegram yesterday afternoon,' said he, 'in which he claimed to have vital information concerning a number of unsolved crimes, including the Gosling Street Bank Robbery.'"

Holmes rubbed his hands, and a flush stole over his face. "This is more like," said he with a chuckle. "And how did Lestrade react to the news of his would-be informant's death?"

"He was thunderstruck," replied Major Yates. "He immediately insisted on examining the scene of the crime, and, in the absence of Inspector Atkins, questioned at length the constable who was still guarding the body."

"Did Lestrade's investigation bear any fruit? He could scarcely have done any worse than that imbecile Atkins."

"Not at first. There were many marks of footsteps in the blood around the body; but most of them had been made since its discovery, and he was unable to learn anything from them."

"If only I had got there first!" cried Holmes, thumping his fist on the arm of his chair in exasperation.

"But on examining the body, Inspector Lestrade did make a couple of interesting discoveries. Clutched in the dead man's grasp, he found a torn scrap of paper on which were inscribed a number of capital letters."

"How were these letters arranged?"

"In groups of two."

"So they might have been the initials of people's names?"

"Quite possibly, yes."

"Excellent. And the inspector's other discovery? You mentioned two."

"Mr. Lestrade searched the victim's pockets, and found his wallet."

"There was nothing unusual about that, surely?"

"Not in itself, no. It was the contents of the wallet that attracted the inspector's attention."

"What do you mean?"

"It contained no less than fifty bank-notes for £10 each, and a similar number of fivers."

Holmes gave a low whistle. "I take it that the money had not come from you, Major Yates?"

"It is many years since I have had access to that sort of sum,

Mr. Holmes. I was utterly unable to explain my secretary's sudden acquisition of so much wealth."

"At this juncture, Inspector Lestrade decided to make a search of the bedrooms."

"Not before time. But at least he has shown more gumption than his Berkshire colleague."

"He found nothing of significance in the chambers occupied by Mr. and Mrs. Montague, Mr. and Mrs. Clunies-Ross, Mr. St. John Bosco or myself. But Ayto's own room had been ransacked: items of furniture had been upturned, drawers dislodged, ornaments smashed and books torn and otherwise vandalized. However, Lestrade's most significant discovery was in the bedroom occupied by Mr. and Mrs. Norton, the paying-guests. There, hidden in the wardrobe, he found a heavy stick covered with blood – undoubtedly the murder weapon. Naturally, Randal Norton became Inspector Lestrade's chief suspect. He was immediately interrogated, but had no explanation as to how the weapon had come to be among his effects. Indeed, things look extremely black for him. I am at my wits' end, Mr. Holmes. Tilstone Court was recommended to the Nortons by mutual friends, and in the short time I have come to know them, I have grown to like and respect them. I cannot believe that they had anything to do with this horrible crime, and yet I am sure that it is only a matter of time before Mr. Norton is arrested. That is why I rushed from my house to come here and beg you to take the case, Mr. Holmes. An innocent man could hang for a crime he did not commit."

"I shall be happy to come down to Tilstone Court tomorrow, Major Yates. The case is not devoid of interest, and it will be a pleasure to work with Lestrade again. However, it would be helpful if first you could furnish me with more information concerning your secretary, John Ayto."

"I had always found him most trustworthy, Mr. Holmes. He was of an age coeval with myself – perhaps slightly older – a quiet, serious, sober man, extremely meticulous and conscientious about his work."

"How long had he been an employé of yours?"

"For more than ten years."

"You say you were surprised by the amount of money in his wallet and by the fact that he had been about to provide Lestrade with information concerning at least one major unsolved crime?"

"Exceedingly so."

"Had Ayto been acting strangely in the days leading up to the murder?"

"Not noticeably so, no, although perhaps he had been a little on edge."

"Thank you, Major Yates. I believe you have told us all we need to know. Until to-morrow, then."

Sherlock Holmes rose to his feet, and held the door open for our distinguished guest, who was somewhat taken aback by the sudden termination of his interview. He departed without a word, and I watched him through the window as he set off determinedly on foot, evidently bent on indulging his prejudice against using cabs in the snow.

"What do you make of our recent client, Watson?" enquired Holmes inscrutably.

"He seemed very concerned about his paying-guests."

"Indeed he did, Watson. Does that not strike you as decidedly odd? He appears to be more worried about a man whom he met only recently, and knows hardly at all, than he does about friends, one of whom went to school with him. If Norton is not guilty of the murder, then suspicion must fall on one of the other occupants of the house. You would think that

that prospect would be less palatable to Major Yates than the imminent arrest of one to whom he is a comparative stranger."

"Unless the guilty person is Mr. St. John Bosco. He was only at the Court on business. And you are forgetting that Mr. and Mrs. Clunies-Ross were at St. George's Chapel at the time of the murder. So they could not be suspected of the crime."

"So I am, Doctor," said Holmes good humouredly. "How foolish of me! Be a good fellow. Make a long arm, and fetch me down Letters W–Z of the index of biographies."

I reached for the requested volume, and handed it to my friend, who turned immediately to the very last page.

"Ah! Here we are. '*Yates, Reculver Merevale Iain, Major*. Lay clerk at St. George's Chapel, Windsor Castle, Berkshire. Formerly First Bengalore Pioneers. Born London, 1842. Son of Sir Frederick Yates, the Conservative politician and Cabinet Minister. Educated Eton and Oxford. Served in Afghan Campaign, Sherpur (dispatches) and Cabul. Addresses: Tilstone Court, Eton, Buckinghamshire; Horseshoe Cloister, Windsor Castle, Berkshire. Clubs: The Anglo-Indian, the Tankerville.' Hum! Most interesting, do you not agree, Watson?"

"I must confess to a feeling of *déjà vu*, Holmes. I seem to recall you reading a very similar biography to me some time in the recent past."

"Bravo, Watson! I refer you to the Adventure of the Empty House. These are deep waters. I suggest an early night, in order that we may be all the fresher for our journey to Buckinghamshire in the morning."

2 : Tilstone Court

When I look at the three bulky volumes which contain our work for the year 1894, I confess that it is very difficult for me, out of such an abundance of data, to choose the cases which are most intrinsically interesting and also most conducive to the demonstration of those talents for which my friend was renowned. As I turn over the leaves, I see my notes upon the repugnant story of the Madagascan cockroach and the horrific death of Fillimore the hatter. Here also I discover an account of the Lansdowne tragedy and the peculiar dentition of the Bermondsey midwife. The famous Stalking Horse case comes also within this period, and so does the arrest, and subsequent hanging, of Polk, the 'Cucumber Frame Murderer' – an exploit for which Holmes was presented with a testimonial from the Cabinet Office as a fitting recognition of his services. Of all these diverse cases, however, I cannot recall any which presented more remarkable features than that which was heralded by the breathless arrival in our rooms of Major Yates a few days before Christmas.

The following morning Sherlock Holmes and I were up betimes. A sharp frost had set in, and the windows were thick with ice crystals, prompting us to draw on our ulsters and wrap cravats about our throats. Having taken a cab to Paddington, we were soon seated in the corner of a first-class carriage. The duns and drabs and slate-greys of London were hidden under a blanket of white as we rattled westward over the flat terrain past Westbourne Park School, the Female Orphans' Home, the West London Gas Works and the military prison at Wormwood Scrubs. Passing through Hanwell, with its Lunatic Asylum, and leaving behind the docks and vitriol works of Southall and the market gardens and brickfields of West Drayton, we eventually pulled up at Slough, where we alighted. It was a crisp, bright morning, and the snow of the night before still lay deep upon the ground, glistening brightly in the wintry sun. Slough Station has a spacious forecourt overlooked by a clock turret. Here we caught a cab which carried us out of the town along the bumpy road which skirts the playing-fields of Eton College. As we turned towards Eton, we caught a glimpse of the lovely grey stone buttresses of the College Chapel, and, nestling beneath them, the homely red-brick buildings of the school itself. Almost at once, we swung sharp left, down the winding lane which Major Yates had described to us the night before, and which I later learned was known as Pocock's Lane, and then right, down a curving, tree-lined drive, before coming to a halt in front of a charming house, girt round with snow-clad lawns.

The magnificent, castle-like gate-house which comprises the main façade of Tilstone Court was built only a few years after Henry VIII became king. The leading features, apart from the central archway already mentioned, are octagonal angle-turrets and a beautiful double-storeyed oriel, in between which and the angle-turrets other windows are pierced, giving a lantern-like appearance to the composition. Battlementing crowns the whole tower as well as the turrets. On either side of the gate-house, stone wings have been added, and, passing through the front part of the building, one emerges into a courtyard which forms a quadrangle completed by the east, west and north wings of the house.

Having alighted from our hansom, Holmes and I walked up to the front door, where my friend pulled at the bell. After a few moments it was answered by a person of gentlemanly bearing with grizzled hair, whom I took to be Porson, Yates's butler. A man of about sixty years of age, he was quietly dressed in a dark-grey suit. "You must be Mr. Sherlock Holmes and Dr. Watson of Baker Street," said he. "Major Yates and Inspector Lestrade are waiting for you in the Library."

We followed him into the Front Hall, where our senses were immediately assailed by the smell of wood-smoke which issued from a mighty log-fire blazing in the hearth. On the opposite side of the spacious chamber, an ornamental stair led to the other rooms in the front part – or south wing – of the house, one of which was the Library. Here we were greeted by our host, whose chubby face lit up as we entered the room.

"Good morning, gentlemen," said he. "You know Inspector Lestrade of Scotland Yard. I am delighted to say that he has not yet arrested Mr. Norton."

"This is not like you, Lestrade," chaffed Holmes. "You have always been very hot on circumstantial evidence, and that stick would be regarded as conclusive by many."

"Perhaps I have taken a leaf out of your book, Mr. Holmes. You will recall the case of the Thor Bridge Mystery. It was not one upon which I myself was engaged, but I have read Dr. Watson's vivid account, and it gave me food for thought. Suspicion fell on a Miss Grace Dunbar, the governess, and there was, as I remember, some very direct evidence. A revolver with one discharged chamber and a calibre which corresponded with the bullet in the victim's body was found on the floor of her wardrobe. Yet you were convinced it was what is termed 'a plant', and that no one would have been so foolish as to incriminate themselves in such a rash manner. Why not simply throw the weapon away? It occurred to me that the same thing applied in the present case. The stick in question – I have it here – is the personal possession of Mr. Randal Norton, and is normally kept in the stand which you, with your keen powers of observation, no doubt noticed to the left of the front door. If Randal Norton killed John Ayto, why did he not simply replace the stick in its usual receptacle – or even leave it beside the body? There would be nothing to prove that the deed had been perpetrated by its owner, whilst to hide it in his own wardrobe – and not even to wipe it clean of the victim's blood – would be an act of such crass stupidity that I am reluctant to give it any credence."

"Bravo, Lestrade. Apparently you are learning wisdom in your old age. May I examine the murder weapon?"

Inspector Lestrade handed the stick to my friend, who examined it minutely with his powerful lens. It was a Penang lawyer weighted with lead, and one end of it was thickly coated with dried blood.

"I believe this was not your only find, Inspector," observed Holmes.

"Indeed not, Mr. Holmes. I discovered two clues on the body itself. The first was this crumpled piece of note-paper found clasped in the dead man's hand. You will see that it is the corner of a much larger sheet, which has been torn from his grasp by the murderer."

Sherlock Holmes held the fragment between his thumb and

forefinger, and subjected it to a keen scrutiny. "There are three pairs of initials listed in a column, but the bottom one is incomplete," said he. " 'J.C.' and 'F.D.' are quite distinct and appear to be grouped together. The third pair, which is separated from the other two by several lines, begins with 'I' and the second letter is almost certainly an 'S', although part of it has been torn away with the rest of the paper. Do you make anything of this, Lestrade?"

"No, Mr. Holmes, apart from the fact that the letters presumably represent people's names."

"Very good. I believe your other 'clue' was Ayto's wallet."

"Yes, Mr. Holmes. As you can see, it contained rather a lot of money for a humble secretary."

Holmes unclasped the proffered note-case and took out its contents – a sizeable wad of five- and ten-pound notes. As with the stick and the torn fragment of paper, he used his magnifying glass to make a close and careful inspection. "Ah, this is interesting," declared he at last. "These bank-notes are forgeries – very good ones, I grant you, but forgeries none the less."

"They seemed perfectly genuine to me," observed Lestrade with a touch of asperity.

"Oh, the draughtsmanship is undoubtedly of the very highest quality. Well, well, Lestrade, I understand that John Ayto had invited you down to Tilstone Court to tell you what he knew about certain crimes that had not yet been cleared up. Perhaps forgery was one of them."

"Who knows, Mr. Holmes? The Gosling Street money was real enough: the thieves got away with eight thousand pounds from the bank, and to this day we have no clue as to their identity."

"Did Ayto explain how he came to have this information?"

"No, Mr. Holmes, but the Gosling Street business alone was

enough to warrant my taking his summons very seriously."

"He did not specify any of the other crimes about which he claimed to have intelligence?"

"Unfortunately not."

Sherlock Holmes then turned to Major Yates.

"Watson and I looked you up in our index after your departure yesterday evening, Major. You have certainly had a very distinguished career. I gather you were in the First Bengalore Pioneers, and served in the Afghan Campaign. You must have known Colonel Sebastian Moran, the one-time Chief of Staff to Professor Moriarty, who was also of the Pioneers. Moran it was who gave me an evil five minutes on the Reichenbach ledge after the death of his leader, and who shot the Honourable Ronald Adair with an expanding bullet from an air-gun through the open window of the second-floor front of No. 427 Park Lane, before attempting to serve me in the same ruthless fashion from an empty house in Baker Street."

"Of course I knew Colonel Moran, Mr. Holmes. He was my commanding officer, although I took my orders more often than not from his second in command, Lieutenant Colonel Carruthers. I also served with Colonel Moran in Sherpur and Cabul, and he was a member of two of the same clubs as I. An honourable man. It was a shame he turned bad. But perhaps you would care to examine Ayto's room now? Inspector Lestrade found it in a state of considerable disorder."

"Would you be so good as to accompany me thither, Lestrade? You can show me the way and direct my attention *en route* to any other little discoveries you have made in the course of your investigation. You, in the meanwhile, Major Yates, will have the kindness to explain to the other occupants of this house that Mr. Holmes of Baker Street wishes to interview them about the unfortunate death of your secretary."

Major Yates gave a nod of assent, and Lestrade led Holmes and me through the maze of rooms to the servants' quarters on the far side – or north wing – of the house.

John Ayto's room was indeed in a state of disarray. There was not one stick of furniture that had not been disturbed, and the carpet was littered with the debris of torn paper and broken china. Sherlock Holmes surveyed the wreckage with a look of bewilderment. "It is clear that someone has been searching for something here, and has not spared the china or the furniture," said he. "But why destroy the books? Unless…"

Here he fell into a brown study, during which he picked up one or two of the mutilated volumes which lay strewn about the floor. "Look here, Watson," he exclaimed. "This is clearly a common-place book, in which were pasted clippings from newspapers. However, most of the pages have been torn out, and, so far as I can tell, removed from the room."

He handed the book to me, which now contained only three or four pages of cuttings, all of them sensational accounts of crimes. One of these in particular caught my eye. "This is a report on the case of the Red-Headed League," I ejaculated. " 'DARING BANK ROBBERY FOILED BY POLICE. A bold attempt to steal a quantity of French gold from the Coburg branch of the City and Suburban Bank has been thwarted by Mr. Peter Jones of Scotland Yard' – I see you chose not to appear in the matter yourself, Holmes."

"Of course not. As you know, I play the game for the game's sake. Celebrity holds no attraction for me."

I resumed my recitation.

" 'John Clay, the murderer, thief, smasher and forger, was apprehended in the very act of purloining no less than thirty thousand napoleons from the vault of the City branch of one of the principal London banks. It appears that Clay had constructed a tunnel from the premises of Mr. Jabez Wilson, a pawnbroker in Coburg Square, who had been duped into absenting himself while the excavations were carried out. There is no doubt that Mr. Jones has detected and defeated in the most complete manner one of the most determined attempts at bank robbery that have ever come within our experience.'"

"I suppose John Clay could be the 'J.C.' on Ayto's piece of paper."

"Although his was not an 'unsolved crime', and none of the other cuttings left in the common-place book refer to an 'F.D.' or an 'I.S.'"

Sherlock Holmes now spent some minutes examining the other objects in the secretary's room. However, there was nothing to hold his interest, and he was on the point of abandoning his search, when a long, bald man of about sixty entered.

"Forgive me," exclaimed the newcomer, who had been taken aback by our presence. "I did not expect anyone to be here."

"Allow me to introduce myself, sir," said Holmes cordially. "I am Sherlock Holmes and this is my friend Dr. Watson. Inspector Lestrade you will already have met. Whom have I the pleasure of addressing?"

"I am Henry St. John Bosco, gentlemen. I am a writer and also the Editor of *Thomson's Miscellany*. I am at the Court to interview Major Yates for a biographical piece I am writing about him for the *Miscellany*. No doubt you are wondering what I am doing poking about his ex-secretary's bedroom."

"Perhaps you would be good enough to enlighten us?"

"The truth is I knew that Ayto had acquired a sizeable amount of information about his employer, in the form of newspaper cuttings and other miscellaneous data. He had promised to lend me this material as useful background to my article, but unfortunately was taken from us before I had the opportunity to avail myself of his generosity. I have come hither to see if I can locate the information for myself."

"I fear that the subject-matter you are seeking has in all probability been destroyed, Mr. St. John Bosco. As you can see, an intruder has been here before us. I myself was examining the remains of his common-place book when you came in, and few pages have been left intact."

"That is unfortunate, Mr. Holmes. It seems I shall have to rely entirely on my interview with Major Yates for my data."

"I understand that you are also engaged in writing your memoirs, Mr. St. John Bosco."

"Indeed I am, Mr. Holmes. In fact, I am close to completing them. I have the manuscript with me here at Tilstone."

"Might I beg that you would have the goodness to furnish me with your version of the events leading up to John Ayto's death?"

"Certainly. My work on the *Miscellany* means that I always have copy to write and edit and proofs to correct. It was upon this that I was engaged on the night in question. I find the Library the most suitable environment for such tasks, and it was thither accordingly that I repaired at about ten past seven, just as Major Yates was about to depart for his concert at St. George's Chapel with Mr. and Mrs. Clunies-Ross. I remained in the Library for the rest of the evening, and only left when Porson came in at about a quarter past eleven to inform me that Ayto's body had been discovered in the Front Hall. I then joined the others to wait for the arrival of the police."

"And you were not aware of any disturbance during the course of the evening?"

"No. The whole place was as quiet as a monastery.

Although, of course, the walls in this old house are extremely thick."

"Have you any knowledge as to the whereabouts of the other guests in the hours leading up to the murder?"

"Only of those who had left for the concert. So far as I know, everyone else was still in the house, though I could not say exactly where."

"Thank you, Mr. St. John Bosco. You are welcome to proceed with your search of Mr. Ayto's effects. However, should you find anything which you consider to be pertinent to my inquiry, I should be grateful if you would let me know. We, in the mean time, will return to the Library, and see if Major Yates has yet located any of the other occupants."

In fact, the Major was waiting for us with Randal and Carolyn Norton, the paying-guests. Mr. Norton was a short man of about 30, dressed in a sombre yet rich style, in black coat, neat brown gaiters, and well-cut pearl-grey trousers. His face was care-worn, and there were dark circles under his eyes. His wife was of about the same age, rather under the middle height, slim with dark brown hair and eyes. She had an anxious look, and seemed very protective towards her husband.

"I have heard of you, Mr. Sherlock Holmes," said she. "If anyone can clear Randal of the dreadful suspicion that hangs over him, it is you. How that stick came to be in our wardrobe I cannot say, but he is as guiltless of this horrible crime as you or I."

"I believe you and your husband were in bed when the murder took place, Mrs. Norton?"

"Yes. Earlier we had been in the Little Drawing Room reading, but according to Inspector Atkins, the state of the body indicated that death had occurred not long before its discovery, by which time we had retired for the night."

"Did you go down to the Front Hall at any stage of the evening?"

"We did not."

"And, so far as you are aware, the murder weapon was not in your wardrobe when you went to bed?"

"I know it was not, Mr. Holmes," interjected Randal Norton. "The stick was discovered on the floor of the wardrobe covered with a piece of cloth. Neither the stick nor the material were there when I hung up my coat and trousers prior to retiring."

"So they must have been placed there after you had gone down to the Front Hall to wait for the police?"

"That's right. Porson raised the alarm at about twenty past eleven, at which point my wife and I dressed and left the room."

"Thank you, Mr. Norton, that is quite clear. Have you anyone else for me, Major Yates?"

"Mrs. Montague is waiting without, Mr. Holmes. If Mr. and Mrs. Norton would care to retire…?"

The paying-guests left, and Celia Montague entered, a golden-haired, blue-eyed woman in her mid twenties, with a perfect complexion.

"I am afraid my husband is out at present," said she. "But he will be back shortly. In the mean time I will be happy to answer any questions on his behalf."

"You are here as personal guests of Major Yates, I understand," remarked Sherlock Holmes affably.

"Yes. My husband and I met him last summer on holiday in the Lake District. He very kindly invited us to stay at Tilstone when he heard that Grafton was writing a book about the history of Windsor. Indeed my husband was working on it when, by all accounts, the murder must have taken place. I myself had already retired for the night with a head-ache."

"But your husband was in the same room?"

"He was. We were both there continuously from about nine o'clock onwards. Grafton had just finished writing, and was preparing to undress prior to joining me in bed, when, at about twenty-five minutes past eleven, there was a knock upon our door, and Porson the butler appeared with the terrible news. I dressed hastily and hurried down to the Front Hall. My husband followed soon afterwards. There is nothing more I can tell you."

At this point the gong sounded for luncheon. We did not have far to go for our meal. Like the Library, the Dining Room opened out of the landing opposite to the ornamental stair which led up from the Front Hall. Lestrade having departed for a somewhat ruder meal in one of the hostelries in Eton, Holmes and I, accompanied by Major Yates and Mrs. Montague, entered the room, where we found Mr. and Mrs. Norton and Mr. St. John Bosco already seated at the table. Moments later, we were joined by a tall, handsome, athletic young man, who immediately took his place next to Mrs. Montague. "This is my husband, Grafton," said she. "Mr. Holmes has been questioning me about the night before last," she continued, addressing her spouse. "I told him that we were in our room after nine o'clock."

"I am sorry I was not here for the interview," said he. "But I am sure my dear wife has told you all you need to know. I have been in Windsor undertaking research for my book. It is a fascinating place."

"Now we are all here apart from Mr. and Mrs. Clunies-Ross," commented Major Yates, who had sat down at the head of the table. "I am reluctant to start lunch without them, but if they do not appear soon…"

After waiting for a further ten minutes, the Major gave the signal for the meal to begin, and Porson appeared with the waiting-maid and a huge tureen of thick, meaty soup. We were eating this, when the door burst open, and the missing couple came in.

William Clunies-Ross and his wife Rosalind made a handsome pair. He was of the middle height, aged about fifty, and smartly dressed in a dark frock-coat with an amethyst pin in his black satin cravat and lavender spats over varnished shoes. Rosalind Clunies-Ross was a strikingly beautiful woman, about ten or twelve years younger than her husband. She had a perfect, clear-cut face, with all the cultured refinement of the Home Counties in her delicate colouring, and was wearing a lavish costume of dove-coloured silk with ostrich feather trimming.

"I must apologize for our tardiness, Major Yates," said Mr. Clunies-Ross earnestly. "We heard the gong, but were not quite ready to come down."

"Mr. and Mrs. Clunies-Ross, may I present you to Mr. Sherlock Holmes, the legendary criminal agent, and his friend, Dr. Watson," replied Major Yates. "They are here to investigate the murder of poor Ayto."

"I shall be glad if you will have the kindness to allow me to question you after luncheon, Mr. Clunies-Ross," said Holmes. "I am trying to build a complete picture of events."

"That will present no problems, Mr. Holmes, although I expect the interview to be a short one since my wife and I were at St. George's all evening."

The company relapsed into silence as the fine Berkshire beef came and went. Randal and Carolyn Norton looked pale and anxious, saying nothing and eating little. Mr. St. John Bosco and the other two couples, by contrast, appeared to have hearty appetites, and, over the apple pie and custard, conversation became animated, Mr. Montague in particular enthusing about the delights of Tilstone Court and its surroundings. I have seldom seen a healthier or a more vigorous young man.

When luncheon was over, Major Yates invited the Nortons and the Montagues to join Mr. St. John Bosco and himself in the Drawing Room for coffee and brandy, leaving Holmes and me with Mr. and Mrs. Clunies-Ross.

"If you will take the chairs by the fire, Watson and I will make ourselves comfortable here," said Holmes, gesturing to the elegant couple with his freshly lighted pipe. "Did you enjoy the concert at the Royal Chapel?"

"Very much so, Mr. Holmes," replied Mrs. Clunies-Ross, her violet eyes shining with pleasure at the recollection. "The choice of music was very seasonable, and the performances were excellent."

"Did you leave the Chapel at any stage during the evening?"

"No. We arrived with Major Yates at about a quarter to eight. He had secured us two seats right in the front, next to Sir Seton and Lady Heatherdene of Eton, and we stayed with them for the duration of the concert, even joining them for mince pies and mulled wine in the interval. We left St. George's with Major Yates at about half past ten, and arrived back at Tilstone Court at about eleven o'clock, when we discovered the body."

"I suppose there had been no sign of forced entrance to the house?"

"No. Major Yates had to unlock the front door, and it is the only means of entrance, as the windows of the gate-house are blocked by old-fashioned shutters with broad iron bars, which are secured every night."

"Very good, Mrs. Clunies-Ross. You and your husband are free to join your friends in the Drawing Room. Watson and I have just one more interview to complete. Come, Watson, I think I noticed Porson's room when we were visiting Ayto's bedchamber in the north wing this morning."

We retraced our steps of earlier in the day, and found the butler relaxing over a glass of port and a cigar. He rose to greet us as we entered, but Holmes was quick to put him at his ease. "Do not trouble to get up, Porson," said he. "There are just a few questions which I should like to ask you, if I may?"

"I shall be glad to answer them," replied the butler, puffing at his cigar, "though I am not sure whether my responses will be of much use to you in your inquiries."

"That remains to be seen, Porson. But you will admit that you are uniquely placed to observe the comings and goings of the occupants of the house."

"That may appear to be the case, Mr. Holmes. But the reality is that I have my duties to perform, and they afford me little enough time for concerning myself with the affairs of others."

"Be that as it may, might I beg that you will give me your version of what happened the night before last?"

"Well, Major Yates left with Mr. and Mrs. Clunies-Ross at about a quarter past seven. I then retired to my room, and did not leave again until just after nine o'clock, when I took a tray round, as is my custom at that hour. At that time, Mr. St. John Bosco was in the Library, and Mr. and Mrs. Norton were in the Little Drawing Room. There was no sign of the Montagues, so they may have gone to bed. However, I did notice that the gas was lit in the Front Hall, and when I peeped over the banister, I could see that Mr. Ayto was down there. He was seated at the table poring over a piece of paper. I called down to him to see if he wanted anything from my tray, but he gestured me away, so I returned to my room again. I stayed there drinking and reading until about eleven o'clock, when I heard this great scream coming from the Front Hall, and rushed down to find the Major and Mr. and Mrs. Clunies-Ross with the dead body of Mr. Ayto. Major Yates then asked me to rouse the guests. Mr. St. John Bosco was still in the Library. I then went to look for the Nortons, but they were no longer in the Little Drawing Room, and had gone to bed. The Montagues were also in their bedroom, although Mr. Montague was still dressed. We all congregated in the Front Hall to wait for the police, one of the maids having been despatched to the police-station in Windsor. Parkin, the gardener, returned to the Court at about a quarter to twelve. He was drunk, as usual. That is all I can tell you, Mr. Holmes."

"Did all the guests arrive in the Front Hall at about the same time?"

"Now let me see. Mr. St. John Bosco came straight down from the Library. The others took longer because – now that is odd when I come to think of it."

"What do you mean?"

"Well, when I entered the Montagues' bedroom, Mrs. Montague was in bed, but Mr. Montague was still up. Yet he was the last person to come down to the Front Hall, arriving some minutes after the others, even though they had had to dress."

"Thank you, Porson. You have been most informative. Come, Watson, let us take a closer look at the scene of the murder."

Unfortunately for Sherlock Holmes, the floor of the Front Hall had been scrubbed clean, and there was nothing for him to examine. Consequently we spent a desultory afternoon pottering around Tilstone Court until dinner, after which most of the house-guests retired to their rooms. All afternoon, a slate-coloured sky had threatened further snow, but at twilight, the clouds had cleared, and, as darkness fell, the stars came out and a great round moon began to cast its silvery light on the snow-draped lawns.

By eleven o'clock, I was ready for my bed. Sherlock Holmes and I had been the last to quit the warmth of the fire in the Front Hall, and I was reading a final chapter in my room prior to donning my night-garb, when I heard a noise, as of someone bumping heavily against a piece of furniture. I listened awhile, and presently there came the sound of soft footfalls upon a flight of stairs. I decided to investigate, and, with my heart thumping in my chest, I grabbed the candle from the mantelpiece and ventured out into the darkness. I began to descend the ornamental stair which led down to the Front Hall, and must have made a noise for down below there came a sudden rush of footsteps and the sound of a bolt being drawn, followed by the creaking of a door. Having reached the Hall, I felt a sudden gust of wind, which caused my candle to gutter and a puff of white smoke to issue from the dying fire. As I progressed into the room, I could see from whence the draught had come, for the front door was wide open. Outside, the garden appeared empty and undisturbed: I could make out nothing apart from the dark loom of the trees and the glint of the ice-crystals in the snow where the moonlight caught them. After a few minutes, my eyes became accustomed to the darkness, but, still detecting no sign of life, I decided to shut and secure the door and return to my bedchamber. However, before quitting the hall, I could not resist drawing back the shutters and gazing out once more at the wintry scene without.

Suddenly I saw it. Next to a giant tree stood the tall black figure of a man clearly outlined against the moon behind it. It was only a fleeting glimpse. Yet I was sure that somewhere, some time in the past, I had seen that long, thin form before.

3: The Horseshoe Cloister

I told Holmes about the shadowy figure in the garden the following morning at breakfast. "You say the man was tall and thin?" queried my friend. "Henry St. John Bosco and Grafton Montague are tall men. Was it either of them, do you think?"

"This man was even longer, Holmes, I am sure of it: about the same height as Major Yates, only much slimmer. Yet I do believe I have seen him before, if not in the recent past."

"Well it will have to remain a mystery for the time being. There has been a fresh fall of snow during the night, so any search for traces would be futile. This morning we will take a walk into Eton and check up on the alibi of Mr. and Mrs. Clunies-Ross and Parkin, the gardener. Then, as I understand our host is at St. George's this morning, and has agreed to receive us, we will pay a visit to his apartment at Windsor Castle for a late luncheon."

It was a cold, sunny morning with no sign of a thaw. We left Tilstone Court through the archway in the centre of the gatehouse, and followed the tree-lined drive which takes the visitor back around the house, away from the river which it faces, and towards Pocock's Lane. From there we trudged through the deep snow, turned left across a bridge which spanned a frozen brook, and soon reached the first red-brick buildings of Eton College. Passing the main entrance to the school, and the elegant exterior of the College Chapel, we crossed the road, and arrived at an archway with plaster casts on the walls, opening into the courtyard of Jourdelays, the house which, as Major Yates had informed us, was the home of Sir Seton and Lady Emily Heatherdene. In its courtyard setting, the house reminded me very much of an old Dutch picture. We crossed the stone flags, which had been cleared of snow and heavily salted, and approached the front door, where Holmes pulled at the ornamental brass bell-knob. After a slight pause, the door was opened by a severe-looking servant, who, on learning of the nature of our business, ushered us into a large, green-papered chamber lined with innumerable volumes.

A few moments later, we were joined by a stately, middle-aged couple, who introduced themselves as the master and mistress of Jourdelays. "Your reputation goes before you, Mr. Sherlock Holmes," declared Sir Seton. "My butler informs me that you are investigating the murder up at Tilstone Court. How may we be of assistance in that connection?"

"Simply by recounting to me your movements on the night in question, Sir Seton," explained Holmes. "I should add that my interest lies not so much in the activities of you and your wife as in those of your companions, Mr. and Mrs. William Clunies-Ross, who are currently guests at the Court."

"We were introduced to them at St. George's Chapel by our mutual friend, Major Yates," replied Sir Seton Heatherdene. "We had adjoining seats. Clunies-Ross is an entertaining fellow. He was educated at the College, you know. Very fond of

Eton and Windsor. His wife is charming too. We had quite a chat over the mulled wine in the interval."

"Did either Mr. or Mrs. Clunies-Ross leave the Chapel at any time during the concert?"

"Oh no. It was far too cold to go outside. Snowing, you know. Heavily."

"At the end of the concert, did you accompany Major Yates and Mr. and Mrs. Clunies-Ross on the first stage of their journey back to Tilstone?"

"Certainly not. I could not have allowed Lady Heatherdene to walk in this weather. We took a cab, but Major Yates has a peculiar aversion to travelling by hansom when there is snow on the ground, and he persuaded Mr. and Mrs. Clunies-Ross to join him on foot. We saw them set off down Castle Hill, and congratulated ourselves on having opted for a more comfortable mode of transport."

"Thank you very much, Sir Seton. That is all I wanted to know. You can confirm, then, that there was no way in which either Mr. or Mrs. Clunies-Ross could have slipped away unnoticed during the course of the evening?"

"I can. They were our constant companions."

Holmes and I took our leave, and resumed our perambulation. Leaving the courtyard of Jourdelays, we passed beneath the archway and turned right towards the bridge over Barnes Pool which marks the end of the College buildings and the beginning of the High Street. Few main streets can have a more fascinating situation than this one, with the massive thirteenth-century Curfew Tower of Windsor Castle blocking the southern sky-line, and the mellow beauty of Eton College to the north. For the main part, the houses that line the street are of graceful late Georgian or early nineteenth-century architecture, but a few are somewhat older, and one of these, not far from the bridge over the River Thames, is the Crown and Cushion, a public house which dates back to the seventeenth century.

Sherlock Holmes and I kicked our feet against the stone steps that led up to the entrance of this building, in order to free them of the snow which we had picked up in the course of our walk, and made our way inside. The Crown and Cushion had a cosy, dark, wood-panelled interior, with a spacious bar-counter and an inviting coal fire, in front of which stood a number of thirsty customers, who were drinking hot toddies and large glasses of black bitter beer. The landlord, whose name we had seen advertised on the board above the front door, was a genial, bald-headed fellow called Edward Urie. He greeted us with a smile of welcome, and we ordered two quarts of the dark brew which was evidently the speciality of the house.

"Could we trouble you for a round or two of bread and some cheese and pickles, landlord?" enquired Holmes, having taken a deep draught from his foaming glass.

"I will tell the girl to prepare them directly," replied Mr. Urie with a beam. "You are strangers around here, I believe?"

"Indeed we are, landlord. I am Sherlock Holmes, and this is my companion, Dr. Watson. We are inquiring into the death of Mr. John Ayto at Tilstone Court. I am told that Sam Parkin, the gardener there, is a regular customer at this house?"

"That he is, sir. In fact, if you look over there in front of the fire, you will see the gentleman in person."

The landlord directed our attention towards a thick-set, burly man, with thinning dark-brown hair, a ruddy complexion and glassy, blood-shot eyes. He was standing next to a rough, uncouth fellow with a shock of grizzled hair, whiskers and a brown, weather-beaten face. Both men were laughing, and quaffing from large pewter tankards, but, at Mr. Urie's words, the former turned to us with a look of hostility in his deep-set, piggy eyes.

"What business do you gentlemen have with me, may I ask?" he enquired belligerently, a further flush of colour coming to his already rubicund complexion.

"It is quite all right, Mr. Parkin," said Holmes diplomatically. "We are guests of your master up at the Court, and are investigating the movements of all those who were in residence at the time of John Ayto's death."

"Well I was here in the Crown and Cushion, and what's more so was this man beside me. He is the gardener at Boveney Court, a mile or so up river, and, like me, unable to do his job when the snow is lying three feet thick on the earth."

Parkin's companion held out his hand, and advanced towards Sherlock Holmes with a grin and a swagger.

"Good morning," said he cordially. "Theodore Bargus. As my friend says, gardener up at Boveney. I was with Sam all night when the murder took place, and if you won't take my word for it, then I am sure Mr. Urie here will back me up."

"It's true, Mr. Holmes. Mr. Parkin came in at about a quarter past eight, and Mr. Bargus shortly afterwards. They stayed until long after eleven o'clock."

The girl came in with two plates of bread and cheese.

"Did you by any chance see Major Yates and Mr. and Mrs. Clunies-Ross passing by on their way back to Tilstone after the concert?" enquired Holmes, addressing Parkin.

"I can't say as I did, Mr. Holmes. But I would have been well gone by then. I had quite a lot to drink that night, didn't I, Mr. Urie?"

"You have quite a lot to drink every night – and during the day too when there's no work for you," said the barman wryly.

"That's true enough, I suppose. Bargus and I enjoy our ale.

In fact, we wouldn't say no to a re-fill now, would we, Theodore?"

Sam Parkin licked his lips, and glanced suggestively at Sherlock Holmes, who, taking the hint, ordered more beer for the thirsty pair.

"Is there anything else you can tell me about John Ayto or the events leading up to his death?" said Holmes, handing Parkin and Bargus their freshly re-filled tankards.

"Not really, Mr. Holmes," replied the gardener, having first taken a huge gulp of his favourite beverage. "Being only the gardener, I tend to keep myself to myself. I don't have much to do with the other servants, and, of course, Mr. Ayto was a man of letters. I saw him about the house and grounds from time to time, but he never spoke to me."

"Thank you, Mr. Parkin, I need not detain you further. Let us finish our bread and cheese, Watson, and then we will resume our most interesting peregrinations around Eton and Windsor."

Having consumed the remains of our light meal, and drained our glasses, we left the cosy surroundings of the Crown and Cushion, and continued our walk along Eton High Street towards the river. The Thames was frozen solid, and several people were skating on it as we crossed the toll bridge into Windsor. From the other side, the main street curves steeply up to the centre of the town, by the western wall of the castle, past the ancient Curfew Tower with its candle-snuffer roof and the smaller drum towers of more recent origin. At the top of the hill, just beyond the entrance to the Great Western Railway Station, and in front of the beautifully proportioned Classical Guildhall, was a disorderly conglomeration of street traders selling their wares from baskets and make-shift stalls. Here, ignoring the earnest entreaties of one such vendor, who was warming his hands at the simple brazier on which he was roasting chestnuts for sale to a largely disinterested public, we turned left, and through the main entrance into Windsor Castle.

In front of us, to our right, we could see St. George's Chapel with its delicate flying buttresses. To its left, across the parade ground which stretched before us, was an archway leading into the Horseshoe Cloister, the home of Major Yates's grace-and-favour apartment. Walking through the archway, we came into a picturesque crescent of red-brick and timber construction, in front of which was a curving, covered passage-way. Out of the Cloister to our right, a flight of wide stone steps led up to the western entrance of St. George's Chapel, whilst about two-thirds of the way around, on the north-west side of the circuit, a small passage led to a narrow flight of steps into the upper level of the great Curfew Tower, the front of which we had been admiring ever since first entering Eton High Street.

Having passed through the archway, we turned left into the passage-way which skirted the terrace, and immediately came to No. 21, above which on a wooden board was painted in gilt letters the name 'MAJOR R.M.I. YATES'.

From inside the house we could hear the sound of a resonant bass voice combined with a halting piano accompaniment, which came to an abrupt end the moment that Sherlock Holmes rapped on the door with the large brass knocker. Seconds later, Major Yates appeared. "Welcome to the Horseshoe Cloister," said he. "I trust you had no difficulty in finding me."

"Indeed not," replied Holmes courteously. "Your directions were most explicit. I should add that we have taken your comments concerning the frugality of your luncheon arrangements to heart and partaken of some light refreshment *en route*."

"I am glad to hear it, gentlemen. My pocket does not stretch to a second set of servants, and so I am compelled to rely on my Tilstone Court staff to fulfil my needs at the Castle. Cook very obligingly ran up with the remains of yesterday's cold beef, and I am afraid that they are all I have to offer."

Major Yates then took us on a short tour of his very comfortable apartment. There were three storeys in all in the narrow yet labyrinthine little terraced house. The front room contained two pianos and a couple of music-stands. Opposite was a small lounge, and a winding flight of stairs led to a pair of bedrooms. But the largest room was in the basement, dominated by a big oak table, on which were set the remains of the cold beef. A small kitchen adjoined this snug dining-room.

Major Yates invited us to sit down before the fire, and offered us some brandy "to keep out the cold". "Did you call on Sir Seton and Lady Heatherdene, as you intended?" he enquired.

"We did," replied Holmes, "and I am delighted to say that they confirmed that Mr. and Mrs. Clunies-Ross were with them throughout your concert at the Chapel. I suppose they did not leave you at any time during your walk back to Tilstone?"

"No, Mr. Holmes. There is only one way back to the Court, and that is across the bridge between Windsor and Eton."

"Normally, yes. But, with the river frozen over as it is, it occurred to me that the most direct route would be to *walk* across it, and then downstream to Tilstone, rather than through Eton and back round to the Court via the drive-way."

"Well that may be the case, Mr. Holmes. But the fact is that none of us went that way. Mr. and Mrs. Clunies-Ross never once left my side, and I certainly came back along the High Street, past the Crown and Cushion, where I saw my gardener."

"Yes, we checked up on him also, Major Yates. It appears

that Parkin was there all evening, although he did not see you pass on your way back to the Court."

"May I assist you to some of this excellent Berkshire beef, gentlemen?"

Without further encouragement, Major Yates cut several slices from the joint upon the table, sandwiched them between some rounds of bread, and thrust them into our hands. "Forgive the absence of ceremony," said he, "but I am not accustomed to receiving guests when I am staying here."

After our rude meal, Major Yates explained that he had choir practice at the Chapel, and Holmes and I took our leave. However, on our way out, Major Yates took us through the archway at the other side of the Cloister, which led to a belvedere terrace. From here we had a clear view of the town of Windsor below us, of the frozen River Thames and of Eton beyond it, dominated by the elegant structure of the College Chapel. I could see the microscopic figures of the skaters on the white surface of the river, but noticed that Tilstone Court, some way over to the right on the far bank, was obscured from sight by a small, tree-covered island, which separated the main channel of the river from the backwater alongside which the house was situated.

Returning to the Cloister, Major Yates was on the point of ascending the stone steps into the western entrance of St. George's Chapel, when Sherlock Holmes enquired if we might be permitted to visit the Curfew Tower.

"I presume there will be no objection," said Major Yates. "Just knock on the door, and the guard will let you in. I am afraid I must leave you now, or I will be late for choir practice."

Major Yates departed up the steps into the Chapel, and Sherlock Holmes and I made our way through the covered passage-way to the narrow alley that led to the oldest tower in the castle. A short flight of steps took us to the door, which was set in the upper part of the rear of the tower. A friendly guard in a dark uniform with a red cap let us in, and took us up the few steps which led into the roof, where we were shown the fine seventeenth-century clock and the eight bells of the chapel, which chime every three hours, by day and by night, at three, six, nine and twelve o'clock. On our way down again, the guard explained that an ancient passage started in an upper room of the tower and descended in the thickness of the wall to an underground level, passing to a point about half-way across the street outside. Apparently, there were two other such "sally ports" in the castle. When we reached the basement, which once housed the dungeons, we were told that here also were the beginnings of a tunnel, through which a prisoner had hoped to escape only to be defeated by the thickness of the masonry.

At the end of our tour, we thanked the guard, and descended the steps back into the Horseshoe Cloister. However, Holmes insisted we could not leave the castle without seeing the interior of St. George's Chapel, and so, having found the western entrance closed, we left the Cloister and entered via the south door.

Once inside, the first impression I received of the Chapel was one of space, light and air, of walls which were almost continuous sheets of glass broken only by slim shafts of stone. The whole Nave is covered by the richest vaulting imaginable with innumerable carved bosses, and, as we walked towards the Choir, I could see that Holmes was enraptured not only by the sublime architecture but by the sweet sound of the singers and the mellow piping of the organ as the Christmas-tide rehearsal progressed. The Choir itself was filled with beautifully carved stalls: indeed, nearly every available space on the woodwork was adorned with carvings depicting the figures of people and animals. At one of these lavish stalls, I could see Major Yates, his portly form illuminated by a large candle in an ornate brass holder. As he sang, his deep bass voice blended sonorously with those of his fellow choristers, and the whole chapel was filled with glorious music. "Tra-la-la-lira-lira-lay," carolled Holmes blissfully as we quitted the chapel and made our way to the castle gate-way.

The sun had gone behind the clouds, and it was bitterly cold as we tramped through the snow and ice down Castle Hill, past the coster's orange barrow and on across the toll bridge once more into Eton. A few flakes of snow began to fall, and so we quickened our pace, and were soon leaving town and College behind as we turned along Pocock's Lane before doubling back towards the river along the main drive into Tilstone.

On arriving at the Court, we let ourselves in with a key that Holmes had obtained from Porson in the forenoon, and entered the warmth of the great Front Hall. A familiar figure was standing in front of the fire, and, as he turned to greet us, we both gave a violent start. "Major Yates!" ejaculated Sherlock Holmes, a look of amazement coming to his normally impassive face. "How did you get home so quickly? I made sure you did not pass us *en route*."

"It was you who gave me the idea, Mr. Holmes. The rehearsal was nearly over when you came into the chapel, and I left soon after you. Well, when I got to the bridge, I thought I would try that short cut you suggested, and walk across the ice. It is by far the most direct route back to Tilstone, and considerably quicker than going by road."

So saying, Major Yates retired to his room to change out of his outdoor clothing. However, I could see that Holmes was far from satisfied with his host's explanation. "Come, Watson," said he. "It is still light. Let us see if Major Yates was telling the truth."

Somewhat puzzled by my friend's words, I followed him straight out again into the icy Buckinghamshire air. As I have mentioned before, the drive-way that leads from the front of Tilstone Court curves round back behind the house and away from the river. Pausing at the point where the drive turned and the lawn down to the river began, Sherlock Holmes dropped to his haunches and examined the blanket of snow which stretched before him. Then, treading carefully, and with his eyes glancing to either side as he did so, he picked his way slowly across the snow-clad grass towards the river – or rather the backwater that ran immediately below the grounds of Tilstone Court. Next, shading his eyes with his hand, he peered across the snow-girt, ice-bound sheet of water before him towards the small, tree-covered island which lay between it and the main channel of the River Thames beyond. The elliptical form of the Round Tower of Windsor Castle towered above the trees in the distance, and to our left, we could see the bridge which carries the South Western Railway across the river from its terminus at the foot of Castle Hill.

"You can see for yourself," observed Holmes. "No one has crossed either the lawn or the river. The skaters have not come this far downstream, and the snow is undisturbed."

"Then Major Yates was lying," said I. "He must have come back to Tilstone by road, and he must have passed us, though I confess I did not see him."

"Neither did I. For some reason he must have been at pains to disguise himself. These are deep waters, Watson. However, there is nothing to be gained by standing out here freezing to death. Let us return to the house without further ado."

Once back inside Tilstone Court, Holmes and I, having deposited our coats in our bedrooms, forgathered in the landing on the first floor of the south wing. Entering the Library together, we received our second shock since returning from Windsor, for there together, deep in conversation, were Mr. William Clunies-Ross and Parkin, the gardener. They made an incongruous pair, Clunies-Ross in his immaculate garb and Parkin in his seedy, coarse-grained smock with the tincture of soil upon it. They sprang apart as we entered, and I could not help but recall Parkin's words in the Crown and Cushion, where he had intimated a sense of social inferiority to the other servants at Tilstone, let alone to its distinguished guests.

William Clunies-Ross was the first to recover his composure. "Good afternoon, Mr. Holmes and Dr. Watson," said he. "I was asking Parkin here about the Christmas decorations. He tells me they are to be put up on Christmas Eve."

"Indeed, gentlemen," stammered the gardener, flushing to the temples. "That is the custom at Tilstone Court – Major Yates's instructions. We bring in the tree and decorate the Front Hall with evergreens every 24th of December. Well, if that is all, Mr. Clunies-Ross, I'll be on my way. It's time I was doing my rounds."

Parkin looked distinctly uncomfortable, and I was unable to shake off the feeling that we had interrupted something far more significant than a mere discussion about Yule-tide embellishment. The feeling of uneasiness remained after his departure, Mr. Clunies-Ross opening a book and starting to read it with an air of ill-feigned nonchalance.

Nothing else of moment occurred until after dinner, when both Holmes and I had retired to our respective rooms for an early night. Having nodded over my novel for about forty-five minutes, I decided to give up the contest, and extinguished the candle. I fell asleep almost immediately, and had been slumbering for a couple of hours when I was awakened by a tremendous commotion. Hastily grabbing my dressing gown and cramming my feet into my bedroom slippers, I dashed out into the corridor, unsure as to where exactly the noise had come from. However, a muffled cry, followed by the sound of a door slamming and a rush of footsteps, pointed me in the right direction, and it was with a thrill of horror that I realized that the scene of the hubbub was none other than my friend's bedchamber.

In a trice I had bounded to his door, and had thrown it open. Holmes was lying on his bed with a ghastly face and a glitter of moisture on his brow. His right hand was clasped to his throat, and he was breathing stertorously, whilst his left hand clawed at a blanket that was draped about his shoulders, and cast it to the floor beside him.

"It was nothing less than attempted murder," he croaked. "Someone has tried to smother me in my sleep."

4: The Eccentric Soloist

"Were you able to ascertain the identity of your assailant?" said I, when Holmes had recovered his composure.

"Alas, no. But the man who attacked me was a young and vigorous animal. I fear, however, that he may have underestimated my own physical strength. Boxing has fitted me well for such work as I have been called upon to undertake this night."

"Could it have been the same man that I saw in the garden last night? He had been inside the house, I am sure of it."

"Quite possibly. But of one thing I am certain. Should the fellow reveal himself to us, he will be unable to disguise his guilt."

"What do you mean?"

"Simply that in the struggle my finger-nails came into contact with his cheek, and drew blood. My attacker will undoubtedly bear the visible signs of his nocturnal encounter."

Whoever he was, the aggressor had clearly disappeared into the night, and there was nothing that either Holmes or I could do about it ere day-break. Consequently, I retired to my room, and the rest of the night passed without incident.

The following morning, I pulled back the shutters to discover fat white flakes descending from a sullen sky. However, the weather had done nothing to dampen my friend's high spirits, and throughout breakfast his conversation and demeanour were marked by an unusual degree of vivacity. In contrast, our only companions at the breakfast-table, Mr. and Mrs. Randal Norton, the paying-guests, were gloomy and withdrawn. I could see that Lestrade's unexpected restraint over the question of the Penang lawyer in the wardrobe had done little to soothe Randal Norton's nerves, and no doubt these were further afflicted by the reflection that, apart from his wife, he had no real alibi for the Ayto murder.

After breakfast, ignoring the fact that it was still snowing heavily, Sherlock Holmes suggested a stroll in the garden. "Let us walk in these beautiful grounds, Watson," said he, "and give a moment or two to the immemorial elms."

A few minutes later, accordingly, wrapped in our long grey travelling-cloaks and sporting close-fitting cloth caps, we ventured once more into the blanched park-land that surrounded Tilstone Court. The traces of our previous expedition, when Holmes had sought to verify the truth of Major Yates's assertion that he had returned to the house via the frozen river, had been entirely covered over by the fresh fall of snow, and as we crossed the whitened sward to the very point where in warmer conditions it would have been lapped by the quietly flowing backwater which bounded it, a ponderous train steamed and rattled over the railway bridge which loomed above us to the east. Invigorating though our perambulation was undoubtedly proving to be, the bitterness of the weather soon prompted us to curtail our constitutional, and so we turned our faces to the biting wind and the swirling snow, and made our way back towards the gate-house.

However, before succumbing to the warmth of the Front Hall, Sherlock Holmes was keen to examine the courtyard on the other side. At first sight, this appeared to be empty, but when we turned back to face the north wall of the gate-house, we were surprised to discover that someone apart from ourselves had elected to brave the harsh weather conditions. For there, standing close to the wall, but still exposed to the driving snow and the wind, was the tall, podgy form of our host, Major Yates. It was clear that he had not yet become aware of our presence, for upon our observing him, he had not moved, but remained huddled against the gate-house wall, apparently talking to himself. There was something strangely furtive about his posture but, as we approached, he straightened and greeted us with a smile. "Good morning, gentlemen," said he. "No doubt you will think me eccentric, but I was practising my singing. I find that performing *al fresco* is beneficial to the vocal cords."

"Indeed?" replied Holmes. "You are a hardy soul, Major Yates. There are not many musicians who would brave a blizzard for the sake of their art."

"That is true, Mr. Holmes. There was a time when my predilection for open-air rehearsal got me into trouble. My neighbours in the Horseshoe Cloister, though musicians themselves, did not take kindly to my unusual habit. I have been forced to confine my practising at the Castle to purely indoor work. But here at Tilstone, where I am master, there can be no one to raise such objections. I do believe, however, that I am now nearly all sung out, and so shall return to the comfort of my front room. Perhaps you would care to join me?"

"Thank you, Major Yates. Physical exercise may be more

conducive than music to warding off the ill effects of bad weather, but there is a limit even to the efficacy of that remedy."

Sherlock Holmes and I followed Major Yates into the Front Hall, and I was on the point of removing my cloak, when Holmes addressed me in a state of suppressed excitement. "Come, Watson. There is not a moment to be lost," he cried. "I believe there is mischief afoot."

"What is it, Holmes?" I replied. "What have you seen?"

"A man running past the front window. I am sure it was Mr. Grafton Montague, the historian, and I am equally certain he was at pains not to be seen. His manner seemed to me to be sly and furtive."

Hastening through the room, and emerging at the front of the gate-house, we were just in time to see the tall figure of Grafton Montague disappearing around the corner of the house. Sherlock Holmes lost no time in following him, and together we ran along the freshly carpeted drive-way which skirted the west wing of Tilstone Court, where a line of footsteps running at a tangent across the snow showed us the direction which our quarry had taken. Following these tracks across the lawn and through a small copse, we eventually came to a sunken formal garden with a frozen pond in the middle and symmetrical beds neatly laid out all around it. At one corner of this garden was a wooden shed, and in front of it stood the impressive physical form of Mr. Grafton Montague. Sherlock Holmes and I withdrew hastily behind a snow-clad bush, and waited to see what he would do next. The historian paused awhile, and glanced anxiously all around him in an attempt to satisfy himself that he had not been followed, before raising his clenched fist and knocking imperiously at the wooden door in front of him. Almost immediately, it opened to reveal the burly figure of Sam Parkin, the gardener.

A muttered conversation then took place, which unfortunately we were too far away to hear, although this became increasingly animated, and quickly developed into a full-scale argument. However, despite their raised voices, we were still unable to make out a word of what they were saying. Sam Parkin was remonstrating with the historian, but the latter appeared resolute and implacable in his response, and eventually the gardener adopted what was evidently a more submissive attitude, and the volume of the conversation returned to its original level. At length, Sam Parkin reached into his pocket and pulled out a thick bundle of white bank-notes. These he started to count, but without waiting for him to finish, Montague grabbed the entire wad from his grasp and thrust it into his trouser pocket. For a moment, it looked as though Parkin was about to protest, but instead, with a shrug of resignation, he returned to the shed and shut the door. Meanwhile, Montague started to make his way back across the garden in the direction of the house. As he passed the bush behind which Holmes and I were concealed, I gave a gasp and grabbed my friend by the arm. "Look, Holmes," I whispered. "His face!"

Sherlock Holmes nodded. Like me he had seen that Grafton Montague's right cheek bore the scar of a recent injury, a deep, red scratch that had surely been of my friend's own infliction.

"What does this mean?" I cried. "Why would Grafton Montague want to kill you?"

"Perhaps because he murdered John Ayto, and feared that I was about to discover the truth. He certainly had the opportunity to commit the crime, assuming that his wife was covering for him."

"Then there is the curious case of Parkin, the gardener. First we see him hob-nobbing with Mr. Clunies-Ross, and now he hands over a substantial sum of money to Mr. Montague. Where would he lay his hands on so much cash, Holmes? Unless…" I had remembered the fake bank-notes discovered on the person of the dead secretary. "Perhaps they were forgeries, like those found in Ayto's wallet?"

"Well if they are, Montague will find out soon enough if he tries to bank them. Those notes of Ayto's might fool a shop-keeper but not an experienced teller. And if Montague is indeed guilty of the secretary's murder, why is it he who is extracting money from the gardener? One might expect to see Parkin taking advantage of the historian, rather than the other way around."

"Unless it was Parkin who committed the crime, and Montague who found out about it?"

"You are forgetting that Parkin could not possibly have murdered John Ayto. He was in the Crown and Cushion at the time, and has witnesses to prove it."

"Well, it is a singular business all the same. Should we now return to the house, Holmes? I confess to being a trifle chilly."

"Certainly, Watson. There is nothing to detain us here."

We retraced our steps to the gate-house entrance, and let ourselves in. There was no one in the Front Hall when we arrived, and Sherlock Holmes took immediate advantage of that fact. Quickly divesting himself of his travelling cloak and cap, he sped over to the north side of the room, and commenced a minute examination of the wall. All four walls of the Front Hall were covered in brown, worm-eaten oak panelling, so old and discoloured that it undoubtedly dated from the original building of the house. Sherlock Holmes placed his ear against one of the panels, and beat upon the wood with his clenched fist. He then repeated the exercise at intervals along the complete length of the north wall of the room, before pulling at each separate panel with his fingers in a vain attempt to dislodge it. I was at a loss to understand the reason for this curious experiment.

"What do you hope to find?" said I.

"I do not believe that any of the panels can be detached," he replied with a touch of disappointment. "However, the exercise has not been entirely devoid of interest."

Having evidently decided not to extend his investigations to the other three walls of the room, Sherlock Holmes took a seat by the crackling fire, and sat for some time with his head sunk upon his breast. Picking up his discarded cloak and cap, I hung them on the stand by the front door and did the same with my own outdoor apparel. I then joined my friend in front of the fire. We had been sitting there in silence for perhaps a quarter of an hour when we were interrupted by Henry St. John Bosco, the editor. He came clattering down the ornamental stair like a man who was half crazed. Then, spotting us in our fire-side chairs, he rushed over to Holmes and stood there palpitating with emotion.

"What a stroke of luck!" he ejaculated. "You were the very person I hoped to find. I have been robbed. My life's work has been horribly desecrated!"

"Calm yourself, Mr. St. John Bosco," said Holmes soothingly. "I take it that something has happened to your memoirs."

"The manuscript has been mutilated, Mr. Holmes. Come and see for yourself. The damage is irreparable."

We followed the unhappy writer up the stair to his room in the east wing. It was immediately obvious that he had been the victim of a determined and conscientious thief. Every drawer in the room had been opened, and the floor was littered with the crumpled remains of half-corrected galley-proofs and copy-edited articles. On the bureau in the corner of the room lay a large, cloth-bound note-book, which was open to reveal the jagged edges of the pages which had been rudely torn from its binding. Of these leaves there was no obvious sign on the carpet thereabouts, suggesting that they had been removed from the room altogether, though the fragments of paper that could be discerned amongst the ashes in the smouldering grate indicated the probability of a different fate.

Sherlock Holmes produced his magnifying-lens, and subjected the room to his usual meticulous scrutiny. "Has anything else been disturbed apart from your writing?" he enquired.

"No, Mr. Holmes," replied the distressed editor. "My valuables are all intact. But, as you can see, my work for the Miscellany has been seriously disrupted. It is the loss of my memoirs, however, that causes me the greatest distress. They are utterly destroyed. What's more, the perpetrator has warned me against re-writing them"

"Indeed. Might I beg that you would have the goodness to be more explicit."

"Here, Mr. Holmes. This paper was left on my desk next to the vandalized document."

Mr. St. John Bosco reached into his inside coat pocket, and pulled out a folded piece of paper, which he handed to Sherlock Holmes with a grimace. "I am not sure if in any case I shall have the heart to re-commence a work on which I have already expended so much time and effort," said he sadly.

Sherlock Holmes examined the proffered sheet with his powerful lens. "The paper is inexpensive stationery of the sort found in any common or garden high street shop," said he. "You will observe that the lettering has been snipped from a newspaper with short-bladed nail-scissors, and pasted in place with gum. The newspaper in question was undoubtedly *The*

Times: the leaded bourgeois type is quite distinctive. I would suggest therefore that if we can find the owner of a mutilated copy of *The Times*, preferably accompanied by a pair of nail-scissors, we will also have located the author of this singular document."

"But what does it *say*?" I enquired with a touch of exasperation.

"See for yourself," muttered Holmes, tossing the folded sheet in my direction.

I opened it, and read the message aloud. "'as You value Your life write about It no more'. It seems clear enough," said I. "The question is why is the person who went to the not inconsiderable trouble of compiling this curious notice so desirous of preventing you from completing your autobiography?"

"Quite so," said Holmes. "Were you perhaps planning to reveal some intelligence which would cause embarrassment or even injury to a person or persons connected with your past life?"

"Not knowingly, Mr. Holmes. My memoirs were merely the reminiscences of a successful writer and editor who has also travelled widely in the pursuit of his profession. But perhaps after all I will not so easily be discouraged from my ambition."

A look of defiance sprang to the writer's face, and he clenched his fists.

"Have you yourself any idea as to who might have destroyed your property and threatened you in this manner?" enquired Holmes with a fleeting smile of commiseration.

"Before this I truly believed I had not an enemy in the world, Mr. Holmes. But there is one whom this morning's incident has led me to regard with suspicion, although I cannot for the life of me imagine what it is that he has against me."

"Of whom are you talking?"

"Of Mr. William Clunies-Ross, the old Etonian. I came across him outside my room immediately before I discovered the damage to its interior. He told me he was looking for Mr. Montague. Something to do with a book about the history of Windsor and Eton by an old school friend of his which he had promised to lend to the historian. I remember thinking it odd at the time because Montague's room is in the west wing, like Clunies-Ross's own."

"And you suspect that Mr. Clunies-Ross was himself responsible for the destruction of your manuscript?"

"I scarcely know what to think. I had never met the fellow before this week. All I know about him is that he was at Eton with Major Yates. It never occurred to me that he would have anything to do with the violation of my property. But afterwards, when I recalled his presence outside my room, and his unsatisfactory explanation as to why he was there, I began to have second thoughts."

"We must interview Mr. Clunies-Ross again, and quiz him on the matter, Mr. St. John Bosco. In the mean time, I can only commiserate with you on the loss of you life's work, and hope that you have not been entirely discouraged from undertaking a second draft."

In the event, William Clunies-Ross and his wife were not in their room, nor were they anywhere on the premises, having taken a cab into Windsor to do some Christmas shopping. As a result, Sherlock Holmes and I spent a desultory morning kicking our heels in the Front Hall, and it was nor until after luncheon that the opportunity arose for the former to interrogate Major Yates's old school-friend.

We came across Mr. and Mrs. Clunies-Ross in the Drawing Room enjoying a round or two of sandwiches and a cup of coffee. "I am afraid that we were too late for lunch," explained Mrs. Clunies-Ross. "But cook very kindly prepared these for us. Would you care for one?"

"No, I thank you. We have already eaten," replied Holmes. "Mr. Clunies-Ross, I was talking to Mr. St. John Bosco, the Editor, this morning. It appears that he has been the victim of a most unfortunate crime."

"Yes, I heard about that. His room was ransacked, and the manuscript of his autobiography destroyed. Very distressing for the poor chap, I am sure."

"I understand that you were seen by Mr. St. John Bosco in the vicinity of his bedroom shortly before he discovered his loss."

"Indeed I was, Mr. Holmes. I was trying to find Mr. Montague, the historian. As you know, he is most interested in this area of the country, and an old friend of mine – a former colleague at Eton College, in fact – has written a book about it. I mentioned this to Montague at supper last night, and he expressed a desire to read the volume, so when I discovered it amongst my effects this morning, I thought I would take it to him forthwith. Unfortunately, I was under the impression that his room was in the east wing, where, as you may know, several of the guest rooms are located. In fact, had I but known it, his sleeping-quarters are only two doors away from my own. Well, I had got as far as the bedrooms in the east wing, and was about to knock on the door of what I believed to be Mr. Montague's chamber, when Mr. St. John Bosco appeared, and I realized my mistake. I had no idea that the room had been vandalized or I would have commiserated with him. We were colleagues at university, you know."

"According to Mr. St. John Bosco, he had never seen you before his arrival at Tilstone Court."

For a moment, William Clunies-Ross was taken aback. But

he recovered quickly.

"When I said we were colleagues, I meant that we were both at Oxford at the same time. However, St. John Bosco was much older than I, and a tutor rather than a student. What's more, we attended different colleges, so I suppose it is possible that he did not know me. I was certainly aware of his existence, but perhaps it is stretching a point to say that we were friends."

"Thank you, Mr. Clunies-Ross. I will leave you to the remainder of your luncheon. I confess I have myself a slight head-ache, and would benefit from another turn in the grounds, especially now that it has finally stopped snowing."

I declined Sherlock Holmes's invitation to join him, and returned to my room, where I put in a useful hour or so reviewing the singular developments of the past few days. Who had killed John Ayto? Apparently Major Yates, Mr. and Mrs. Clunies-Ross and Sam Parkin were to be discounted, as they were not on the premises when the murder took place. But what was behind the apparent intimacy between Clunies-Ross and the gardener, and what had the old Etonian been doing near St. John Bosco's bedroom around the time that it had been vandalized? Of those who could have committed the crime, perhaps the most suspicious was Mr. Montague, the historian. It seemed likely that it had been he who had attacked Holmes in his bed. But why had he been extracting money from Parkin, the gardener, and, for that matter, whence had Parkin obtained the cash to pay him? Then there were the paying-guests, Mr. and Mrs. Randal Norton. Lestrade had concluded that finding the murder weapon in such an obvious place as their wardrobe was proof of their innocence. But what if they had panicked after committing the crime, and had simply concealed the stick in the first place that came to hand? Or, alternatively, what if they were playing a game of double-bluff, assuming that the discovery of the blood-stained cudgel would divert suspicion away from, rather than towards them? Of the remaining suspects, it was clear that the murder could have been committed by Mr. St. John Bosco, the Editor, or even Porson, the butler. But what motive could either have had for the crime? Finally, there was the mysterious figure in the garden at night. Apart from the altogether more corpulent Major Yates, he was taller than any of the known occupants of the house, and had undoubtedly been inside it at some point. Could it have been this unknown person who had murdered Major Yates's secretary?

The rest of the day passed without incident. However, mindful of the events of the previous two nights, on retiring to my room, I sat up for some time with a candle, listening intently for the slightest sound. Notwithstanding my determination to stay alert, I found my attention wandering, and my thoughts had turned once more to the question of the identity of John Ayto's murderer, when the noise of a furtive footfall on a creaking floorboard brought me to my senses, and I felt the hairs stand up on the back of my neck.

Pausing only to grab the dark lantern without which Holmes and I would have been powerless to undertake many of our nocturnal adventures, I crept silently out of my room, and made my way along the corridor to the chamber which was occupied by my friend. Holmes was still up when I entered, but quickly sprang to his feet, and, upon my placing a warning finger to my lips, followed me noiselessly out into the corridor. From here it was but a short step to the landing above the Front Hall, where a winding stair in the north-west angle-turret led to what is known as the Tower Room. Disappearing up this staircase was the bowed figure of an elderly man, carrying a guttering candle in one hand and what looked like a bag of some sort in the other. "Surely it is Porson, the butler," I whispered. "Indeed it is," replied Holmes. "Let us follow him."

Treading cautiously to avoid making any noise which might alert the butler to our presence, we ascended the stairs behind him, coming to a stop immediately outside the Tower Room. "Unless he has gone up on to the roof, he must still be in there," said Holmes in my ear. "We cannot risk going in. I suggest waiting for him downstairs."

We retraced our steps, and slipped into the Dining Room, where we concealed ourselves behind the door and waited for Porson to return. After a short while, the butler's shuffling footfalls could be heard descending from the tower, and we observed him passing along the landing in the direction of the east wing. In his hands, he continued to carry the candle and what we could now see was a large canvas bag. As soon as he had disappeared from view, Holmes beckoned to me, and with the aid of the dark lantern, we made our way up to the Tower Room once more.

The chamber we had entered was small and unfurnished, and like the Front Hall beneath it, was covered in brown oak panelling. Sherlock Holmes took the dark lantern from my hand, and made a cursory examination of the empty room. He then crossed to the door in the corner of the outer wall, before opening it and ascending the short flight of wooden steps which led to the roof outside. I followed him, and soon we were standing on a narrow, battlemented walk-way which looked down into the courtyard at the centre of Tilstone Court. This walk-way led directly to the top of the north-east angle-turret on our right, and I realized that, if Porson had indeed met anyone on the roof, he or she could easily have descended since by an alternative route.

"There is no one here," said Holmes with a touch of disappointment. "But that is not to say that Porson did not meet somebody, possibly he whom you observed the other night in the garden. I suggest that we return hither in the day-light, when we may hope to find some tangible clue as to that person's identity."

5: Christmas Eve

The next morning Lestrade came up to the Court, eager to be brought up to date with the latest developments. He listened to Sherlock Holmes's account of the previous day's incidents with the keenest interest, before announcing: "I have been turning the case over in my mind, Mr. Holmes, and I am not now so certain of Mr. and Mrs. Norton's innocence. It may seem inconceivable to you or me that anyone could be so bone-headed as to commit a murder and then hide the murder-weapon in their own bedroom, but there is no accounting for the recklessness of the desperate man – or woman. I believe I should like to interview Mr. Randal Norton again."

As Holmes had no objection to Lestrade's suggested course of action, we made our way up the ornamental stair from the Front Hall, and headed for the east wing, where Mr. and Mrs. Norton's bedroom was located. However, on our arrival, the paying-guests were nowhere to be seen, and we were about to retrace our steps, when Lestrade declared his intention of searching their room. "If they were so foolish as to incriminate themselves once, might we not find fresh evidence to cast suspicion at their door?" said he with a look of grim determination, as he entered the comfortable chamber in which Mr. and Mrs. Norton had been accommodated for their sojourn at Tilstone Court.

It was a homely little room, with a low ceiling and a gaping fireplace, after the fashion of old country houses. In one corner was the wardrobe in which I assumed the bloodstained Penang lawyer had been discovered. Lestrade immediately strode over to this cupboard, and flung open the doors, before rummaging around in its interior. "The stick was on the floor covered by a piece of cloth," he remarked, turning away with a grunt of disappointment. "But there is nothing here now."

Sherlock Holmes meanwhile had begun to open a chest of drawers which stood next to the bed. The next moment he uttered a cry of triumph, and turned to us with the remains of a newspaper clutched in his right hand. "I believe we have found the copy of *The Times* from which was clipped that singular warning to Mr. St. John Bosco," said he. "See for yourself."

He tossed the mutilated newspaper to me. It had been folded so that the leader was face forward, and I could see clearly that a number of words had been removed from that article with a pair of scissors. "This, if I am not mistaken, my dear Watson, is the very implement with which the deed was done," said Holmes, pulling a pair of short-bladed nail-scissors from the same drawer of the chest from which he had recovered the newspaper.

"And could this be the gum with which the lettering was affixed to the paper?" added Lestrade, who had turned his attention to the contents of a suit-case which had been placed atop the wardrobe.

"One for you, Lestrade," said Sherlock Holmes. "The evidence would seem to be mounting against Mr. and Mrs.

Randal Norton, the paying-guests. Yet it is still all circumstantial."

"None the less, I should very much like to question them on this latest discovery," commented Lestrade grimly.

At this juncture, the very people of whom we had been talking came into the room. They seemed more surprised than shocked to find us there and puzzled rather than alarmed by the objects which we had found in their room.

"I had not expected to find you gentlemen in my bedroom," exclaimed Randal Norton with a suggestion of irritation in his voice.

"Obviously not," replied Lestrade sternly. "Can you explain the presence of this spoiled newspaper in your chest of drawers? We believe it to be the source of a threatening message to Mr. Henry St. John Bosco."

"I have never seen it before," said Mr. Randal Norton. "If it was found among my possessions, I can only assume it was placed there by the same hand that planted the murder weapon in my wardrobe."

"You deny, then, that you were responsible for stealing and destroying Mr. St. John Bosco's memoirs?"

"I do. I have never so much as set foot in his room, even though it is but three doors away from my own. And I have certainly not threatened him in any way. There is a conspiracy against me, and the sooner I leave this accursed house the better."

"I am afraid we cannot allow you to do that," said Sherlock Holmes. "But you can rest assured that we will get to the bottom of this business, and that, if indeed you are innocent, then no harm will befall you."

"That is all very well, Mr. Holmes. But can you guarantee that I will not be arrested on the basis of the evidence that appears to be piling up against me?"

"No, I cannot, Mr. Norton. But I can promise you that personally I do not suspect you of any crime, and that I will caution Mr. Lestrade against any rash move to take you into custody. The evidence of which you speak is purely circumstantial, and there are others whom I believe are more deserving of our suspicion than yourself. In that connection, Lestrade, I shall be glad if you will join me in seeking out our friend Mr. William Clunies-Ross, the old Etonian. I wish to interview him further."

"You cannot suspect him, Mr. Holmes. He was at Windsor Castle at the time of the murder."

"I want to interview him about another of Tilstone Court's guests, Lestrade. I refer to Mr. Grafton Montague, the historian. He had every opportunity to kill John Ayto, and it was he, I believe, who attacked me in my room the night before last."

Mr. William Clunies-Ross was in the Little Drawing Room when we caught up with him. He seemed surprised that Holmes wished to question him again so soon after his previous interview. "I thought I had explained that mix-up over St. John Bosco's room," said he. "It was a simple enough mistake. I told you, I was looking for Montague."

"It is about Mr. Montague that I wish to quiz you," explained Holmes. "When you talked with him the previous evening and mentioned the book about Windsor and Eton, did you notice if he had a scratch on his face?"

"No, he did not. But when I finally caught up with him to give him the book late yesterday afternoon, I noticed the mark to which you refer. Upon my enquiring if he had met with an accident, he explained that the abrasion had been acquired just before he had retired to bed. He had stumbled in his bedroom, and in her attempt to break his fall, Mrs. Montague had flung out her arms to support him, accidentally scratching his face in the process."

"On the night of John Ayto's murder, while you were waiting in the Front Hall for the police to arrive, did you notice anything unusual about Grafton Montague's behaviour?"

"Only that he was the last person to come down after Porson had raised the alarm. Mrs. Montague arrived almost immediately, so perhaps she was already dressed, and Mr. Montague had to change out of his night-attire."

"I observe that you are friendly with Sam Parkin, the gardener: you were conversing with him the day before last in the Library when Watson and I returned from Windsor."

"I had met him on my way in from the garden, and, merely out of politeness, engaged him in conversation about the first topic that entered my head. That, as you may remember, was the question of the Christmas decorations which are to be carried out to-night in the Front Hall."

"Be that as it may, Mr. Clunies-Ross, can you explain why Sam Parkin should pay money to Mr. Montague?"

"This is the first I have heard of such a thing. What money? When?"

"Parkin was observed handing over a substantial amount of cash to Grafton Montague in the garden yesterday morning."

"But Parkin has no money. What little he earns, by all accounts, he squanders in the Crown and Cushion. I am sorry, Mr. Holmes, but I cannot explain it."

"Thank you, Mr. Clunies-Ross. Unless Lestrade has any further questions, that will be all for the time being. I believe it is time to return to the Tower Room and see if any light can be thrown on our recent nocturnal adventures. Come, Watson, Lestrade. It is only a short step."

We crossed the landing above the Front Hall, and ascended

the winding stair in the north-west angle-turret to the Tower Room. Producing his powerful magnifying lens, Sherlock Holmes dropped to the floor, and searched for any clues which might explain the butler's curious expedition of the previous night. "The floor seems to have been brushed recently," said he with disgust. "There are no traces even of our own footprints, let alone those of Porson or of anyone he may have met."

Opening the door in the corner of the room, Sherlock Holmes then climbed the steps to the walk-way on the roof outside, and subjected this to a similar scrutiny. Slowly he made his way along to the north-east angle-turret, where, having descended the wooden steps which matched those leading from the north-west turret, he paused at the door which led to the twin of the Tower Room. On attempting to open this door, however, Holmes discovered that it was locked, and so he returned to the room in which Lestrade and I were waiting, and together we descended once more to the landing. The stair-way at the eastern end was identical to that which led to the north-west turret, and we were soon in the second Tower Room, which, like the first, was empty and had recently been scrubbed clean. "Tut! Tut!" muttered Holmes with chagrin. "It seems we are none the wiser. The question remains: why did Porson climb the tower in the middle of the night? Did he have an assignation with some person who returned to his or her room via this second tower room? The outer door is locked now, but was that the case last night? Or was Porson's object perhaps to signal to someone from the roof? I would give five shillings to discover the contents of that canvas bag of his."

Shortly after our abortive expedition to the upper extremities of Tilstone Court, Lestrade returned to Windsor Police Station, and the remainder of the day passed without further incident. It being Christmas Eve, however, the Front

Hall was a hive of activity once the sun had set and preparations for the Yule-tide festivities had begun. Parkin had brought in many bundles of evergreens, and was engaged in decking the walls with the shining branches. A great yule block had been kindled in the hearth and was soon burning hotly and odorously, the ivy, holly and rosemary flashing and flickering in the blaze. Meanwhile, in one corner of the hall, a young fir, about eight feet high, had been set up, and was being decorated by the two maids: on each tier of branches they had arranged a dozen wax tapers, which had been lit, with the result that the whole tree sparkled and glittered with bright objects. For pendant from its branches were elegant trays, baskets, *bonbonnières* and other receptacles for sweetmeats. Fancy cakes, gilt gingerbread and eggs filled with sweetmeats were also being suspended by variously coloured ribbons from the branches, whilst on the summit of the tree stood the small figure of an angel with outstretched wings. While all the work of decoration was going on, the cook was arranging plates of mince-pies on the big oak table, and Major Yates was stirring a huge bowl of wassail – native ale, heightened in its flavour by Eastern spices and hissing with a wealth of roasted apples. There was also a bowl of reeking punch, a caste of mulled wine and a large serving-plate on which had been placed a rich and delicious-looking plum-cake. Finally, at about eight o'clock, the waits arrived and commenced to sing their carols outside the gate-house. Porson opened the front door to reveal a group of about half a dozen well-gloved songsters – two or three of them with lanterns – and a couple of instrumentalists, who were struggling to keep warm in the steadily falling snow. After they had completed their first carol, Major Yates invited them in, and they shuffled into the great entrance-hall with a stamping of feet and a flurry of snowflakes, before helping themselves to the odoriferous wassail and the mouth-watering mince-pies.

When they had left, Major Yates invited Parkin and the servants to join him in a toast, and we all raised glasses of steaming punch to the success of the festive decorations. The plum-cake had been cut, and a fresh supply of hot mince-pies brought up from the kitchen, when a sudden loud report from upstairs jerked us from the heady effects of our Yule-tide celebrations.

"Great scott!" ejaculated Major Yates. "That sounded like a gun being fired."

Without a moment's hesitation, Sherlock Holmes slammed his glass down on the table, and set off up the ornamantel stair which led up from the Front Hall. I followed him, and was quickly joined by Major Yates, Parkin, the gardener, and Porson, the butler. As we quitted the room, the cook was having hysterics in front of the fire, whilst the two maids fanned her assiduously with the tea-cloths they had used to convey the trays of hot mince-pies from the kitchen.

On the first floor, we observed Mr. William Clunies-Ross, about to enter the Drawing Room, which, like the Dining Room and the Library, opened out of the landing at the top of the staircase. Apart from the small cupboard outside the Library, and the few portraits and landscapes which adorned the walls, the only other features of the landing were the winding stairs in the two angle-turrets at either end, and the passage-ways which led respectively into the west and east wings of the house.

"The shot came from one of the rooms, I am sure of it," exclaimed Clunies-Ross. "I was returning from my bedroom in the west wing when I heard it. I looked in the Dining Room, but it was empty. Now let us try the second room."

Together we entered the Drawing Room, which was brilliantly lit, and which also appeared empty at first sight.

However, almost immediately our eyes were drawn to a large shape lying in the far left-hand corner of the room, partially obscured by a richly upholstered arm-chair.

Sherlock Holmes beckoned to me, and together we pushed the chair out of the way, to reveal the lifeless body of a tall, bald man of about 60.

"St. John Bosco!" I vociferated.

The dead editor was lying face-up, with an expression of absolute horror frozen on his ashy features. In the middle of his forehead, a small, round, red hole showed where the bullet had passed into his head, which lay in an ever increasing pool of blood, indicating the freshness of the mortal wound. In an instant, Holmes had whipped out his lens, and was examining the body and its surroundings with his customary thoroughness. "Shot with a revolver from a distance of about two feet," said he at last. "But no sign of the weapon."

Suddenly he spun round on his heel, and looked William Clunies-Ross full in the face. "Where is Mr. Grafton Montague?" cried he with a note of urgency.

"He was with me earlier," replied the old Etonian. "As were our wives. We were all four next door in the Library. My wife and I left them there some minutes ago to return to our bedroom."

"And where is your wife now?"

"Still in our bedroom, I suppose."

"Let us see if we can find the Montagues. If you would be good enough to wait here, Watson and I will take a look next door."

Leaving Major Yates, Mr. Clunies-Ross, Porson and Parkin in the Drawing Room, we hastened out on to the landing, and turned left towards the Library. On entering this room, however, we found only one member of the couple for whom we were searching. Cowering on the sofa was the golden-haired, blue-eyed figure of Mrs. Celia Montague, her young face blanched with terror. "I heard the report," said she with a quaver in her soft voice. "But I was too frightened to come out. If only Grafton had been here…"

"I understood from Mr. Clunies-Ross that your husband was present until recently," said Sherlock Holmes. "May I ask what has become of him?"

"He was indeed here, Mr. Holmes. But shortly after Mr. and Mrs. Clunies-Ross retired to their room, he heard the sound of the waits in the Front Hall, and resolved to join the party downstairs. I was engrossed in my book, and so decided to stay where I was."

"I can tell you, Mrs. Montague, that your husband never arrived in the Front Hall. Watson and I have been down there all evening, together with Major Yates and the servants. However, it is imperative that we find Mr. Montague as soon as possible, in order to rule him out of our inquiries. That report which you heard, Mrs. Montague, was the sound of a revolver being fired in the Drawing Room next door. Mr. Henry St. John Bosco, the editor, has been shot dead."

Mrs. Celia Montague clapped her hand to her mouth, and uttered a wordless cry of horror. "But why should you suspect Grafton?" said she.

"Nobody is above suspicion at this time," replied Sherlock Holmes sternly. "Do you think that he may have returned to his bedroom?"

"It is possible, I suppose."

"And where, pray, is that room located?"

"In the west wing, two doors away from the chamber which is occupied by Mr. and Mrs. Clunies-Ross. Come, I will show you."

Mrs. Montague led us out of the Library, and along the landing, past the Drawing Room – where Major Yates, Mr. Clunies-Ross, Porson and Parkin were waiting with the body of the unfortunate editor – past the Dining Room and the stair in the north-west angle-turret, and on to the west wing. Having passed the Little Drawing Room, we soon arrived at the bedrooms, outside the door of one of which Mrs. Montague came to a halt. "This is our room," said she, leading us into a plainly furnished little chamber with a grey carpet.

Against one wall was a tall wardrobe, on top of which were piled two or three suit-cases, while in the window, there was a large dressing-table with a mirror. But what attracted our attention was the great four-poster bed which dominated, and indeed practically filled, the diminutive room in which the Montagues had been accommodated. For lying on its coverlet was a revolver.

"What do you make of this, my dear Watson?" enquired Holmes, handing me the weapon with a muffled cry of satisfaction.

"An Eley's No. 2 with one discharged chamber," I replied. "It should be a comparatively easy matter to establish whether or not this was the weapon used to kill Mr. St. John Bosco."

Mrs. Montague looked aghast, but said nothing.

"I am afraid things look very black against your husband," observed Sherlock Holmes gravely. "Is this his gun?"

"I b...believe it is, Mr. Holmes. But why would Grafton want to kill Mr. St. John Bosco? Somebody must have stolen it."

"None the less you do not deny that the revolver belongs to Mr. Montague?"

"No. But he kept it in his suit-case. Surely if he was the murderer, he would have at least tried to conceal it?"

"Perhaps he did not have time to do so. When we eventually catch up with Mr. Grafton Montague, no doubt he will be able to shed some light on the matter. In the mean time, Mrs. Montague, can you tell me which bedroom is occupied by Mr. and Mrs. Clunies-Ross?"

"Yes, Mr. Holmes. It is the next but one down the corridor from here."

Holmes exited the scene of our dramatic discovery, and made his way quickly to the room in question, where he paused and knocked on the closed door. Receiving no response, however, he pushed it open and went in, with me following closely behind him. The bedroom was empty.

"Strange," muttered Holmes with a puzzled expression. "I understood from Mr. Clunies-Ross that he and his wife had both returned to their room. We know that Mr. Clunies-Ross came back to the south wing – though he has not yet explained why he did so – but his wife, surely, should still be here?"

Sherlock Holmes returned to the corridor, and addressed Mrs. Montague, who was waiting for him outside her room. "Come, Mrs. Montague," said he briskly. "We must join the others at the scene of the crime, and see if your husband has yet made an appearance."

Back in the Drawing Room, however, there was still no sign of Grafton Montague. Nor were the Nortons or Mrs. Clunies-Ross anywhere to be seen.

"In view of our discovery in Mr. Montague's bedroom, perhaps I should examine the body?" I suggested, placing the revolver in my coat pocket.

"Indeed, Watson," replied Holmes. "I suppose there is no doubt that Mr. Grafton Montague's gun was the murder weapon?"

In order to facilitate my inquiry, I had moved the arm-chair which had originally partially obscured the body further into the centre of the room, and as I did so, I noticed a small object glinting on the carpet. "This was under the chair," said I, picking it up and handing it to Sherlock Holmes.

"A waist-coat button," observed Holmes. "This may or may not be germane to the case, but more likely than not it has lain amongst the fluff and dust for months. The button is evidently from a waist-coat of the highest quality, however. I shall retain it for future reference."

Sherlock Holmes popped the dainty accoutrement into his own handsome coat pocket, and addressed the assembled company with a note of authority.

"Has anything been heard of the whereabouts of Mr. and Mrs. Randal Norton, the paying-guests?" said he.

"I believe they are in their room, Mr. Holmes," volunteered Mrs. Montague. "After supper this evening, when the rest of us withdrew to the Library, they expressed their intention of taking an early night."

"Perhaps you would be so good as to fetch them, Porson?" requested Sherlock Holmes, at which the butler gave a bow of assent, and departed the room.

I, in the mean time, had been studying the corpse of the unhappy editor. "It will require an officially approved surgeon to remove the bullet from his skull," said I. "But I am satisfied that the hole in the forehead of the deceased is exactly commensurate with the calibre of a bullet fired from an Eley's No. 2. I would say that Mr. Montague's gun was almost certainly the weapon used."

As if on cue, the owner of the revolver suddenly walked into the room, his bland expression immediately giving way to surprise and then horror, as he registered the disturbing contents of the room into which he had strolled. I could not help noticing again the livid, red weal on his cheek.

"Celia, my dear!" exclaimed Grafton Montague, solicitously hastening towards his fair wife. "What has been happening here? Has St. John Bosco met with an accident?"

"Mr. St. John Bosco has been murdered," said Sherlock Holmes gravely. "And with your gun, Mr. Montague. Might I enquire where you have been all this time?"

"Certainly, Mr. Holmes. There is no mystery about it. My wife may have told you that when I heard the carol-singers in the Front Hall, I expressed a desire to go down and join in the festivities. However, no sooner had I left the room than I heard a noise which appeared to be coming from the north-west tower room. It sounded like a door being opened, and as I believed the room in question to be empty, I was intrigued, and could not resist climbing the stair to investigate. There was no one in the room, but while I was up there, I went out on to the roof, and lost all sense of time. At one point, I even believed I was locked out."

"You did not hear the shot, then?"

"No. I was probably on the walk-way at the top of the house when it was fired."

At this point, Porson returned with the paying-guests. Mr. and Mrs. Norton appeared deeply disturbed by the tragic turn of events.

"I hope you do not think we had anything to do with this horrible affair," said Mrs. Norton nervously. "We have been in our bedroom all along."

"Is there anyone who can corroborate that fact?" enquired Holmes with a keen glance.

"I am afraid not," replied Mr. Norton. "We have been quite alone. However, Porson tells me you have the murder weapon."

"We do indeed, Mr. Norton, and this time it does not belong

to you. Nor does there appear to be anything to connect you with it. Did you hear the report?"

"No, Mr. Holmes. Our bedroom is some way away in the east wing of the house, and we had our door shut."

Mrs. Clunies-Ross then came into the room. She was dressed in a richly embroidered dressing-gown of the finest silk, and her clear-cut face was pale and agitated. "William, darling," said she, addressing her husband with a tremulous voice. "What has been going on? When you did not return, I began to worry that something was afoot, and now I see that poor Mr. St. John Bosco has met with a grave misfortune."

"It is murder, no less, my dear," replied William Clunies-Ross, placing his arm protectively around his wife's shoulders. "The question is what are we to do now?"

"As we are all present at last," said Sherlock Holmes decisively, "I think perhaps that we might send for Mr. Lestrade. He will need to be notified of the murder, and will undoubtedly wish to interrogate everyone concerned. Parkin, I wonder if you would be so good as to fetch the Scotland Yard inspector. If I am not mistaken, you will find him at Windsor Police Station."

6: The Face at the Window

By the time Parkin had returned to the Court with Lestrade, everybody had repaired to the Front Hall, the presence of St. John Bosco's corpse having proved both too disturbing and too distasteful, especially for the ladies. Following Sherlock Holmes's detailed account of the evening's events, the inspector was thus free to examine the body on his own. "You say you have found the murder weapon, Mr. Holmes?" said he. "Is that it?"

Holmes had produced the Eley's No. 2 from his jacket pocket.

"The bullet will need to be extracted from the victim's forehead," said I. "But there seems no doubt that it was fired from this gun, which was discovered in Mr. Grafton Montague's bedroom, and which, by his wife's admission, belongs to her husband."

"If it was indeed Montague who shot Henry St. John Bosco, then he must have been a very cool customer," observed Lestrade grimly. "How was he to know that the sound of the gun suddenly being discharged would not bring the other guests running into the room to catch him red-handed?"

"I have been considering that point," replied Sherlock Holmes. "You will notice that the Drawing Room has a connecting door to the Dining Room but not to the Library on the other side. If the murderer had satisfied him or herself that the Dining Room was empty, then he or she could easily have made their escape by that route. We also discovered this button under the arm-chair by the body," he added, handing the shiny object to the police inspector. "It may not be relevant to the case, of course."

"A police doctor will be along to examine the body shortly," explained Lestrade. "In the meanwhile, I should like to interview all persons on the premises, including the servants."

We descended the stair-case to the Front Hall, where guests and staff alike were huddled together in front of the blazing yule-fire, surrounded by the remains of the festive food and drink.

"I think we will start with the butler," said Lestrade, inviting Porson to join him at the big oak table, which bore the half-empty wassail-bowl and what was left of the plum-cake.

"Porson, are you able to account for your movements this evening?" enquired the Scotland Yard inspector cordially.

"I have been down in the hall supervising the arrangements," relpied the butler. "I am sure that Major Yates – and indeed Mr. Holmes himself – can corroborate this. I may have left the room to assist cook with the comestibles, but otherwise I was here all the time."

"I presume the food and drink were fetched from the kitchen?"

"Yes, sir. In the basement."

"And neither you nor the other servants detected anything

unusual during the course of this activity?"

"We did not. We certainly had no occasion to go upstairs where the murder took place."

"I can vouch for the servants, Lestrade," said Sherlock Holmes. "They never left the hall except to visit the kitchen. Indeed, the maids were fully occupied with dressing the Christmas tree. I am interested to know, however, what it was that Porson was doing in the tower last night. The room at the top was empty, and yet he was observed entering it with a canvas bag."

"There is no secret about that, sir," replied the butler, it seemed to me with a touch of nervousness. "I was doing my late-night round. I check all parts of Tilstone Court to make sure that they are secure and that nothing is amiss."

"And the canvas bag?"

"Merely contained the keys to various doors around the house and a few spare candles."

"Your movements could reasonably be described as furtive."

"It was late at night, and I did not wish to awaken any of the guests. I was at pains to make as little noise as possible."

The cook and the maids confirmed Porson's – and Holmes's – account of their activities, and could add nothing material to the evidence which Lestrade was seeking to compile. The inspector then called over Sam Parkin to deliver his statement.

"I was hanging up the decorations all evening," said the gardener. "Then the waits came in, and we all stopped for some refreshment. The shot went off while we were eating and drinking."

"Pardon me for interrupting," said Sherlock Holmes with a steely glance at the thick-set man in front of him. "But the other morning you were seen handing over a substantial amount of money to Mr. Grafton Montague, the historian. May I ask why you did this, and where you obtained so much cash in the first place? I do not believe you can have earned it."

Sam Parkin looked at my friend with an unblinking gaze. "I can see that nothing gets past you, Mr. Holmes. Well, I suppose it had to come out sooner or later. The truth is I used to be employed by Mr. Montague's father."

"As his gardener?"

"As his under-gardener. He had a large etstate in Northamptonshire. My twin weaknesses have always been drinking and gambling – not that either of these vices has ever affected my work, you understand. The elder Mr. Montague valued my scrvices highly – very highly indeed. Alas, my constant gambling landed me heavily in debt. So much so, in fact, that I became desperately impecunious, and my very life was threatened by the money-lenders. The situation became so dire that I was forced to resort to stealing from my employer in order to keep my head above water. Worse still, I was actually on the point of extracting the money from Mr. Montague's safe, when my master came into the room, and caught me red-handed. 'You blackguard!' he exclaimed. 'Is this how you serve me for the trust I have bestowed upon you? Now you will pay for your wickedness. The police must be summoned directly!' I did not wait for him to act upon his words, but, seizing a statuette from the mantelpiece, I struck him a fearful blow on the head, which sent him reeling to the floor. Then, taking the proceeds of my crime with me, I fled the house. As to remain in the neighbourhood was now forbidden me, I saw no reason to pay off my debt, but kept the money, and used some of it to sustain me whilst I established a new life for myself in Buckinghamshire. My undoubted skills in horticulture helped me to obtain a new billet soon enough, and a good one at that.

Here I have remained for several years, unmolested by my former employer, and, whilst it may seem that I squander all my lucre, I have had a fair run of luck with the horses of late, and the money I stole from Mr. Montague has actually grown rather than dwindled. Imagine my shock, however, when Mr. Montague's son turned up on the premises, having befriended my new master while he was on holiday in the Lake District. Of course, I expected Mr. Grafton Montague to expose me immediately. He was only a young lad when I worked for his father, but I could see straightaway that he recognized me as the man who had both robbed and injured his beloved parent. But it seems he had some compassion after all, for he assured me that if I returned the money I had taken, he would keep mum about the crime I had committed all those years ago. He saw that I was now living a respectable life, and that my misdemeanour, whilst unpardonable, had clearly been only a solitary lapse. What you observed the other morning in the garden, Mr. Holmes, was Mr. Montague exacting his dues. I wasn't happy at first, because Mr. Montague seemed to think I owed him interest. I argued with him, and believed we had come to some sort of compromise, but when I started to count out the amount I thought we had agreed, he made a grab for the cash. For a moment, the pulses on my temples beat like sledgehammers, and I believe I would have attacked him just as I did his father, but then reason returned to me. I realized that, if he wished, Mr. Grafton Montague could easily have me arrested for assault and burglary, and that, after all, he was entitled to some sort of compensation for the forbearance he was showing toward me. So I let it pass. That is the complete explanation of what you witnessed."

"I am obliged to you for your candour, Parkin," said Sherlock Holmes with a quick smile. "And since the money has now been restored to the family from which it was taken, I do not believe any further action against you needs to be taken. Whom do you wish to interview next, Lestrade?"

The inspector opted to interrogate Major Yates, the master of Tilstone Court. Our plump host had become somewhat flustered by the recent turn of events, his florid face appearing even more rubicund than usual. "I do not believe I can shed any light on the matter," said he. "I observed the servants coming and going, but so far as I could see, nobody ascended to the first floor. I spent most of my time organizing the beverages. It is my custom always to stir the wassail-bowl on Chrsitmas Eve. I also mix the punch, and make sure the mulled wine is coming along nicely."

"Apart from Porson and the cook – to go to the kitchen – did anyone leave the Front Hall at all?" enquired Lestrade.

"I am certain they did not."

"Not Parkin, for instance?"

"No. He spent the whole evening hanging up the decorations."

"Are you aware that your guest, Mr. Grafton Montague, is acquainted with Parkin: indeed, that his father once employed him?"

"I did not know that."

"It seems that Parkin not only worked for Montague's father, but that, having incurred debts which he was unable to pay, he attacked and robbed his master before fleeing the area. When you employed him, he was in point of fact a fugitive from justice."

"If I had known that, I would most certainly not have given him a billet. All I can say is that, since he has come here, apart from his tendency to drink rather too much at times, his conduct has been exemplary. He has been an excellent gardener, and, so far as I know, an honest one."

"Thank you, Major Yates. I do not believe I have any further questions. Perhaps you would be so good as to ask Mr. and Mrs. William Clunies-Ross to come over to the table?"

The handsome couple seemed composed and unruffled. "How may we help you, Mr. Lestrade?" said Clunies-Ross ingratiatingly. "My wife and I have been deeply saddened by St. John Bosco's demise. I shall ever regard him as an old university colleague, even though we were never intimately acquainted."

"I understand that you and your wife withdrew to the Library after supper this evening?"

"That is correct. With Mr. and Mrs. Montague. The Nortons went straight to their bed, I believe."

"But you were not in the Library at the time the shot was fired?"

"No. My wife and I had gone back to our room by then."

"Yet I believe you were returning to the south wing when you heard the report?"

"Yes. When I reached my bedroom, I found that I had left my book in the Library. I was returning to fetch it when the gun went off."

"Where exactly were you at this point?"

"I had just turned the corner into the south wing. I was passing the stair in the north-west angle-turret. I knew that the sound had come from one of the three rooms which open out of the landing, so as soon as I reached the Dining Room I looked in there first. But it was empty and in darkness."

"You are sure that it was empty, even though it was unlit?" interpolated Holmes.

"As certain as I can be. If there was somebody in there, they must have been hiding behind an arm-chair or something."

"And what did you do next?" enquired Lestrade.

"Well, I was about to enter the next room – the Drawing Room, where it turned out the murder had been committed – when Major Yates and the others came rushing up from the Front Hall. The rest you know."

"I observe that there is a button missing from your waistcoat, Mr. Clunies-Ross," said Sherlock Holmes quietly. "Is this perchance the fastening you have mislaid?" He produced the shiny object which I had found under the arm-chair next to the body, and handed it to the surprised old Etonian.

"Yes, Mr. Holmes. This is mine all right. I had no idea I had lost it. Where was it discovered?"

"Under the arm-chair next to the body of Mr. Henry St. John Bosco."

"I suppose it must have worked loose, and rolled under there at some time. I hope you do not believe that it implicates me in the murder, Mr. Holmes?"

"It proves nothing, Mr. Clunies-Ross. But I am surprised that you did not miss it."

"I must have lost it to-day. It was certainly in place when I dressed this morning. I am somewhat fastidious about my appearance, as you may have remarked."

"I wonder if you would be so good as to describe your movements, Mrs. Clunies-Ross?" enquired Sherlock Holmes.

"Certainly, Mr. Holmes. I left the Library at the same time as my husband, when we returned to our bedroom in the west wing. We decided that we would not go to bed until later, but would sit up for some time reading. However, as he explained, my husband discovered that he had left his book in the Library, and so went back to fetch it. I myself remained in my room."

"Then how do you explain the fact that you were absent when we came to call on you following our visit to the

Montagues' bedroom immediately after the murder?" exclaimed Sherlock Holmes jubilantly.

I thought that Mrs. Clunies-Ross was somewhat taken aback by the question, but she recovered almost immediately.

"I was absent for a few minutes, Mr. Holmes. You must have arrived while I was gone."

"And where, pray, *did* you go?"

"My husband will attest to the fact that I have been sleeping rather poorly of late, and I fancied that a night-cap would prove efficacious. Rather than put Porson to the trouble of coming to our room, only to be sent off on another errand in search of brandy, I elected to seek out the butler for myself. It was only when I reached his room in the north wing that I remembered he was in the Front Hall helping with the Christmas-tide preparations, so I helped myself to the decanter, and returned with it to my bedroom. Later, when my husband did not come back, I made my way to the south wing to see what was afoot."

"Thank you, Mrs. Clunies-Ross. You have been most helpful."

"If you have no further questions, Mr. Holmes," said Lestrade, "I should like to call Mr. and Mrs. Norton."

The little couple seemed as anxious as ever as they came over to the oak table and took their places beside Lestrade, Holmes and me.

"And where were you two at the time of the murder?" said Lestrade, glaring suspiciously at the uncomfortable pair of paying-guests.

"In our bedroom," replied Mr. Randal Norton, running a finger nervously under his collar. "We decided on an early night, and went there immediately supper was over."

"And you have no witnesses who can verify your story?"

"I am afraid not. We are not accustomed to keeping

company in our bedchamber."

"I need hardly remind you that a note which might be interpreted as a threat to Mr. St. John Bosco's life – what did it say? Let me see..." Mr. Lestrade opened his leather-covered note-book and read the message out verbatim: "'As you value your life, write about it no more.' As I say, this note was constructed using lettering that had been cut from a newspaper discovered in your bedroom. And now Mr. St. John Bosco is dead. That is highly suggestive, is it not?"

"I cannot deny that it appears to be so, Mr. Lestrade. But, as I said before, I am unable to explain how that newspaper came to be in our room. I would suggest that whoever placed it there was also Mr. St. John Bosco's killer."

"That's as may be. But can we be sure that that person was not you or your wife? Very well, Mr. and Mrs. Norton. You may go. Kindly ask Mr. and Mrs. Montague to take your place."

The tall historian and his wife now joined us at the table.

"Mr. Montague," said Lestrade. "You and Mrs. Montague repaired to the Library with Mr. and Mrs. Clunies-Ross at the conclusion of your supper. Yet by the time the body was discovered in the Drawing Room, you had disappeared. Mr. and Mrs. Clunies-Ross, so they inform me, had retired to their bedroom, and your wife remained alone in the Library. So where were you?"

"I have already explained to Mr. Holmes," said Grafton Montague impassively. "When the waits came into the Front Hall, I decided to go down and listen to them. I was feeling in a festive mood, and I knew there was good food and drink to be had down there. In fact, I was on the point of descending the stair, when I heard a noise in the north-west tower. Well, I wondered who it was, and what their business could possibly be in such a remote corner of the house. So I decided to find out."

"But there was nobody up there, I understand?"

"I was sure I had heard a door being opened, and when I reached the Tower Room, the outer door leading to the roof was indeed ajar. Even as I entered the room, I could hear footsteps on the walk-way outside, so I immediately went out myself. Just as I did so, I heard another door being closed to my right. I am positive it was the outer door of the north-east angle-turret at the far end of the walk-way, and when I went along there to try it, I found it was locked. Of course, I could see what had happened. I had surprised whoever it was that had been in the Tower Room, and they had made their escape along the walk-way and down through the angle-turret at the other end of the wing, locking the door behind them."

"I fear something very similar may have happened to us only the other night," observed Holmes gravely. "What did you do next, Mr. Montague?"

"Finding the door locked, I had no option but to retrace my steps along the walk-way and return to the north-west Tower Room," replied the historian. "Unfortunately the door had slammed shut, and I was unable to open it at first. In fact, I thought for a moment that I had been locked out. However, it was merely jammed, because I was able to free it at last by dint of main force."

"You did not hear the shot being fired?" enquired Lestrade.

"No. As I told Mr. Holmes, I must have been shut outside when the murder took place, and I heard nothing."

"And then you came back down from the angle-turret?"

"I did. And as soon as I heard the kerfuffle in the Drawing Room, I hastened thither, where I found Mr. Holmes and the others with the body of Mr. St. John Bosco."

"I gather from Parkin, the gardener, that you were acquainted with him before your arrival at Tilstone Court?"

"That is correct. He was my father's under-gardener at our estate in Northamptonshire."

"In which capacity, I am told, Parkin assaulted him and stole some money which you have since recovered?"

"Yes. But I do not wish to take the matter further. I consider that sufficient reparation has now been made."

"In fact, you extracted more cash from Mr. Parkin than he took in the first place, as the price for your continued silence. Are you aware that technically you are guilty of balckmail?"

"Perhaps so, Mr. Lestrade. The truth is that I am desperately in need of money, and the arrangement was advantageous to both of us: Parkin retained his freedom and his position; and I am enabled to meet the pressing demands of my creditors. I do not believe you have anything to gain from arresting either the gardener or me. As I say, we were both beneficiaries from the transaction."

"I suppose so, Mr. Montague. And indeed none of this is strictly germane to the present case. Is there anything further you wish to ask, Mr. Holmes?"

"I have just two more questions, Lestrade," said Holmes quietly. "First, there seems to be little doubt that Mr. Montague's gun was the murder weapon. Can he explain how it came to be on his bed shortly after Mr. St. John Bosco was found shot?"

"No, I cannot," replied the historian frankly. "I do not deny that the weapon belongs to me. But I had not set eyes upon it since packing it in my suit-case prior to travelling to Tilstone Court."

"Very good. My second question concerns that scar on your cheek. May I ask how you came by it?"

"It was a mishap in the bedroom," said Montague coolly. "I tripped over a rug on the floor, and my wife accidentally scratched my face while attempting to prevent me from falling."

"Thank you, Mr. and Mrs. Montague. Well, I believe that completes the questions, Lestrade. What do you propose to do now?"

"Wait for the police doctor to come for the body, then return to Windsor, Mr. Holmes. It is nearly mid-night after all."

"Precisely," said Major Yates. "Which means that Christmas Day is fast approaching. It may seem inappropriate given the circumstances, but I always see in Christmas Day with a glass of something seasonal. I invite you to join me in a toast."

Porson removed the silver ladle from the half-empty wassail-bowl, and began to fill several glasses with the odorous, spice-and-apple-flavoured liquid. The maids then ferried trayfuls of the brimming goblets to the assembled guests, before helping Porson and themselves to what was left.

The people gathered in the great Front Hall of Tilstone Court that night were a subdued bunch. By the table were the diminutive figures of Randal and Carolyn Norton, the paying-guests, pale and nervous in the flickering light of the Christmas-tree tapers. Next to them stood William and Rosalind Clunies-Ross, more composed than the Nortons, and resplendent in their fine clothes; to their right, the athletic form of Grafton Montague and his beautiful, golden-haired young wife, Celia; and in the background, framed by the copious branches of evergreens which he had himself hung up on the walls earlier, Parkin, the burly, ruddy-cheeked gardener, together with Porson, the butler, and the diffident figures of the cook and the two maids. Finally, in front of the fire, and flanked by Lestrade, Holmes and me, stood the portly master of the house, Major Reculver Yates. As he was in the act of raising his glass in a toast to the onset of Christmas Day, the major paused, and said: "I wonder if it is still snowing. Porson, do you remove the iron bars from the shutters, and then we can see."

The butler walked over to one of the windows on the southern side of the hall, which looked out on to the garden above the ice-bound river, and pulled back the heavy wooden shutters. But instead of a moonlit garden, what we saw, if only for the briefest of moments, was the face of a man – a man whose forehead domed out in a white curve, and whose two eyes were deeply sunken in his head. It was a clean-shaven, pale and ascetic-looking face, which slowly oscillated from side to side in a curiously reptilian fashion.

Sherlock Holmes gave a gasp, and the glass fell from his nerveless fingers. "It cannot be," said he, his voice dropping to a hoarse whisper. "Watson, we have just seen the ghost of Professor Moriarty!"

7: A Close Shave

"Quick, Holmes, we should follow him," said I urgently, hastening towards the door in my excitement.

"I fear it would be to no avail," replied Sherlock Holmes dreamily. "He will have disappeared into the night, and we should be hampered by the heavy fall of snow. No, let him go. There will be time enough to pick up the trail of Professor Moriarty in the morning."

"But I do not understand, Holmes. Surely you saw him fall to his death. Or perhaps I have been labouring under a misapprehension."

"No, Watson. I truly believed he was dead. There was a moment as we two tottered together upon the brink of the fall when I wondered if I would be the one to disappear into that boiling pit. But, as you know, I was saved by my knowledge of baritsu – the Japanese system of wrestling. I evaded his grip, and watched him as he lost his balance, and fell into the abyss. I could see the look of horror in his puckered eyes as he descended into the thick, flickering curtain of spray which hissed for ever upwards through that fearful chasm. Then he struck a rock, bounded off, and splashed into the water. It is a miracle he survived."

"Now I know why the figure I observed in the garden a few nights ago was familiar. I have never seen Professor Moriarty close up before, but I did catch a glimpse of his long form on Victoria Station when we eluded him at the start of that continental excursion which was to end in what until now I have always believed to be a fatal contest – at least for him. And I espied him again when I was hurrying back from the Reichenbach Falls to Meiringen, upon the urgent but, in the event, spurious entreaty of Peter Steiler the elder. I remember that as I neared the bottom of the descent I looked back, and saw the energetic black figure of Moriarty clearly outlined against the green behind him, as he walked rapidly along the curving path which wound over the shoulder of the hill to the fall. I now realize that that was the same figure I saw silhouetted against the moon in the garden."

"So it would seem, my dear Watson. I am not easily surprised, but I must confess that this turn of events has left me absolutely dumbfounded."

"Who would have believed that the murderer was Professor Moriarty, a man whose evil influence we all thought had been for ever obliterated from the face of the earth?"

"No, Watson. Amazed though I am to discover that the professor is still alive, I shall be even more astonished if it turns out that he has personally done away with John Ayto and Henry St. John Bosco. You do not know the man as I do. He sits immobile, like a spider at the heart of its web. He does little himself. He merely schemes. But his agents are myriad, and wonderfully organized. I believe that one of those agents is present in this house, and that it is to him or her that we must look if we are to find our murderer. But at the same time, there can be little doubt that Moriarty is the driving force behind the horrible crimes that have been committed here this Christmas."

The clock had struck half past twelve before the police doctor turned up to examine the body of the dead editor. Within a few minutes, he had extracted the bullet from the victim's skull, and verified that it had been fired from Grafton Montague's revolver – or one identical to it. Two burly police officers then removed the body from the Drawing Room, and Lestrade and the police doctor took their leave. There being nothing further that either Holmes or I could do, we retired to our beds, with Christmas morning already considerably advanced.

By eight o'clock, it had finally stopped snowing, and the grounds of Tilstone Court were shimmering brightly in a watery sun. The absence of any footprints on the freshly covered lawns, however, testified to the fact that there had been a degree of precipitation since the sighting of Moriarty shortly after midnight. Despite this, Sherlock Holmes was philosophical. "An old hand like the professor would make sure to leave a false trail in any event," said he. "So I do not believe we are much worse off for all that."

Considering the awful events of the previous night, spirits were fairly high around the breakfast table. Major Yates, in particular, seemed eager to instil a certain amount of Yule-tide warmth into the proceedings, humming snatches of Chrtismas carols as he sliced a giant ham with elaborate flourishes of his old-fashioned carving-knife. After breakfast, the major announced his intention of walking to St. George's Chapel, where he was due to fulfil his choral obligations as a lay clerk of Windsor Castle. Holmes and I immediately volunteered to accompany him, and we were joined by Mrs. Clunies-Ross, who had evidently enjoyed her previous visit to the royal chapel. She duly arrived at the front door warmly clad in a thick coat, woolly muffler and heavy boots.

It was a bracing walk into Windsor that Christmas morning. The snow was extremely deep in the grounds of Tilstone Court, and scarcely less so once we reached the main road into Eton. A row of glittering icicles hung from the archway outside Jourdelays, and Barnes Pool was the setting for a large snowman, which three or four ragged children were decorating with pieces of coal and a large, mis-shapen carrot. A few of the residents of Eton High Street had made some small attempt to clear the snow from their allotment of pavement, but in the main, our passage through the dignified town made heavy going. Divers towns-people passed us by on their way to the parish church, which stood to the east about half-way down the street, and several of these ruddy-cheeked folk nodded to us in a friendly manner, and wished us the compliments of the season. Major Yates led us across the Thames bridge and up the hill to Windsor Castle. Soon we were seated in the airy Nave of St. George's Chapel, with the sunlight streaming through the rich tints of the glass in the great West Window and casting exquisite spangles of colour on the elaborate lace-like stonework. The service progressed, punctuated with music from the choir and hymns to which the congregation were permitted to add their own, less sophisticated vocal talents. Eventually, the priest intoned the parting benediction, and, as the sound of the organ swelled to fill the whole chapel with its melodious sweetness, the choristers, each holding a silver dish containing a guttering candle decorated with a sprig of Christmas holly, processed down the Nave and out through the west door of the chapel, before descending the steps into the Horseshoe Cloister.

Mrs. Clunies-Ross rose to her feet, but was immediately

checked by Sherlock Holmes. "I know that we are invited to drinks at Major Yates's apartment," said he, "but that gentleman will need time to change out of his surplice and prepare for our arrival. Let us tarry awhile, and enjoy this magnificent organ music."

The great detective sank back into his pew with a sigh of contentment, and closed his eyes. A malefactor, observing him now in his ecstatic reverie, would no doubt have considered him an innocuous-looking adversary; but such a villain would have done so at his peril. For I knew that, however serene and imperturbable my friend might appear, his was a character capable of sudden and intense energy. Indeed, no sooner had the last chords of the organ echoed into stillness, than he sprang to his feet. "Come, Watson, Mrs. Clunies-Ross," he cried, seemingly heartily refreshed after his spiritual intermission. "I believe the major will be ready to receive us now."

Together we left the chapel via the west door, and walked down the wide flight of steps which led to the Horseshoe Cloister. However, as we neared No. 21, we became conscious of raised voices – three of them, if I was not mistaken – issuing from within. Uncertain as to how to proceed, we came to a halt at the entrance to the passage-way which skirted the crescent. "It appears that Major Yates's visitors are causing him some consternation," said Holmes quietly. "Perhaps we had better postpone our visit."

Even as he spoke, however, the front door of the major's apartment flew open, and Grafton Montague came out, seemingly unruffled by the furious argument of which we had been unintentional auditors. "Ah, Mr. Holmes, Dr. Watson," said he gruffly. "And Mrs. Clunies-Ross too. The snow keeps off. We will speak of this matter again, Major Yates. Good morning to you." Placing his hat on his head, Mr. Montague turned and marched stiffly off in the direction of the castle gate-way.

There was an embarrassed silence before Major Yates, perceiving our presence at his threshold, invited us in. "I hope you enjoyed the service," said he cordially. "If you will take a seat in my lounge, I will fetch some refreshment. I trust that sherry-wine will be acceptable? Christmas dinner will be served at Tilstone Court on the stroke of three."

When we were comfortably seated with large glasses of a most superior sherry, Sherlock Holmes finally broached the subject which had been uppermost in my mind ever since our arrival at the Cloister. "I gather that you and Mr. Montague have had some sort of disagreement, Major Yates," said he. "I trust that your friend will not use it as an excuse to absent himself from Tilstone Court. He cannot be permitted to leave until we know the identity of the murderer."

"The argument was a comparatively trifling one, Mr. Holmes. I do not believe Montague has been greatly offended. But the truth is I am disappointed in the man. He should have informed me straightaway about the character and history of my gardener, Parkin. At least then I should have been on my guard in case there was some repetition of his criminal behaviour. I consider it dishonest of Montague to have concealed the truth, and I told him so in no uncertain words. The fact that Parkin appears to be a reformed character is neither here nor there."

"I can appreciate your feelings on the matter, Major Yates. What was Mr. Montague's response to your criticism?"

"He said – and with some justification, I suppose – that once he had realized that Parkin had not erred since leaving Norhamptonshire, and now appeared to be leading a respectable life, he saw no reason to expose him, and no immediate danger to me or my estate. My argument was that I should have been given the opportunity to make up my own mind on the matter."

When we had finished our drinks, the three of us took our leave, Major Yates having expressed his intention of following us back to Tilstone Court in time for Christmas dinner. It was not long after one o'clock, but the wintry sun was already low in the sky as we descended Castle Hill and crossed the bridge into Eton. Thin sprays of smoke were issuing from the chimneys on the snow-capped roofs of the houses, and a hard frost was setting in as we crunched our way along the near-deserted street. Outside the Crown and Cushion, we paused, and peered through the window at the dimly lit interior and the few people who preferred a convivial glass of ale to the warmth of their own hearths. Amongst them, we could see Sam Parkin, the gardener, and William Clunies-Ross, the old Etonian, deep in conversation and apparently the best of friends. In order to obtain a clearer view, Sherlock Holmes rubbed his coat-sleeve against the ice-encrusted window-pane, an action which must have been audible within the room, for William Clunies-Ross looked up suddenly, and, catching sight of my friend and me, hurriedly drained his glass, before rising to his feet. Then, with a valedictory nod to his erstwhile companion, he grabbed his coat and made his way to the door, where he joined the three of us in the freezing street outside. "Hello, my dear," said he, addressing his shivering wife. "Did you enjoy the service? You will forgive me my Christmas Day tipple, I am sure."

"I can never persuade my husband to come to church on Christmas morning," explained Mrs. Clunies-Ross apologetically. "Every year it is the same. I go to church; he goes to the public house."

"That fellow Parkin was in there," added the old Etonian

carelessly. "Indeed I believe he is seldom out of the place, especially when there is nothing to be done in the garden. Still, he is an agreeable enough companion, if the consumption of alcoholic drink is your game. But should we not be returning to the Court? I am told Christmas dinner is at three sharp, and, by all accounts, it is a meal not to be missed!"

We had not been back at the house for long before Major Yates arrived, and by the time the clock struck three, the whole party was seated around the oak table in the Front Hall – which was evidently preferred to the Dining Room for large, formal meals – eager to partake of the Yule-tide feast. It was a festive scene indeed. Our host was in a nostalgic mood, and seemed bent on re-creating the gaieties and chaff of the mess table. The fire blazed and crackled fragrantly in the hearth. The illuminated tapers on the richly decked Christmas tree added their flickering light to that of the fire, causing the evergreens on the walls to coruscate and scintillate amid the dark shadows of the ancient chamber. At five past the hour, the butler entered bearing a huge goose on a silver platter. He was followed by the two maids with bowls of mashed potatoes and green vegetables, a jug of hissing gravy and a large dish of sweet-smelling apple-sauce. Major Yates himself plunged the carving-knife into the plump breast of the goose, and a cascade of sage-and-onion stuffing gushed out. When we had eaten our fill of the main course, washing it down with copious draughts of ale or wine, cook came in with a gigantic cannon-ball of a pudding, flaming in half-a-quartern of burning brandy, and with a sprig of holly in the top.

After dinner, apples and oranges were placed upon the table, and a shovel-full of chestnuts on the fire. Major Yates helped his guests to glasses of hot punch, and silence reigned throughout the hall, broken only by the intermittent sputtering and crackling of the chestnuts in the hearth and the occasional grunt of satisfaction from the sated diners.

At last, I was myself overcome by the stultifying effect of the heavy meal, and decided to repair to my room for a much-needed sleep. Holmes, by contrast, had only picked at his food, consuming no more than a few morsels of goose and a spoonful or two of mashed potato, whilst he had declined the pudding altogether. He now sprang to his feet with a burst of nervous energy. His eyes twinkled, and there was a touch of colour upon his sallow cheeks. "Ah, Watson," said he playfully. "I see you are fatigued after your alimentary excesses. No, do not trouble yourself. Sleeping it off may well be the best medicine for a man in your present condition. I myself rather fancy a brief but bracing constitutional in these lovely grounds. There is a theory which I wish to test."

"If you would rather that I joined you, Holmes…?"

"Certainly not, Watson. I will see you later."

Sherlock Holmes donned his heavy coat and gloves, and opened the front door, causing a cold blast of icy air briefly to invade the cosy interior of the Front Hall. As my friend disappeared into the steadily gathering gloom, I rose wearily to my feet, and dragged myself laboriously up the ornamental stair to my room in the east wing, where I was soon fast asleep on my comfortable bed.

I awoke two hours later to find that it was now completely dark, although the snow had still not returned, and the sky was dotted with a multitude of twinkling stars. I rose from my bed, and made my way back to the south wing. However, on arriving in the landing above the Front Hall, I was stopped abruptly in my tracks by Sherlock Holmes, who was standing outside the Library, the index finger of his right hand held to his lips, and his left arm raised in an attitude of warning. "Hush, Watson," he hissed in an urgent undertone. "There is trouble afoot, if I am not mistaken."

From within the Library there came the sound of a frantic scuffle. It was clear that blows were being exchanged, and violent ones at that. Muffled curses were interspersed with the occasional crack of breaking furniture and the smacking sound of fist against flesh. As the noise increased, there was a sudden rush of footsteps on the stair-case, and Major Yates appeared, puffing heavily, and crimson in the face from his unwonted exertion. "Whatever is the matter, Mr. Holmes?" cried he breathlessly. "Is there a fight in progress?"

"So it would appear," replied my friend calmly. "And from what I can tell, the contest is between Mr. Grafton Montague and Mr. William Clunies-Ross."

"But they seemed to be on such friendly terms at dinner. And indeed throughout the time that they have been together at the Court."

"I suppose we shall have to intervene," muttered Holmes without enthusiasm, opening the Library door to reveal a scene of devastation within. William Clunies-Ross, the old Etonian, was lying on the floor, his nose bloody, his hair dishevelled and his shirt ripped to the waist. Astride his chest was the equally bedraggled figure of the historian, his livid face a picture of savage and uncontrollable ferocity. As Clunies-Ross lay powerless and whimpering on the floor, his frenzied adversary was pummelling his head with flailing fists, and bombarding him with a fusillade of horrid imprecations.

Sherlock Holmes stepped forward, and pulled the hysterical assailant from his hapless victim. "Come, come, Mr. Montague," said he, in an admonishing tone. "This will not do. Break it up there, gentlemen! Whatever has caused such an unseemly display of naked animosity?"

"Mr. Clunies-Ross was harassing my wife," cried Grafton Montague, spitting out the words with unalloyed venom. "Not that she would deign to have any truck with his loathsome attentions."

"In that case, you had no cause to assault me in this wanton fashion," retorted the furious old Etonian. "Besides, I was merely being friendly towards her. You have over-reacted monstrously, my good sir!"

"Calm yourselves, gentlemen," said Sherlock Holmes soothingly. "Mr. Montague, would you be so kind as to tell me exactly what has happened here, without recourse to contumely or recrimination?"

Grafton Montague eased himself into a large arm-chair by the window, and lit a cigar. William Clunies-Ross rose to his feet, dusted himself down, and took a seat near the desk. "It was in this way," said Mr. Montague, with a long, sensual draw on his cigar. "We were all replete after our excellent dinner, and disinclined to any sort of activity. Mr. and Mrs. Norton expressed their intention of going up to the Little Drawing Room in the west wing, which has become their favourite haunt since coming to stay at Tilstone Court. Major Yates remained in the Front Hall dozing by the fire. Meanwhile, Mr. and Mrs. Clunies-Ross and my wife and I decided to come up here to the Library, but almost at once, Mrs. Clunies-Ross complained of being fatigued, and left to go and lie down in her room. Well, there is a fine collection of books in this room, many of them dealing with the history of the area, in which, as you know, I have a particular interest. I quickly became absorbed in a volume about Windsor Castle in the Middle Ages, and Clunies-Ross clearly thought he would take advantage of my preoccupation to make his contemptible advances towards my wife. It is disgusting. He must be at least twenty-five years her senior!"

"At any rate, I do not act as if I were fifty years older, by ignoring her for a dusty old history book!" exclaimed William Clunies-Ross indignantly. "She is a beautiful young woman. I was only paying her the attention which such a creature deserves."

"It was an attention that she neither sought nor invited. I could see by her manner that she was embarrassed and repulsed by your behaviour, and wanted nothing to do with you."

"On the contrary, she was upset by your obvious and unnecessary jealousy. The truth is that she was flattered by my gallantry, and only left the room because she could see the effect that her manifest enjoyment of my company was having upon a mean-spirited and possessive husband."

"That is a lie, Mr. Holmes. She was revolted by Clunies-Ross's conduct, and consequently returned to her room on the pretext of a head-ache. As soon as she had left, I took Clunies-Ross to task, and a fight ensued. I am not sure that I have any desire to remain in a house which numbers a libertine amongst its occupants."

"As to that, I fear you have no choice, Mr. Montague," said Holmes firmly. "Until my investigation, not to mention that of the official police force, is complete, no one can be allowed to leave. I suggest that you join your wife, Mr. Montague, and that you, Mr. Clunies-Ross, go for a walk in the fresh air. We will put this unfortunate incident down to an excess of wine and punch during and after an excellent dinner."

Both men then left the room rather sheepishly. "Personally, I believe that the whole affair is a storm in a teacup," said Major Yates when they had gone. "I am sure that Clunies-Ross meant nothing by his friendly manner towards Mrs. Montague. I have known him for most of his life, and he is above all a gentleman." Shaking his head sadly, he made his way to the door, and waddled out, leaving Holmes and me with the Library to ourselves.

"Well, Watson," cried Holmes excitedly. "While you have been sunk in lethargy, I have been having an exciting time of it. You recall that I said I had a theory to test? That theory has been tested and proven."

"I am all ears, Holmes."

"When I left you to go for a walk in the grounds, I had a specific destination in mind. You will remember how earlier in the week, when we ventured into the courtyard at the centre of this wonderful old building, we observed Major Yates standing by the north wall of the gate-house, apparently practising his vocal skills. I believe you considered his behaviour rather eccentric?"

"I did indeed, Holmes. It was snowing at the time, as I recall."

"Apart from that, did anything else strike you as odd about what he was doing – or what he claimed to be doing?"

"It is odd to be practising singing in the open air when the temperature is below freezing."

"Yes, but I do not believe he was singing. Did you observe the choristers in St. George's Chapel at this morning's service?"

"Not especially, Holmes."

"Their performance was distinguished by two particular characteristics: first, they opened their mouths very wide in order to enunciate as clearly as possible; and secondly, the music being stately and solemn in nature, in keeping with its devotional character, their oral movements were correspondingly slow and drawn out."

"What is your point, Holmes?"

"Since Major Yates was himself shortly to be participating in the Christmas morning service at St. George's Chapel, one could reasonably presume that, if he claimed to be practising his singing, he was doing so in order to prepare himself for that particular event. One would therefore have expected his mouth movements to be slow and expansive. Yet they were not. They were rapid and sloppy. In other words, he was not *singing* at all; he was *talking*. And unless he is even more eccentric than he himself would have us believe, he was not *soliloquising*. He was, in fact, *holding a conversation*. Acting upon this premise, I sought to examine more closely the setting for Major Yates's unusual vocal performance. The idea occurred to me before, when we returned to the Front Hall following our encounter with the major in the courtyard. It was for that reason that I examined the panels on the north wall of the room for evidence of a concealed hiding-place which might contain a person or persons whom Major Yates had been secretly addressing from outside. I could find no entrance to such a chamber, but I did detect that one or two of the panels had a hollow ring, suggesting that a priest-hole or some such small room might be hidden therein, albeit not accessible from the hall itself.

"Since then, two incidents have occurred in the Tower Room or on the roof of the gate-house. First, Porson was seen visiting the north-west angle-turret at night, carrying a mysterious canvas bag. He claims to have been performing his normal duties, but his manner was furtive, and I suspected him of having an assignation, probably with the man whom you, Watson, had seen in the garden at night. At the time, it did not occur to me that the Tower Room might contain the entrance to the scret chamber. I thought only that it was the chosen place for their clandestine meeting. Secondly, Grafton Montague told us how, on the day of St. John Bosco's murder, he had heard a noise in the tower and gone up there to investigate. We know now that the person he was pursuing was in all likelihood Professor Moriarty, the man whom you had glimpsed in the garden and whom we were all to see fleetingly at the window around mid-night on Christmas Eve. I believe the sequence of events that occurred was as follows: when Montague heard a door being opened in the Tower Room, it had been Professor Moriarty letting himself out on to the roof. Indeed, the outer door was open when Mr. Montague arrived in the Tower Room, and he heard footsteps on the walk-way outside. At this point, Professor Moriarty, having realized that he was being pursued, hurried along to the north-east angle-turret, went in, and locked the door behind him, before disappearing into the depths of the house, and eventually into the garden. Later, wishing to return to the warmth of the building, he was endeavouring to find out if the guests had gone to bed, by peering through the chink in the shutters on the windows of the Front Hall, when they were unexpectedly flung open by Porson, revealing his presence to everyone in the room.

"It was when I was reviewing this sequence of events that it occurred to me that the entrance to the secret chamber in the Front Hall – as I say, most probably an ancient priest-hole – was in the Tower Room. The north-west angle-turret is located immediately above the Front Hall, and could easily be reached by a passage-way down through the thickness of the wall. It was in order to test my theory that there was indeed a secret room in the hall, and that a speaking-hole was located in the wall outside, that I embarked upon my post-prandial expedition to the courtyard. I quickly found the place where Major Yates had been observed 'practising his singing', and found a small hole in the masonry which connected with the interior of the Front Hall. I then looked up to the north-west angle-turret above, and was convinced that I had indeed found the point of access to the concealed room below. However, even as my eyes scanned the roof, I caught a glimpse of a dark figure on the walk-way which runs along its edge, and the next thing I knew a large slate had come hurtling down, and was shattered to fragments at my feet. It was the second time that an attempt had been made upon my life since arriving at Tilstone Court. I did not linger, but hastened back to the Front Hall, where I refreshed myself with brandy, and sat for some considerable time mulling over the case and all its ramifications. One thing is for sure: my would-be assailant could not have been Major Yates himself, for he was fast asleep in the Front Hall when I returned to the house."

"Perhaps it was Moriarty who threw the slate?"

"I very much doubt it. Now that he has been exposed, he would surely not risk returning to his hiding place in the house."

"So Major Yates is the agent who has been working for Moriarty in Tilstone Court."

"He and, I suspect, Porson, the butler, who has undoubtedly been keeping the professor well victualled for the duration of his concealment."

"Do you suspect either the major or his servant of being the murderer of John Ayto and Henry St. John Bosco?"

"No, I do not. Major Yates was singing at St. George's Chapel when Ayto was killed, and there are any number of eminent witnesses who can vouch for that fact. Similarly, both the major and Porson were clearly visible in the Front Hall when the shot was fired that despatched Henry St. John Bosco."

"In that case, Holmes, whom do you suspect?"

"Let us marshal the facts. First, the murder of Ayto, Yates's secretary. His body was discovered with a torn fragment of paper and a number of forged bank-notes, whose presence we have, as yet, been unable to explain. Neither Major Yates nor Mr. and Mrs. Clunies-Ross could have killed him, since they were at the concert. Sam Parkin, the gardener, was at the Crown and Cushion, a fact which can be verified by his friend Bargus and the landlord. However, Randal Norton and his wife, the paying-guests, could have committed the crime, and the murder weapon was discovered concealed in their wardrobe. But, far from implicating them, this has all the hall-marks of being a plant. For why not simply leave the stick at the scene of the murder or dispose of it anywhere but amongst their own effects? Let us turn now to Grafton Montague and his wife, Celia. Montague certainly had the opportunity to kill John Ayto. And what's more, it is very likely that he was the person who attempted to smother me in my sleep.

"Now, to the second murder: that of Henry St. John Bosco, the editor. Again suspicion would seem, at least superficially, to fall on Randal and Carolyn Norton. The copy of *The Times* from which had been fashioned the threatening message left in St. John Bosco's room on the occasion when his memoirs were destroyed was discovered in their room. They also had the opportunity to commit the crime, and no alibi. Once more, however, their carelessness in leaving such incriminating evidence in their own room would seem to point to the possibility of a plant.

"Grafton Montague, on the other hand, is even more heavily implicated. He has no real alibi, and the gun with which the crime was committed was discovered on his bed. But here again there are possible objections. First, if we discount the stick in the case of the first murder, on the grounds that it was placed in Norton's wardrobe in order to incriminate him, can we not do the same for Montague's gun? If Montague did indeed shoot Henry St. John Bosco, why did he go to the trouble of taking the weapon back to his room and then leave it in a place where it could be seen by anyone who entered?"

"Perhaps he was intending to conceal the gun, but simply did not have time to do so?"

"But why take it there in the first place? If he had simply left it at the scene of the crime, there would have been nothing to suggest its ownership. Which brings me to the second problem, if we are to consider Montague as the perpetrator of these crimes. If he was indeed the murderer of John Ayto, then his wife must have been lying when she said that he was with her in the room at the time when the crime was committed. Yet, in the case of the second murder, she made no attempt to deny that the gun on the bed belonged to her husband. If she had done so, we might have been led to believe that it had been planted by the real murderer in an attempt to incriminate Montague. But by admitting that the revolver was his, she damned him even as she exonerated him in the case of the first murder.

"Furthermore, there is that about Grafton Montague's own account of his whereabouts at the time of St. John Bosco's death which has the ring of truth about it. And yet, if it is true, and he was side-tracked by a suspicious noise in the Tower Room, not only was he elsewhere when the crime was committed, but it would also imply that he was not aware of Moriarty's presence in the house, and therefore was unlikely to have been working for him."

" – Though he may have been working for his agent, namely Major Yates."

"That is true. In conclusion, then, Watson, it seems that, while Grafton Montague is the most likely suspect, there are certain drawbacks to that theory, and there is still the possibility that Randal Norton is our man. After all, a criminal may be incompetent – or capable of a very clever double bluff."

"Have you yet been up to the Tower Room to see if you can find the entrance to the priest-hole?"

"No, Watson. I believe that can wait until to-morrow. As I said before, I am certain that, by now, the nest will be empty, and the bird will have flown."

8: The Two Diaries

By the following morning, it was snowing again. A sharp wind had blown up, causing the fat flakes to scurry and dance through the air like a swarm of angry white bees, and a thick accumulation to form on the lower parts of the windows, almost concealing the view of the garden without.

It was obvious from the first that today was to be no ordinary day at Tilstone Court. For a start, the great table in the Front Hall was set with all manner of dishes not normally to be seen at breakfast-time. There were any number of cold meats and cheeses, dishes of cold potatoes, loaves of bread, jars of pickles, and other assorted delicacies, together with flagons of ale, castes of wine and a freshly heated bowl of wassail, bobbing with apples. Moreover, the servants, usually in the background, and seen only when called upon to serve the food or bring in a fresh pot of coffee, were lined up in a row in front of the Christmas tree, and all dressed in their finest clothes rather than the drab, workaday apparel to which they were accustomed.

"At Tilstone we celebrate Boxing Day by presenting our servants with 'boxes' of money and gifts, and letting them have the day off," announced Major Yates cordially. He then stepped forward, and handed a small parcel to each of the five persons standing before him: Porson, the butler; the cook; the two maids; and finally, Parkin, the gardener. The two men bowed and touched their foreheads deferentially; the women curtsied; after which they were all presented with brimming cups of wassail to see them on their way. They then trooped out of the room, to spend the day with their respective families in Windsor and Eton, or, in the case of Parkin, as I suspected, with his drinking companions in the snug of the Crown and Cushion.

Once they had departed, despite the early hour, we all partook of the heady beverage, and Major Yates explained that the food on the table would have to last until to-morrow, the servants not being due to return to the Court until eleven o'clock the following morning.

Sherlock Holmes, meanwhile, had nudged me in the ribs, and indicated his desire to pay a return visit to the Tower Room. "Come, Watson," said he. "Let us see if we can locate Professor Moriarty's hiding-place."

Together, we ascended the ornamental stair, and crossed the landing to the winding stair-case which led to the Tower Room at the top of the north-west angle-turret. Once inside, Sherlock Holmes immediately set to work examining the panelling, just as he had done some days earlier in the Front Hall below. With his ear close to the wall, he beat on each panel in turn with his fist, listening for the tell-tale hollow sound which would betray the presence of the secret chamber he was seeking. At length, about half-way along the northern wall of the room, he came to a halt. "Listen, Watson," said he, tapping the wall several times with his clenched fist. "Do you notice the difference? It has a distinct ring, quite unlike that of the other panels. I believe the entrance to Moriarty's priest-hole is behind here."

Wedging his fingers into the edges of the panel, he then attempted to dislodge it, and eventually, with a slight grating sound, it came away from the wall, revealing a dark aperture just large enough to admit a normal-sized adult. "As I said to you before, Watson, I do not believe we will find anybody down there, but it would be rash to venture inside. Anyone descending into that hole would be very vulnerable to attack from below, and I know too much of Moriarty's evil intentions towards me personally to risk my back in that way. We will exercise caution, and replace this panel, at least for the time being."

"But surely, Holmes, we cannot give up now. I have my army revolver with me."

"I appreciate that, Watson. But I would prefer to load the dice even more in our favour. It is improbable that Professor Moriarty is still in there, but it remains a possibility. Let us make absolutely certain that the chamber is empty before making our entrance. Do you recall our adventure at Yoxley Old Place last month?"

"It is too recent for me to have forgotten it, Holmes: you mean the case of young Willoughby Smith, who was found fatally stabbed in the neck, and with a golden pince-nez clasped in his right hand. I have a mind to chronicle the story one day, under the title of 'The Golden Pince-Nez'."

"Then you will remember that the solution to the crime hinged upon my realization that the murderess was hiding in a recess behind the book-case. Do you also recollect how I flushed her out?"

"Yes, Holmes, I do. You smoked a great number of cigarettes, and dropped the ash all over the space in front of the suspected book-case. Then, when you saw, from the traces upon the cigarette ash, that the guilty woman had, in our absence, come out from, and returned to, her retreat, you were able to force her to reveal both herself and her hiding-place."

"In the event, it transpired that she was guilty not of premeditated murder but only of being involved in an unhappy accident. However, the material facts remain. A recess did exist, and it was occupied by the responsible party. In the present case, we have already been able to ascertain the former. If you will be good enough to join me in smoking as many of these excellent cigarettes as you can stomach, Watson, we will endeavour to verify the truth of the latter as well."

After ensuring that the floor in front of the relevant panel was covered with a film of ash, we retreated from the room and descended once more to the Front Hall, where we found that – the continuing heavy snow having deterred anybody from venturing outside – something of a party had developed. The comparatively subdued mood of past days, which had been the natural result of two unsolved murders, had been replaced with a frenzied conviviality which seemed at times to border on the hysterical. Major Yates was at the heart of the throng. He was standing behind the great oak table, pouring wassail into a series of goblets by means of a large silver ladle. Seated to his left were Grafton Montague and Rosalind Clunies-Ross, deep in conversation; while in front of the fire, William Clunies-Ross was entertaining Celia Montague, who was laughing uproariously at what was clearly an amusing anecdote of some description. Even Randal and Carolyn Norton, who were standing close to the ornamental stair, each with a half-empty glass of wine, seemed to be enjoying themselves, and to have lost the nervousness which had been their chief characteristic ever since the murder of Major Yates's secretary.

Refusing the offer himself of a drink, and gesturing to me to do likewise, Sherlock Holmes took me aside, and addressed me in a loud whisper. "I think you will agree that now would be an ideal time to search the rooms for clues," said he earnestly. "It looks to me as if the party is set to last well into the afternoon. Well, Watson, are you game?"

I nodded my agreement, and together we moved swiftly up the stairs to the landing above. At the top I looked down into the hall, and saw with some satisfaction that none of the occupants seemed to have noticed our surreptitious departure.

"Where first, Holmes?" said I eagerly.

"To the rooms nearest to our own in the east wing," replied my friend. "I believe I am now quite *au fait* with where everybody is based. Let us make the Nortons' bedroom our first port of call. If past experience is anything to go by, we can expect to find rich pickings indeed."

It was not long before we arrived at the paying-guests' homely little room. "Do you take the wardrobe where the Penang lawyer was discovered," ordered Holmes, "while I search the chest of drawers in which I found the mutilated copy of *The Times*."

In the event, it was I who made the discovery. This was not in the wardrobe, but in the suit-case which lay on top of it – the same from which Lestrade had recovered the gum we believed had been used to construct the threatening message left for St. John Bosco. "Look, Holmes," said I excitedly. "It is a diary – a diary belonging to…" I opened the book, and read the owner's name, which was inscribed in large letters on the fly-leaf. "…Henry St. John Bosco!"

"Strange!" exclaimed Holmes. "That was not there when Lestrade searched the suit-case earlier."

"But Lestrade made his discovery before St. John Bosco was murdered," said I. "Suppose Norton was the killer after all, and recovered the diary from his room later, believing it to incriminate him in some way."

"Let me examine the book," said Holmes. "Why, almost every page is blank. But wait…there are one or two entries for July, and a couple more for December: some initials, and a few cryptic comments."

"Anything for the days leading up to Christmas?"

"Yes. The entry for the 17th of December reads: 'To T.C. for interview with R.Y.'"

"Presumably: 'To Tilstone Court for interview with Reculver Yates'?"

"Indubitably. But the entry for the 19th – the day when John Ayto was murdered – is more interesting: 'R.N. must be watched. V. dangerous man, as know to cost.'"

"Well, there you are, Holmes. R.N.: Randal Norton! Is there anything else?"

"Not much. There is something for the 20th of December: 'J.A. dead. Inevitable in circs.' That clearly refers to John Ayto. Then nothing apart from a brief entry recording the loss of St. John Bosco's memoirs on the 23rd."

"All these initials remind me of the piece of paper found clasped in John Ayto's hand, Holmes. Do you think there is a connection?"

"The hand-writing is quite different, Watson. I believe that, in all probability, the letters on the fragment of paper held by the dead secretary were in his own hand – but that is something it will be easy enough to verify. It will also be possible to check if these diary entries were indeed written by Henry St. John Bosco. His room is quite close to this one, and no doubt contains other examples of his hand-writing. However, that does not explain why we should discover the diary here in Norton's suit-case."

"But surely that is obvious, Holmes. The diary entries implicate Randal Norton directly in the murder of John Ayto. He could not risk the volume being discovered amongst St. John Bosco's effects."

"There was evidence that St. John Bosco's memoirs were burnt in his fire-place," said Holmes. "So why not burn the diary as well?"

"As I suggested before, Holmes, perhaps Norton did not know of the diary's existence at that time, but only found it later after the murder. He may have felt it was too risky to start a fire in the grate of a dead man's room."

"Then he could have burnt it in his own. Randal Norton seems to go out of his way to furnish us with evidence of his guilt. However, let us at least see if we can authenticate this singular document."

Henry St. John Bosco's room was a short way down the corridor from the Nortons' bedroom, and presented a far more orderly appearance than it had done on the occasion of our last visit. Then the floor had been littered with crumpled paper, and the furniture disarranged. Now someone had tidied up what remained of St. John Bosco's manuscripts, and shut all the drawers and the cupboard doors.

Sherlock Holmes walked over to the bureau, on which a pile of galley-proofs and copy-edited pages had been neatly stacked. He then produced the diary, which he had brought with him from the Nortons' bedroom, and proceeded to compare the hand-written entries therein with the blue-pencilled corrections on the proofs. "Unless the diary is a clever forgery," he pronounced, "it has been written by the same hand that made these marks of correction. And look here, Watson. These notes that St. John Bosco has penned for an article in the *Miscellany* present a number of distinctive features which exactly match the writing in the diary. Note, in particular, the weak t's of 'the' and 'that'. They are quite decisive."

A cursory examination of the rest of the furniture in the editor's room produced nothing of further interest. At length, Holmes, having pocketed the diary for a second time, together with two or three sheets of paper containing further examples of Henry St. John Bosco's hand-writing, turned to me and said: "The west wing, I think, Watson?" We then re-traced our steps past the Nortons' bedroom, and sped along the landing above the Front Hall to the west wing, where more of the guest bedchambers were located.

Our first stop was the room which was currently being used by Grafton Montague and his wife, Celia. The room was dominated by the four-poster bed on which we had discovered the Eley's No. 2 used to kill Henry St. John Bosco, but was otherwise furnished very simply, with nothing more than a dressing-table and a large wardrobe. It was to the former of these articles that Sherlock Holmes turned his attention first, and he was immediately rewarded with success. For, on opening the drawer, he discovered that it was stuffed full of bank-notes.

"This must be the money which Montague extracted from Sam Parkin," said I. "Only it seems to have grown somewhat."

"More than a little," replied Holmes. "There must be at least four times as much here as he got from the gardener."

"Forgeries, Holmes?" I enquired, remembering once more the spurious contents of John Ayto's wallet.

"Certainly not. These notes are real enough, and one wonders whence they came. But let us see what else we can find. Watson, do you take a look in that wardrobe, whilst I examine the contents of the suit-cases which sit atop it. Halloa! Surely you have struck gold already."

I had indeed, and literally so. For nestling on the floor in a corner of the wardrobe was a small glittering object, which pricked my finger when I attempted to pick it up. "A lady's brooch! by the living Jingo!" I ejaculated. "Presumably the property of Celia Montague."

"Quite probably," replied Holmes, taking the bright object from my hand. "It may have fallen from one of these dresses which we see hanging here. And yet…"

"Yes, Holmes?"

"I have not noticed Mrs. Montague wearing any jewellery before. Mrs. Clunies-Ross, yes. Even her husband is not averse to sporting a flashy amethyst in his cravat. But I have a suspicion that Mrs. Montague is rather of the view that all she requires by way of golden ornamentation is her lustrous hair."

"But if it is not *her* brooch, then whose is it?"

"I cannot say. But I shall keep it for the nonce. If it turns out, after all, to be the property of Mrs. Montague, I shall gladly return it to its owner. If it does not, however, its discovery here may yet prove to have a more sinister significance."

Sherlock Holmes then resumed his search of the Montagues' bedroom by lying flat on his stomach and peering under the bed. Having found nothing there but a chamber pot and a few balls of fluff, he turned instead to the grate, the contents of which were clearly of much greater interest to him, since he immediately dropped to his knees and began to sift through the ash with his fingers. "Something other than wood or coal has been burned here," said he excitedly. "Ha! A singular discovery indeed!"

My friend rose to his feet, a small fragment of charred paper clutched between his finger and thumb. "It is part of the first page of a diary," said he. "And what is curious about it is that it appears to be the first page of a diary belonging, not to Grafton or Celia Montague, but to Henry St. John Bosco."

"Perhaps it is from an old diary, Holmes?"

"No, Watson. The date – 1894 – is clearly visible."

"But we have already found St. John Bosco's diary for this year in Randal Norton's suit-case."

"None the less, his name and the date are unmistakable."

Sherlock Holmes crouched down before the fire-place, and resumed his painstaking probe of the burnt remains. At length, he uttered a cry of triumph, and his fingers emerged from the ash grasping a second, tiny scrap of blackened paper, on which were inscribed two or three words of spidery hand-writing. He then whipped out St. John Bosco's other diary from his pocket, opened it and laid it flat on the carpet beside him. "Just as I thought, Watson," said he jubilantly. "The writing is identical. Behold! The same weak t's."

"But surely St. John Bosco did not keep two diaries?" said I, stunned by this latest development.

"He must have done," replied Holmes. "Perhaps one was to record material he wished to include later in his formal memoirs; and the other was for more personal and private observations. I cannot say. The salient question is: why was the one in Randal Norton's suit-case; and what are the burnt remains of the other doing in Grafton Montague's grate?"

Sherlock Holmes put the scorched pieces of paper in an envelope, and slipped that between the leaves of the diary, which he then replaced in his coat pocket. "I seem to remember that Clunies-Ross's room is close by," said he. "Let us continue our most interesting and, so far at least, exceedingly fruitful investigation."

The room occupied by the old Etonian and his wife was larger than the one which had been given to the Montagues; it had a huge old-fashioned fire-place with an iron screen behind it, and it was to this that Sherlock Holmes turned his attention first. "What have we here?" said he, pulling a piece of half-burnt cloth from the ash. "It appears that Grafton Montague is not the only person who has a taste for burning unusual things. This, if I am not mistaken, is part of a man's handkerchief – a common-place enough object, you might think, but one which in this instance is by no means devoid of interest. Look, Watson. What do you make of that?"

Sherlock Holmes handed me the singed portion of linen, which despite its blackened edges none the less retained something of its original whiteness, albeit a whiteness that had itself been partially tainted with another colour. For across the centre of the fragment there was an unmistakable blotch of crimson. Having moistened the tip of my index finger and applied it first to the stain and then to my tongue, I was left in no doubt as to the individuality of the substance with which the material had been impregnated. "Blood, Holmes," said I.

"Indubitably," observed my friend. "This handkerchief has been used to soak up blood. If I were to hazard a conjecture, I would say that the murderer of Henry St. John Bosco wiped his face with it when, having shot the unhappy editor from a distance of no more than two feet, he found himself unavoidably sprayed with his victim's gore."

"Do you mean William Clunies-Ross?"

"Not necessarily, Watson. After all, we found the Penang lawyer in Randal Norton's room; and the Eley's No. 2 in Montague's. Yet in each case we were forced to consider the possibility that the weapon had been planted there. Who is to say that the same thing does not apply to this blood-stained cloth?"

Sherlock Holmes placed the rag in another of the envelopes which he habitually carried around with him for the protection of vital pieces of evidence, and stuffed it into his coat pocket. He then resumed his examination of the room, an operation which led him in turn to the wardrobe, the chest of drawers, the corner-cupboard and the under-side of the bed. At last, however, having unearthed no clues in any of these locations, he expressed himself satisfied with his search, and announced his intention of proceeding to the room of our host, Major Reculver Yates.

The major's bedchamber was, not surprisingly, the largest of all the rooms which we had visited, but it was as simply furnished as the others. It had a high ceiling, and a broad fireplace, and like many of the rooms in Tilstone Court, was panelled with dark woodwork. A chest of drawers of the same hue as the panels stood in one corner, a wide green-counterpaned bed in another, and a dressing-table on the right-hand side of the window. These articles, together with two small wicker-work chairs and a bureau, made up all the furniture in the room, save for a square of moth-eaten carpet in the centre.

Sherlock Holmes headed straight for the bureau, but found it locked. However, he was able to open one of the drawers, which contained a number of envelopes, several hand-written sheets of paper, a bottle of ink and a couple of pens. "This is interesting," said he, brandishing one of the pages of manuscript. "It appears to be an *apologia* of some sort for Moriarty."

He handed the document to me, and I saw straight-away that it was indeed a defence of the professor's memory.

"This is not altogether surprising, Holmes," I remarked. "We knew already that Major Yates was an agent of Moriarty and that he has been communicating with him in secret ever since our arrival at the Court. By this account, however, the professor died at the Reichenbach Falls, and the author seeks only to defend his reputation against what he claims has been 'an absolute perversion of the facts by the criminal agent Mr. Sherlock Holmes, by whose hand he unhappily perished'. The document refers to Moriarty's good birth, excellent education and phenomenal mathematical faculty. It mentions his treatise upon the Binomial Theorem, his ascendancy to the mathematical Chair of Durham University and his career as an Army coach. It says nothing, however, of the dark rumours which gathered around him in the University town, or of the criminal organization over which he ultimately presided. It is a curious thing, Holmes, but as I peruse this testimonial, I am struck, not for the first time in this case, by an overwhelming feeling of *déjà vu*."

"For myself, Watson, I think it would be as well if we were to keep quiet about this latest discovery. We do not want to put Major Yates on his guard. There is, however, another document of interest amongst his papers."

"Really, Holmes. What is that, pray?"

"It appears to be a memorandum of sorts written to Major Yates by his secretary, John Ayto."

Sherlock Holmes handed me the sheet of paper, which comprised a series of hand-written instructions in connection with the major's forthcoming engagements. "Note the strong capital letters," said he. "They are quite different from those penned by Henry St. John Bosco. This is the hand-writing of a person at least ten years younger. I have here in this envelope the fragment of paper which was found in the dead secretary's hand. Even though there is very little to go on, you can see clearly that the capital C's and D's are identical in both documents."

"That would certainly seem to be conclusive, Holmes."

"I suggest that we return now to the Front Hall, before Major Yates, noticing our absence, decides to institute his own enquiries, and discovers us ferreting around amongst his personal belongings. It is imperative that he has no inkling of our suspicions, particularly those concerning his connection with Professor Moriarty."

Back in the Front Hall, the wine and the wassail were still flowing freely. Lunch had already been taken, as was evidenced by the number of empty or depleted dishes on the old oak table. Major Yates was snoozing in front of the fire; and the Nortons were seated close by, tucking into the remains of cold beef and pickles. Of Celia Montague, there was no sign, she having apparently retired to her room: I was very glad that we had long since completed our search of that chamber. Grafton Montague, however, was still engaged in intimate conversation with Mrs. Clunies-Ross, while the latter's husband stood by the mantelpiece, glaring at them with ill-concealed jealousy.

"I am not quite sure whether Mr. Montague is genuinely attracted to Mrs. Clunies-Ross, or whether this is his way of gaining revenge for Clunies-Ross's attentions to his own wife," said Holmes. "But if he is seeking to make William Clunies-Ross jealous, then he is certainly succeeding."

"There is no doubt that Rosalind Clunies-Ross is a very beautiful woman," I replied. "But, then, so is Mrs. Montague – and she is a good ten to fifteen years younger."

Suddenly the man by the fire seemed to snap. Smashing his glass down on the mantelpiece, he stormed over to where the historian was flirting with his wife, and, grabbing the latter roughly by her wrist, said in an imperious voice: "Enough!"

"William!" exclaimed Mrs. Clunies-Ross, her cheeks flushed, and her eyes blazing. "If you use that word in reference to my consumption of drink, as I hope and trust that you do –

since the alternative would be simply too distressing to contemplate – I can assure you that I have consumed barely two glasses of wine."

"I did not mean to comment in any way on your behaviour, my dear," retorted William Clunies-Ross, his brow crinkled with anger, and the veins standing out at his temples with passion. "I am sure that you have acted with the propriety that befits a loving and faithful wife. I was referring to this!"

He turned to Montague with venomous eyes, and prodded him sharply in the chest with his outstretched finger.

"I meant nothing by it," responded Grafton Montague sullenly. "At least, no more, I trow, than did you when you were entertaining my wife in the Library yesterday afternoon."

There was a long pause.

"In that case," replied William Clunies-Ross at last. "I have nothing to reproach you with. Come, my dear, let us seek some more sober entertainment."

He marched stiffly from the room, followed by a reluctant Mrs. Clunies-Ross – whose red face and angry eyes showed that she was far from being placated – and calm descended once more on the ancient hall.

"I think, perhaps, a little less wassail, and a little more of this excellent pork, would do us all a world of good," declared Sherlock Holmes, helping himself to meat and bread from the still amply stocked table. "Further questions can wait until to-morrow, when, with any luck, heads, if sore, may at least be somewhat cooler."

9: The Spoilt Pillows

Breakfast on the morning of the 27th December was rather poorly attended. This I ascribed to a combination of over-indulgence on the previous day, and the fact that the cold collation on the table in the Front Hall had dwindled somewhat. By nine o'clock, Sherlock Holmes and I were still the only people to have made an appearance. However, with the servants due to return by eleven o'clock, I anticipated a rather better attendance for luncheon.

The weather had improved since Boxing Day. A welcoming sun was casting shafts of light across the hall floor, its bright warmth inviting me to don my hat and coat and venture out into the sparkling brilliance of the Tilstone gardens. But Sherlock Holmes had other plans. "Let us see if we can find Mr. William Clunies-Ross," he declared. "I would very much like to have his explanation for that blood-stained handkerchief we found in his grate."

Clunies-Ross was seated in the Library, reading a book. "Ah, Mr. Holmes, Dr. Watson," said he carelessly, laying his book down on the arm of his chair. "It is a fine morning, is it not?"

Sherlock Holmes, however, was not listening. Instead his attention was fixed on the wall opposite the fire-place, which was hung with a great number of portraits, including one of Sir Frederick Yates, Major Yates's father. The other pictures too, I assumed, were of family members, past and present. However, a rectangle of exposed wall-paper in their midst, brighter than the paper which could be seen all around it, indicated that one of the portraits had been recently removed, and it was this that had caught Holmes's attention. "One of these portraits is missing," he observed, indicating the space in question, which was about 18 inches high, and a foot wide.

"Not a portrait. A landscape, I understand," replied William Clunies-Ross. "I was asking Major Yates about it earlier. He said it was a view of the south front of Windsor Castle from the Long Walk, although I cannot say I recall it from my previous visits to Tilstone. Apparently it was rather dirty, and Major Yates has arranged for it to be cleaned."

"Odd," remarked Holmes, a puzzled expression appearing on his normally impassive features. "One would not expect a landscape – and especially one depicting such a broad structure as Windsor Castle – to be painted in a format normally reserved for portraiture."

"You are right, Mr. Holmes. But, as I say, I do not remember ever seeing the work in question. Perhaps it was chosen to fit in with these other pictures, which are, as you see, all portraits?"

"Quite probably. However, it was not about art that I wished to talk to you, Mr. Clunies-Ross. Watson and I took the liberty yesterday of searching all the rooms, and we found this in your fire-place. As you can see, it is a fragment of a gentleman's handkerchief, stained with blood. Do you know how it came to be there?"

Mr. Clunies-Ross's eyes widened with surprise. He took the scrap of cloth in his fingers, and examined it closely, pursing his lips and shaking his head incredulously as he did so. "I have not the slightest idea," said he at last. "I have never seen it before in my life."

"You do not claim ownership of the handkerchief of which this is a part?"

"I do not, Mr. Holmes. You say you found it in my grate, and clearly someone has been attempting to burn it. I can only say that that person was not I."

He handed the fragment back to my friend, who pocketed it. "Thank you, Mr. Clunies-Ross. I should add that this was not the only item of interest that we discovered in the course of our search yesterday, though it it was all that we found in your room. I shall, of course, let you know if we are able to shed any light upon it."

Having left the Library, and found both the Drawing Room and the Dining Room to be empty, Holmes turned to me and said: "I wager that we shall find the Nortons in the Little Drawing Room. I believe that, outside of their bedroom, it is their favourite place in Tilstone Court."

A visit to the west wing proved him right. Mr. and Mrs. Norton were indeed in the room Holmes had suggested, reading the yellow-backed novels to which they were both partial. "Pray do not bother to get up," said Holmes as he entered the room, adding: "I am afraid that I have some further questions concerning the murder of Mr. St. John Bosco."

"Surely not, Mr. Holmes," said Mrs. Norton in a tremulous voice. "We have already told you everything we know."

"Do you recognize this?" enquired Holmes, producing the diary I had discovered in the paying-guests' suit-case.

"No. What is it?" replied Randal Norton, taking the volume,

and opening it at random.

"It is Henry St. John Bosco's diary. It was discovered yesterday in your bedroom, and what's more, if you look at the entry for the 19th of December, you will see there is a cryptic reference to an 'R.N.'. Your initials, Mr. Norton."

Randal Norton froze in his chair. "This is preposterous!" he exclaimed. "I said before there was a conspiracy against me, and now I am sure of it."

"You will also note that the 'R.N.' in the diary is described as a very dangerous man. Do you still deny that you had anything to do with the deaths of John Ayto and Henry St. John Bosco?"

"Of course I do. I had never met either of them before I came to Tilstone Court as a paying-guest. I have never seen this diary before in my life, and I certainly can't explain the apparent references to me. Are you sure that the diary is genuine?"

"We cannot be absolutely certain, Mr. Norton. But why should anyone want to forge a journal of this description?"

"Why, that is obvious, Mr. Holmes. To make it seem as if I was the guilty party. I have already had a murder weapon and a spoiled newspaper planted on me. So why not a doctored diary?"

"If you are telling the truth, Mr. Norton – and I must confess that I am strongly inclined to believe that you are – then someone has gone to extraordinary lengths to divert suspicion away from themselves. You will be glad to hear, however, that yours was not the only room in which we found traces of a diary belonging to Mr. St. John Bosco."

"Well there you are, then. The one you discovered in my suit-case was a forgery after all. Where did you unearth the real one?"

"In the bedroom occupied by Mr. and Mrs. Grafton Montague. But it is always possible, of course, that Henry St. John Bosco kept two diaries."

"If one refers to me, then it is definitely a forgery," said Randal Norton with certainty. "Unless there is somebody else with the initials R.N."

"Thank you, Mr. Norton. I am very much obliged to you for your opinion. Let us see if Mr. Montague has anything to say about the remains of the diary discovered in his bedroom."

As luck would have it, Grafton Montague was in the Drawing Room by the time we arrived back in the south wing, and Sherlock Holmes lost no time in questioning him about the various items which we had found. "Dr. Watson came across this brooch on the floor of your wardrobe," said he. "I presume it belongs to your wife?"

Grafton Montague observed the glittering object with bulging eyes. "I...I suppose it must do," he replied uncertainly. "Although my wife does not possess a great deal by way of jewellery, and I do not recall...unless..."

"Unless what, Mr. Montague?"

"It occurred to me that it might have been a gift to Mrs. Montague from...from William Clunies-Ross."

"You do suspect your wife of a vulgar intrigue, then?"

"No. I can't believe it. The other day in the Library, I was mistaken. I am sure of it."

"We will assume, then, that the brooch was purchased by Mrs. Montague herself, and that you were simply unaware that she was in possession of it."

"That is the most likely explanation."

"We also found traces of Henry St. John Bosco's diary in your grate."

"What? Are you sure?"

"Absolutely, Mr. Montague. The scraps of paper had been badly burned, but there was enough to show that they originated from Mr. St. John Bosco's journal for the current year. The hand-writing matched examples found in his room."

"I cannot explain it, Mr. Holmes."

"You deny, then, that you obtained possession of Mr. St. John Bosco's diary, and attempted to destroy it in your fire?"

"Most vehemently. I have never even seen Mr. St. John Bosco's diary, let alone stolen it or tried to burn it."

"Well, then. Do you also deny that you are in possession of a great deal of cash, which you have concealed in the drawer of your dressing-table?"

"Of course not. You know that I obtained that money from Parkin, the gardener, as reparation for what he stole from my father."

"I am afraid that is not good enough, Mr. Montague. There was far more cash in your drawer than can be accounted for in that way."

"That is true. But what you do not know is that Major Yates borrowed a substantial sum from me when we were in the Lake District. We were staying in a remote part of Cumberland, and there were no banks nearby. We decided that the best solution was for me to lend him the money, and for him to pay me back when I came to stay with him at Tilstone. This he has now done, and that is why there is so much cash in my dressing-table drawer at present."

"It might be a good idea to have it transferred to Major Yates's safe."

"Indeed, Mr. Holmes. I shall act upon your advice directly."

As we were leaving the Drawing Room, we almost collided with Mrs. Montague, who had been about to join her husband. However, Sherlock Holmes insisted on having a word with her in private, and ushered her into the adjacent Library. William Clunies-Ross had departed by now, and so we had the room to ourselves. "I wonder if you recognize this brooch, Mrs. Montague," said Holmes, producing the object in question, and showing it to the historian's wife.

"No, I have never seen it before," replied she. "Whose is it?"

"That we have yet to ascertain," said Holmes quietly. "But it may interest you to know that it was discovered on the floor of the wardrobe in your room."

"Well, it is not mine. Though I have a good idea to whom it does belong," said Mrs. Montague grimly.

"To Mrs. Clunies-Ross perhaps?"

"Indeed. And I shall be interested to find out exactly what that woman has been doing in my wardrobe."

"You suspect your husband and Mrs. Clunies-Ross of conducting a clandestine affair?"

"I hope and pray it has not gone as far as that, Mr. Holmes. But there is undoubtedly a partiality on both sides."

"And likewise between Mr. Clunies-Ross and you, Mrs. Montague?"

"Oh no. Nothing like that."

"But your husband thinks it to be so, does he not? He even attacked Mr. Clunies-Ross in a fit of jealous rage the other day in the Library."

"I cannot believe that that had anything to do with me, Mr. Holmes. No, it must have been for some other reason."

"Thank you, Mrs. Montague. At least we have established that the brooch does not belong to you."

At this point, the gong was sounded for luncheon, which, as expected, was very well attended by virtue of being the first cooked meal to be served since Christmas Day. Indeed, there were no absentees at all at the Dining Room table. The Nortons seemed to have recovered their equanimity following Holmes's dramatic revelation concerning the discovery of Henry St. John Bosco's diary in their suit-case; but there was a distinct chilliness between the Montagues and the Clunies-Rosses. This was not helped by Grafton Montague's constant attempts to continue his flirtation with Rosalind Clunies-Ross, actions which drew sharp glances of recrimination from a stony-faced Celia Montague. However, I could detect no such covert familiarity between Mr. Clunies-Ross and Mrs. Montague, rather bearing out what the latter had told us concerning the altercation in the Library between the old Etonian and her husband, even if it did not exactly correspond to their own account of the incident.

I knew that Sherlock Holmes was keen to interview Mrs. Clunies-Ross on her own, but at the conclusion of the meal she and her husband left together, causing my friend to turn his attention to the matter of the secret chamber. "Let us see if our trap has been sprung," said he, his eyes kindling and a slight flush springing into his thin cheeks.

However, as we approached the stair in the north-west angle-turret which led to the Tower Room, Mrs. Clunies-Ross came hurrying around the corner from her room in the west wing. She was warmly clad, and evidently about to embark upon an excursion into the grounds, or even further afield. "Ah, Mrs. Clunies-Ross," cried Sherlock Holmes. "I should esteem it a great kindness if you would agree to postpone your walk for a short while, and answer one or two questions in private. I believe the Drawing Room is empty at present."

Rosalind Clunies-Ross followed us into the aforementioned room without a murmur, and seated herself in a comfortable arm-chair. "Well, Mr. Holmes. What is it that you wanted to know?"

"Have you seen this brooch before?"

Once more Sherlock Holmes produced the item of jewellery which I had found in the Montagues' wardrobe.

"Oh, you have found it!" exclaimed Mrs. Clunies-Ross delightedly. "I mislaid it three days ago, and I had begun to think it would never turn up. Where was it?"

"On the floor of the wardrobe in Mr. and Mrs. Montague's bedroom."

Mrs. Clunies-Ross gave a violent start, and dropped her gloves. "And I suppose you are wondering how it came to be there?" said she at length, colouring deeply.

"Indeed," replied Holmes. "Mrs. Montague suspects that there is, shall we say, an affinity between you and her husband."

"I cannot deny it, although it is nothing more than that. Mr. Montague is a young and vigorous animal, but I love my husband dearly, and would never betray him."

"You have still not explained how the brooch came to be in Grafton Montague's wardrobe."

"Well, it was like this. I had always thought history a rather dry and dusty subject until I met Grafton. But he makes even the story of this old place seem thoroughly enchanting. For instance, did you know that the family who lived here in the sixteenth century were involved in a plot to murder Elizabeth I and make Mary of Scots Queen in her stead. The same family also played an indirect part in the Gunpowder Plot, since they lent the house to Sir Everard Digby, a relative, and from the gate-house on the 5th of November 1605, Lady Digby and other ladies, together with the Jesuit Fathers Garnet and Testimond, anxiously awaited the news. This was brought to them at dead of night, whereupon the disappointed party made their escape. Grafton told me he had found a book all about it in the Tilstone Court Library, and I went to his room after dinner to see if he would lend it to me. Well, when I knocked on his door, and there was no answer, I let myself in, and decided to wait. But as soon as I entered, I saw the book in question on the dressing-table. I picked it up, and was about to leave, when I heard Mrs. Montague in the corridor outside. I realized she was about to come in, and it suddenly dawned on me that I was in a very compromising position. I knew that Mrs. Montague was not happy about the friendship that had sprung up between her husband and me, and would be alarmed if she were to find me in her bedroom. On the spur of the moment, therefore, I decided to do what I quickly came to appreciate was a very foolish thing indeed: I hid in the wardrobe. Of course, if Mrs. Montague had only opened the cupboard door, my position would have been that much worse, since the fact that I was hiding would imply guilt on my part. But fortunately, she left almost immediately without realizing that I was there, and I was able to make my escape. The brooch must have become detached while I was in hiding."

"I apologize if the question is indelicate, Mrs. Clunies-Ross, but is your friendship with Mr. Montague perhaps nothing more than a reaction to the intimacy which you have observed between Mrs. Montague and your own husband?"

"Oh no, Mr. Holmes. I do not believe Mr. Clunies-Ross is capable of intimacy with another woman. He is too reserved when it comes to matters of the heart."

"Yet Mr. Montague was driven to assault him in a fit of jealous rage because of his flirtatious behaviour towards Mrs. Montague."

"Are you sure about that?"

"Mr. Montague accused your husband of being a libertine."

"And my husband did not contradict him?"

"He said that he was merely being friendly towards Mrs.

Montague, and that Mr. Montague over-reacted."

"I am quite certain that William was telling the truth. Grafton must have been mistaken. Either that or the fight was for some other reason entirely."

"No alternative explanation was put forward by either Mr. Montague or your husband. And Mr. Clunies-Ross did say that he thought Mrs. Montague was a beautiful young woman."

"That does not sound like him at all."

"At any rate, I do not think we need detain you any longer from your walk, Mrs. Clunies-Ross. Thank you for your candour. You may rest assured that we will not reveal anything you have told us to your husband."

"I am grateful for that, Mr. Holmes," said Mrs. Clunies-Ross with a sigh of relief. "He would undoubtedly be very angry if he found out that I had been hiding in Grafton's wardrobe."

When Mrs. Clunies-Ross had left for her ramble, Sherlock Holmes and I resumed our expedition to the Tower Room. It was immediately clear that no one had either come out from or entered the secret chamber, since the layer of cigarette ash that we had dropped on the floor in front of its entrance remained undisturbed. "In that case, we are free to proceed with our investigation," said Holmes, rubbing his hands gleefully, before applying them to the removable wooden panel which covered the entrance to the old priest-hole.

The dark passage which lay behind descended into the depths of Tilstone Court through the thickness of the wall, and was hung with a flimsy-looking rope-ladder. Pausing first to light a candle, since the foot of the shaft was completely invisible from above, Sherlock Holmes lowered himself into the abyss, and started to climb easily downwards towards the hidden chamber; I followed closely behind him. At the base of the passage, it opened out into a small chamber in which, by the flickering light of the candle, we were able to make out a palliasse bed, three altar stones and a folding leather altar. "These objects confirm that this was a hiding-place for recusant priests in times of trouble," said Holmes. "By my calculation, we are now immediately behind the north wall of the Front Hall, and – ha! yes, I thought so. Here is the speaking-hole which connects with the other hole on the wall outside. This was the point where Moriarty was communicating with Major Yates when the latter was pretending to be practising his singing on the day before Christmas Eve."

"This place seems to have been used as a chapel," said I. "Look. Here is a tomb."

Sherlock Holmes shone his candle over the stone structure to which I had alluded, which stood in a corner of the chamber, to the right of the folding altar. "This is not just any tomb, Doctor," said he, thrilling with excitement. "It is a tomb for the living. See the inscription, man!"

He handed me the candle, and by its light, I read the inscription that had been carved into the stone lid of the mysterious sepulchre: 'IN MEMORIAM R.M.J. YATES'.

"But surely that is not quite right, Holmes," said I. "If Major Yates has indeed made preparations for his own burial, then the mason who carved his name upon this tomb has made a mistake. According to the sign above his apartment in the Horseshoe Cloister, the major's initials are R.M.I., not R.M.J."

"Excellent, Watson! You are scintillating this afternoon. Could this perhaps, then, be the tomb of a forebear? Or has it some more sinister significance? Well, there is only one way to find out."

With a burst of energy, Sherlock Holmes gripped the heavy stone lid of the sepulchre, and endeavoured to pull it free.

Slowly, and with a dull grating sound, it slid away, upon which Holmes and I sprang forward, and shone our candle into the dark hole which was thereby revealed. But the tomb was empty.

"Curious," remarked Holmes as he stared into the void. "But perhaps not as curious as *these*."

The flickering candle had illuminated what appeared to be a number of pieces of linen on the floor near the base of the empty tomb. I bent to pick one of these up, and found that it was the remains of a pillow, which had been slit through the middle and emptied almost entirely of the feathers with which it had been stuffed. A few of the remaining feathers fluttered to the floor as I raised the damaged cloth bag to the light. "What do you make of this, Holmes?" I cried, eyeing the mutilated object with perplexity. "There appear to be three of them in all, two of which have been entirely emptied of their stuffing. Who would want to spoil perfectly good pillows in this way?"

"Without further data, I cannot say," replied Holmes. "But one thing is certain. We must question Major Yates about this empty tomb."

So saying, Sherlock Holmes began to climb the rickety rope-ladder out of the shaft, and I followed behind him, carrying the guttering candle. "When we find Major Yates," said Holmes, clambering through the hole in the wall of the Tower Room and dusting himself down, "say nothing which would indicate that we know he is collaborating with Professor Moriarty. We are sure to learn more if he believes we are ignorant of that fact."

Before we left the Tower Room, Holmes and I rapidly smoked several cigarettes, and left a fresh deposit of ash in front of the entrance to the priest-hole.

We found the major in the Library. "I am glad you are alone," said Sherlock Holmes, "as there is something rather delicate which I need to discuss with you. What do you know about Professor Moriarty?"

"The man whose face we saw at the window at midnight on Christmas Eve? Nothing apart from what you told me about his connection with my former commanding officer, Colonel Sebastian Moran. You said he was a very dangerous man, and he must be if he has murdered two people."

"I do not think he has – at least, not personally. But he is indeed a ruthless criminal, and I have reason to believe he has been hiding in your home."

"Surely not. How could he have infiltrated into Tilstone Court without my knowledge?"

"We think he has an accomplice, who has granted him access to the house, and that he has been hiding in an old priest-hole, whose entrance is in the Tower Room at the top of the north-west angle-turret."

"And whom do you suspect of being his confederate?"

"Your butler, Porson? He has been seen creeping about the tower at night."

"Impossible, Mr. Holmes. Porson has been a good and faithful servant to me for years. I do not believe he would betray my trust."

"Mr. Montague, then? I am pretty sure it was he who tried to murder me in my bed."

As Major Yates mulled over my friend's suggestion, I could see from his changed expression that it had struck a chord. "It is true that I have only known Mr. Montague since meeting him in the Lake District last summer, and he has already lied to me about my gardener, Parkin. He is also a keen historian, and has no doubt read about the existence of our priest-hole."

"I am sure that he has, Major Yates. Mrs. Clunies-Ross has been telling us about a book that Mr. Montague found in this very room which would almost certainly contain information about the secret chamber."

"Well, then. I suppose he must be your man. But how did you yourself come to know about the priest-hole? Have you been reading my books too?"

"I deduced its existence. And this afternoon, Dr. Watson and I visited the chamber for ourselves."

"Did you find any traces of the intruder?"

"We found a tomb. An empty tomb with your name upon it – or, at least, something which approximated to your name."

"That must have come as something of a shock, Mr. Holmes. But I can explain it. You may have noticed that there is no chapel either adjacent to, or contained within, Tilstone Court. The priest-hole, when I discovered it, was already furnished more or less as you saw it this afternoon: with a folding altar and some altar stones that date back to the time when the chamber was constructed. That secret room is the closest thing I have to a private chapel, and indeed it was used as such by the people who built it. Can you wonder, then, that I came to think of it as the place where I should like to be buried when I pass away? I had a tomb made, and a simple inscription carved upon it by the local stone-mason. Then I arranged for part of the north wall of the gate-house to be temporarily dismantled so that the tomb could be installed in the priest-hole, after which it was bricked up again, in order that the chamber could once more only be reached from its original, concealed entrance. Unfortunately, it was not until the work had been completed that I realized the mason had misread my writing and carved the initials 'R.M.J.' instead of 'R.M.I.' It is a nuisance, but I am in no hurry to depart this life, Mr. Holmes. You can rest assured that the correction *will* be made eventually."

"I see. Well, it is a curious story, Major Yates. But I sympathize with your desire to be buried in your own home, especially when the place in question has such a strong religious association."

The remainder of the day passed without incident, and it was not long before we were all gathered togther again in the Dining Room for supper. This time Grafton Montague seemed determined to ignore Rosalind Clunies-Ross, but this did not stop Celia Montague from treating her rival with a frosty disdain, and at the end of the meal both ladies departed to their rooms without a word, and without even acknowledging each other's existence. Major Yates had been similarly cold towards Grafton Montague, and he rather pointedly asked the historian if he knew about the existence of the priest-hole. Mr. Montague replied that he had read about it, and Major Yates referred him to a book about the early history of Tilstone Court which sent his guest scurrying off to the Library in search of it. Major Yates himself announced that, the evergreens in the Front Hall having become somewhat damaged during the recent party, he had arranged to meet Parkin there with a view to replacing them. The Nortons went off to the Little Drawing Room, as was their wont; and William Clunies-Ross invited Holmes and me to join him in a game of billiards.

The Billiard Room was situated in the east wing of the house, and I quickly discovered that Clunies-Ross was an indifferent performer at the game. But I found the activity congenial, and started to relax after the excitement of the afternoon's expedition to the secret chamber. William Clunies-Ross had enlisted Sherlock Holmes's services as a scorer, a responsibility which he discharged without enthusiasm, preferring to spend most of the time watching the game from the comfort of his chair, his hands buried deep in his trouser pockets, and his chin sunk upon his breast. Silence had descended upon all three of us, broken only by the intermittent clicking of the billiard balls and the padding of our feet upon the soft carpet.

Which is why the explosion, when it occurred, sounded like the end of all things.

10: *An Impossible Murder*

The gunshot – for I was convinced that such was the explosion we had heard – reminded me irresistibly of the report which had heralded our discovery of Henry St. John Bosco's body in the Drawing Room on Christmas Eve; only this time the noise seemed louder, and closer to hand.

William Clunies-Ross flung down his billiard cue and dashed from the room, closely followed by Holmes and me. When we reached the landing above the Front Hall, we found Parkin standing in front of the closed door of the Library and endeavouring to open it. "The noise came from in here," said he. "A gunshot, I am sure of it. But the door is locked."

At this point, Major Yates came running up the stairs from the Front Hall, and joined him. "Montague was in the Library," he gasped. "We must break the door down without delay." So saying, he and the gardener put their shoulders to the door and pushed. Almost immediately, with a crack and a splintering sound, it gave way and swung open, causing the two men to stumble into the room, propelled forward by their own momentum.

A truly terrible sight greeted us. Lying on the floor in a pool of blood near the desk was the body of Grafton Montague, his face horribly distorted, his throat slashed from ear to ear, and his chest a bloody mass of ragged lacerations. The knife with which these gruesome injuries had clearly been wrought was lying on the carpet next to the body, but of the gun whose firing had alerted us to the crime there was no sign.

Major Yates walked over to the corpse of his guest in stunned silence, and I turned to find Holmes busily engaged in studying the door and the carpet in front of it. The key was in the lock on the inside of the door, and it was evident that the bolt had also been drawn across, since it was still housed in its socket, which had been wrenched from the door-frame by the force which had been applied to it by Major Yates and Parkin. Sherlock Holmes examined both the socket and the damaged part of the door-frame with his powerful magnifying-lens. "What do you make of this, Watson?" said he, handing me the glass. On close inspection, I was able to see that the wood on the frame of the door where the socket had originally been screwed in place, whilst flush with the wood all around it, was none the less cracked and splintered, damage which had clearly been caused by the forcible opening of the door. A number of splinters of wood upon the carpet below testified to the truth of this observation. "There can be no doubt about it," I concluded. "The door was locked and bolted on the inside at the time when the murder was committed."

By now, Sherlock Holmes had moved across the room, and was examining the body of the unfortunate historian. "This was a particularly vicious assault," said he. "The cut to the throat alone would have killed him instantaneously, yet the murderer has also stabbed him in the chest, not once but repeatedly."

"I suppose this is the murder weapon," said I, pointing to the knife on the carpet beside the body. "But we heard a gunshot."

"If Mr. Montague was shot in the chest," observed Holmes, "the wound may have been disguised by the lacerations, although, of course, we should still find a bullet. In the mean time, let us see if we can locate the gun."

Sherlock Holmes then proceeded to subject the room to a rigorous scrutiny. It quickly became clear that, not only had the door been fastened and bolted upon the inside, but, as in the Front Hall below, the windows were all blocked by old-fashioned shutters with broad iron bars. In addition, the walls were carefully sounded, and found to be quite solid all around – there were no secret chambers behind this room – while the flooring was also thoroughly examined with the same result. The fire-place too, while wide, offered no possibility of a hiding-place or a means of ingress or escape. Moreover, an exhaustive search of every corner of the room, and every item of furniture within it, revealed no trace of the gun which we had heard moments before arriving outside the locked room.

"This is a mystery indeed," said William Clunies-Ross, turning away from the corpse with a shudder of revulsion. "A man is shot and stabbed to death in a room which is locked and bolted from the inside, and which offers no means of escape. And yet there is nobody here except the victim, and no sign of the gun. I defy even you to explain that away, Mr. Holmes."

"On the face of it, it does seem impossible," replied Holmes. "And yet I am not without hope of reaching a solution. There are certain aspects of the affair which are distinctly suggestive."

At this juncture, Mr. and Mrs. Norton burst into the room, accompanied by Porson, the butler. "We heard the shot from the Little Drawing Room," said Randal Norton breathlessly. "Great God! Don't look, my dear! It is horrible, horrible!"

Mrs. Norton uttered a scream, and buried her head in her husband's chest. Porson too appeared deeply affected. "You must go and fetch Inspector Lestrade," said Holmes, addressing the distraught butler. "He will want to investigate this crime for himself, and I will postpone any further enquiries on my part until his arrival. In the meanwhile, kindly instruct one of the maids to fetch Mrs. Clunies-Ross and Mrs. Montague from their rooms. Clearly they did not hear the shot."

By the time Lestrade had arrived from Windsor Police Station with the same doctor who had examined the body of Henry St. John Bosco, everyone had repaired to the Front Hall. Sherlock Holmes directed the two men to the murder scene, and explained what had happened, allowing Lestrade to peruse the evidence for himself, while the doctor examined the corpse. "This man has not been shot," concluded the latter. "There is no sign of a bullet. I would say that he was killed by having his throat cut, and that the wounds to the chest were inflicted afterwards"

"What makes you say that?" enquired Sherlock Holmes.

"The victim's hands are uninjured, indicating that he made no attempt to ward off the attack. It is probable, therefore, that he was already dead when these chest injuries were received."

"They could not have been self-inflicted, I suppose?" murmured Lestrade, eyeing the key in the lock and the drawn bolt."

"Unlikely," replied the doctor. "Unless the victim wanted to cause himself unspeakable agony before dying."

"This is a poser, to be sure," said Lestrade, scratching his head. "You say there was nobody in the room when you broke in, Mr. Holmes?"

"Not apart from the victim, no."

"Then how...? Ah, well. Perhaps the other occupants of the

house will be able to shed some light on the problem. I noticed that they were all assembled in the Front Hall."

Downstairs, the atmosphere was decidedly subdued. Porson had distributed brandy to the worst affected, chief amongst whom, understandably, was the bereaved wife, Mrs. Celia Montague, who looked weary and haggard. Dabbing her red eyes with a handkerchief, she was being comforted by Mrs. Clunies-Ross, all trace of animosity between the two rivals seemingly having been wiped out by the enormity of the tragedy which had hit the younger woman.

"I believe Sam Parkin, the gardener, was the first to arrive at the murder scene," said Lestrade formally. "Would you be so kind as to ask him to step over to the table, Doctor?"

The burly gardener shuffled towards us, his ruddy face bearing an expression of utter fear and confusion. "I will help you if I can, sir," said he tremulously, addressing the formidable Scotland Yard inspector. "But I know no more about the affair than Mr. Holmes or Dr. Watson here, who arrived on the landing only seconds after I did."

"Where were you when the shot was fired?"

"I was half-way up the ornamental stair, sir, affixing fresh evergreens to the banisters, as the original ones had come adrift during the Christmas festivities. I heard a loud bang just above me, and when I reached the top of the stairs, the Library door was shut, which was unusual, so I assumed the noise had come from there."

"Pardon me for interrupting," said Sherlock Holmes quietly. "But was the report louder or softer than the one you heard when Mr. St. John Bosco was shot in the Drawing Room on Christmas Eve?"

"Oh, I don't know, sir. About the same, I should say."

"And what did you do next?" urged Mr. Lestrade.

"I tried the Library door, but it was locked. Then Mr. Clunies-Ross came running on to the landing with Mr. Holmes and Dr. Watson, and they were followed almost immediately by Major Yates, who had been down in the Front Hall helping me with the decorations. The rest you know. We broke down the door, and found Mr. Montague dead on the floor."

"You saw no sign of a gun anywhere in the room when you entered the Library?"

"No, sir. Only the body and the knife."

"Very good. Please remain on hand in case we need to question you further. In the mean time, you may go."

The next person to be interviewed was the tall, corpulent figure of our host, Major Reculver Yates. He looked hollow-eyed with anxiety, and his normally rosy features were as white as cheese. "This is a terrible business, gentlemen," said he, wringing his hands fretfully. "Three people have been murdered in my house in the space of a few days. Surely now, Mr. Holmes, you must acknowledge the hand of Professor Moriarty in all this?"

"I have no doubt he was the prime mover," replied Holmes. "But, as I told you before, I do not believe he committed the crimes himself."

"Indeed," observed Inspector Lestrade grimly. "On the contrary, it is evident that the murderer was a magician. For who but a sorcerer could have caused the death of Grafton Montague in a room that was both locked and bolted from the inside? Your gardener said you were in this room when the shot was fired, Major Yates?"

"Yes. I was assisting him in the work of re-decoration. In fact, I was standing on a chair, nailing some ivy to one of the panels, when the explosion occurred. It gave me quite a jolt, I can tell you. I dropped the hammer, and fell off the chair, stunning myself rather in the process. It took me a few moments to come to my senses, but when I did, I wasted no time in joining my gardener, who had raced up the stairs the moment he had heard the shot. The Library door was locked, and so together we forced it open. That is all. Come to think of it, there can be only one possible explanation."

"Yes, Major Yates?"

"As Montague was entirely alone in the room, he must have killed himself."

"That does not explain the gunshot: no bullet was found on the person of the victim or indeed anywhere in the room. Nor does it explain how Mr. Montague's body came to be so badly mutilated, apparently after his throat had been cut."

Next to be interrogated was Porson, the butler, who had been busy administering brandy throughout our interview with his master and the bibulous gardener. "I had been in my room in the north wing," observed the grizzled servant, "when the bell rang, and I realized I was being summoned to the Little Drawing Room in the west wing. Well, I knew that was where Mr. and Mrs. Norton had retired after supper, and, anticipating that they required liquid refreshment, I decided to take a tray of decanters and glasses along with me."

"On your way to the Little Drawing Room, you must have passed the bedrooms occupied by Mrs. Clunies-Ross and Mrs. Montague," said Sherlock Holmes keenly. "Were you aware of any activity in either room?"

"There were raised voices coming from Mrs. Montague's room," replied Porson. "I believe both ladies were in there together, and they appeared to be arguing. When I reached the Little Drawing Room, I discovered that I had been right in supposing that Mr. and Mrs. Norton wanted a drink, and I was in the process of pouring whisky when we heard the shot."

"Was it a loud shot?"

"Quite loud, yes. Louder than the one we heard when Mr. St. John Bosco was killed. We all three then made our way to the south wing, where we found Major Yates and the other gentlemen endeavouring to gain access to the Library."

The Nortons confirmed Porson's story in every particular. "We have come to prefer the Litle Drawing Room as a retreat," explained Randal Norton. "As the only paying-guests at Tilstone Court, we feel rather like outsiders, and prefer to keep ourselves to ourselves. On this occasion, we fancied a drink, and decided to ring for one. The shot occurred shortly after Porson's arrival. I imagine the reason why we heard it, and Mrs. Montague and Mrs. Clunies-Ross did not, was that their rooms are further away from the south wing than the Little Drawing Room."

Mrs. Clunies-Ross seemed quite composed when Inspector Lestrade questioned her. She explained that she had retired to her bedroom after supper, and had been reading a book, when Mrs. Montague had burst in upon her, and accused her of conducting an illicit liaison with her husband. It transpired that her suspicions were largely based on the discovery of the brooch in Mrs. Montague's wardrobe, which she rightly suspected of belonging to Mrs. Clunies-Ross. Mrs. Montague had subjected the old Etonian's wife to a tirade of angry abuse, before storming out of the room without allowing her rival the opportunity to deny the allegations. Mrs. Clunies-Ross had then followed Mrs. Montague to her room, and, after a furious argument, had finally succeeded in getting across her version of events. Mrs. Clunies-Ross had admitted that the brooch belonged to her, and had given the same explanation to Mrs. Montague that she had given to us, namely that she had gone to Mrs. Montague's room to borrow a book which had been recommended to her by Mr. Montague, and that, fearing discovery in a compromising position by Mrs. Montague, she had taken temporary cover in the wardrobe, where the brooch had become detached. Mrs. Clunies-Ross had at last been convinced of the truth of Mrs. Montague's account, and had returned to her room in a somewhat mollified condition. She had not heard the gunshot, and had not realized that anything was amiss until the maid had come to her room in tears, requesting her presence in the south wing.

Mrs. Montague was in a bad way when she came over to the table to be interviewed. Her face was gaunt and troubled, and any vestige of colour had been driven from it by the trauma of her husband's sudden and terrible demise. "I am sorry to intrude upon your grief at this time," said Inspector Lestrade gently. "But there are one or two questions that I feel compelled to ask. I understand that you suspected your husband of having an affair with Mrs. Clunies-Ross?"

"Oh, that is all cleared up now," replied the distressed widow. "Mrs. Clunies-Ross has explained it to me, and I believe her. It was the brooch that had convinced me of their guilt. When I heard that it had been discovered in our wardrobe, I was sure that it must be hers."

"So you went to her room, and had it out with her?"

"Yes. I called her every name under the sun, and told her to leave my husband alone."

"What happened next?"

"I slammed the door, and returned to my room. But moments later, she followed me in, and there was a further altercation."

"That must have been when Porson passed the room on his way to the Little Drawing Room," said I.

"When I had calmed down a little," continued Mrs. Montague, "Mrs. Clunies-Ross explained how she had come to be hiding in the wardrobe. My husband had not been in the room, and she had only gone there in the first place to borrow a history book. When she said that, I finally began to believe her. My husband was obsessed with history, especially the history of this area, and the idea of his promising to lend her a book about it rang true. She told me that she hid in the wardrobe because she was worried that if I found her in my bedroom, I would suspect the worst." Mrs. Montague wiped away a tear, and lapsed into silence.

"So Mrs. Clunies-Ross and you were reconciled, and she went back to her room?" prompted Lestrade.

"Yes. Nothing else happened then until the maid arrived with the dreadful news. I still cannot believe it. Who could possibly want to kill my husband? Unless…"

"Yes, Mrs. Montague?"

"I was thinking – perhaps Mr. Clunies-Ross? He was very jealous of the attention Grafton was paying his wife, however innocent that may have turned out to be."

"Mr. Clunies-Ross could not have murdered your husband," said Holmes. "He was playing billiards with Doctor Watson at the time."

For that very reason, Lestrade's interview with the old Etonian was perfunctory, and when it was over, I could see that the Scotland Yard inspector was baffled. "Not only does everybody have an alibi," said he moodily, "but the murder would seem to have been impossible anyway. Or do you disagree, Mr. Holmes?"

"I believe I know how it was committed – and by whom –" replied Holmes. "But I am still in the dark about the deaths of John Ayto and Henry St. John Bosco. As soon as you have returned to Windsor, it is my intention to devote considerable thought to the matter."

Sherlock Holmes was as good as his word. When everybody else had gone to bed, I left him seated in front of the smouldering fire in the Front Hall, his clear-cut, hawk-like features wreathed in the acrid smoke which was issuing from his black clay pipe, and I knew that he would be there long into the watches of the night, pondering over the strange problem which he had set himself to unravel.

The morning of the 28th of December was crisp and bright. Holmes's room, which I visited the moment I had completed my toilet, was empty, and it was evident that his bed had not been slept in. Sure enough, I found him still down in the Front Hall, scarcely visible behind a malodorous miasma of taobacco smoke. However, on closer inspection, I could see, from the drawn look upon his ascetic face, and the brooding of his deep-set and lack-lustre eyes, that his long vigil had failed to provide him with the inspiration he had been seeking. "It is no good, Watson," said he testily, confirming the truth of my observation. "I confess I have been unable to make the breakthrough I had anticipated."

"Yet you have solved the mystery of Grafton Montague's death," said I, remembering what he had said to Mr. Lestrade the previous night. "Surely that is something?"

"As to that, Watson, have you a moment or two to spare before breakfast?"

"Of course, Holmes."

"Then come with me. There is a theory which I wish to test, and which I was unable to follow up yesterday when others were present. Perhaps I should have done so during the night, but I was perfectly confident as to the outcome, and considered there to be no urgency about the matter."

With these enigmatical words, Sherlock Holmes led me up the ornamental stair to the landing from which opened out the

Dining Room, the Drawing Room and the Library, and began to conduct an intricate search of the wooden panelling which lined its walls. After some moments, he uttered a cry of triumph, and, extracting a small knife from his jacket pocket, he prised a tiny object from the section of the wall which stood between the door-ways leading, respectively, to the Drawing Room and the Library. "*Voilà!*" he exclaimed, clasping the diminutive item between his thumb and forefinger. "The bullet whose firing alerted us to the death of Mr. Grafton Montague!"

"So the report came from the landing and not the Library," said I excitedly, "and Montague was stabbed to death, not shot."

"Well, we knew that already, since no bullet was found on the body," replied Holmes. "Now, to find the gun from which it was fired."

There was only one article of furniture on the landing, and that was the small cupboard which I had noticed before outside the Library. Sherlock Holmes approached this, and opened the doors, only to utter a sigh of disappointment. The cupboard was completely empty. "There is nowhere else around here where the weapon could have been concealed," said he ruefully. "Never mind. It may yet turn up."

"What I cannot understand", said I, "is why a gun was fired at all. It only served to draw attention to the fact that a murder had taken place, albeit one that had actually been committed with a knife."

"And one which, apparently, had occurred in a room that was locked from the inside."

"I suppose the person who fired the gun may have been shooting at somebody who had witnessed the murder, and was escaping across the landing."

"But how could such an individual have seen what happened? The door was locked shut, and the keyhole was blocked with a key. And, in any case, how did the murderer get through that locked door afterwards?"

"Yet, from what you say, you know the answers to these questions."

"Do I? Perhaps they are the wrong questions."

Sherlock Holmes refused to be drawn further, and after the brief spurt of enthusiasm he had exhibited during his search of the landing, lapsed into his former state of depression. Over breakfast, he picked moodily at a plate of kedgeree, before pushing his plate away practically untasted. Refusing the offer of a cup of coffee, he left the Dining Room through the connecting door which led to the Drawing Room, and it was there that I found him later, sitting in an arm-chair, his chin sunk upon his breast, and his hands thrust disconsolately into his trouser pockets.

I picked up a newspaper, and started to read it in a desultory fashion. Meanwhile, Major Yates, who was seated at the desk in the window which overlooked the courtyard at the heart of Tilstone Court, was busily engaged in writing a letter. After some minutes reading about the latest events in the world of politics and current affairs, I chanced to look up at Sherlock Holmes, and saw immediately that a great change had come over him. He was sitting bolt upright in his chair, his eyes shining, and his cheeks flushed with exhilaration. Following his gaze, I saw that he was staring with rapt attention at the window immediately in front of Major Yates, and it was clear that whatever it was he had seen through those ice-encrusted panes had at last provided him with a solution to the problem. Surprise and satisfaction were both etched upon his eager face.

Sherlock Holmes sprang from his chair, vibrating with nervous energy and the pressing need for action. "Ah, Watson," said he with feeling. "What a blind beetle I have been, to be sure! But it will not be long now before the chain is complete. It is necessary for me to make a trip to London. There is a considerable amount of research which I must carry out ere I can bring this extraordinary case to a conclusion. Do you arrange for Major Yates, Mr. and Mrs. Clunies-Ross, Mr. and Mrs. Norton, Mrs. Montague, Porson and Parkin to meet me in the Front Hall at eight o'clock to-morrow evening. Tell Inspector Lestrade to be there too, accompanied by at least two large constables. I would also recommend that, as a precautionary measure, policemen be stationed at all exits to Tilstone Court. But I must be on my way. There is not a moment to be lost."

Sherlock Holmes turned upon his heel and left the room. I, meanwhile, assumed his former position on the arm-chair facing the window, and attempted to discover what it was that had constituted this remarkable epiphany. However, the window in front of Major Yates was of such an elevation that, from where Holmes had been seated, the only thing visible was the upper floor of the north wing on the other side of the courtyard, and even that was indistinct because of the ice-crystals which had formed on the glass: if somebody had appeared at one of the windows opposite, I was sure that it would have been impossible to see them. And yet it was clear that Holmes had descried something: an object passing through the air, perhaps; or something on the roof.

Whatever it had been, there was no trace of it now.

11: The Innocuous Intruder

My first thought, after Holmes's departure for London, was to re-visit the Tower Room. The ash in front of the entrance to the priest-hole remained undisturbed, so I knew that the chamber would be empty. But I was determined to re-enter it. Perhaps I would be able to uncover some clue which Sherlock Holmes had missed, and which would shed some light on the mystery.

Holding a lantern in one hand, I descended the rickety rope-ladder into the depths of the hole. Then, having arrived at the base of the shaft, I shone my light all around me to gain my bearings. The palliasse bed, the altar stones, the folding altar and the tomb were all exactly as they had been before. But the spoilt pillow-cases, which had lain next to the empty tomb, had now been folded, and moved over to the wall. And, on closer examination of the floor nearby, I detected traces of cigarette-ash, the stub of a cigarette and a number of bread-crumbs which I felt sure had not been there during our previous visit to the chamber. I marvelled at these discoveries, since the fact that the film of ash which we had left at the entrance to the priest-hole had remained unblemished seemed to indicate extraordinary powers of observation on the part of Moriarty, who must have taken great care when he entered the shaft. Perhaps, having detected the tell-tale layer of ash, he had simply replaced it with a fresh one. Remembering Holmes's methods, I extracted three envelopes from my jacket pocket, and, with the aid of my pen-knife, scraped samples of the cigarette-ash and the bread-crumbs which I had found on the floor of the chamber into two of them, before securing the cigarette-stub and depositing it in the third. I then rose to my feet, and continued my exploration of the secret chamber.

From the depth and location of the shaft, I calculated that the room must be situated behind the panelling at the north-west end of the Front Hall. Beyond the eastern wall of the priest-hole, by that token, were the small corridor and the flight of steps leading down to the kitchen in the basement of Tilstone Court which were reached from the Front Hall by means of a door in its north wall. This was the door through which Porson and the other servants had passed on Christmas Eve when bringing up the wassail and the other refreshments from the kitchen below. The kitchen was, therefore, presumably immediately beneath where I was standing, and it seemed to be the case that, unless there was a secret door in the outer wall of the chamber, the only entrance to the hole was the shaft which led down from the Tower Room. I examined the north wall of the chamber at some length, and quickly located the speaking-hole which connected with the hole on the wall outside. But it was clear that no hidden doorway existed. A difference in the texture of the wall indicated where a section had been removed at some time to enable the tomb to be installed, as Major Yates had explained, but it was evident that this aperture had been blocked up, and that the wall was now as solid as it had ever been.

Having exhausted the possibilities of the priest-hole, I climbed back up, and emerged once more into the Tower Room. Feeling in need of a breath of fresh air after the cramped and stuffy conditions of the secret chamber, I crossed the room, and opened the door from which a flight of steps led up to the walk-way on the roof of the gate-house. As I stepped out on to this, I espied a figure in the courtyard below, and realized with a shock that it was William Clunies-Ross, running furtively across the flagstones towards the well which was situated in the centre of the yard. I leaned over the battlements to obtain a better view. The old Etonian appeared to be carrying a small object in his right hand, and, as he approached the well, there was a sudden flash of metal in the sun-light, and I perceived that it was a gun. I uttered a wordless cry. Was this the weapon that had been used to shoot Grafton Montague – or, rather, the gun that had been fired on the landing outside the room in which Grafton Montague had been stabbed to death? The next thing I knew, William Clunies-Ross had come to a halt next to the well, and, with a sudden movement, had dropped the weapon into the shaft. Then, just as furtively as before, he hurried back across the courtyard and into the door which led to the servants' quarters in the north wing of the house.

I lost no time in descending from the north-west angle-turret. Leaving the gate-house through the door in the north wall of the Front Hall, I entered the courtyard which I had just been observing from above, and made my way to the well at its centre. As soon as I looked inside, I knew that it would be no easy task to retrieve the gun. The shaft was so deep that a pebble dropped into it took several seconds to reach the bottom. I turned away in disappointment – confident none the less that the evidence concealed by the well would still be there when the time came eventually to recover it – and made my way back to the house.

In the Front Hall, I found Randal and Carolyn Norton warming themselves in front of the fire. "You seemed in a hurry, Dr. Watson," said Randal Norton. "Yet you were not outside for long."

"No indeed," I replied. "I thought I saw Mr. Clunies-Ross in the courtyard when I was up on the roof just now, and I needed to speak to him. Which reminds me. Please make sure that you are here in the Front Hall to-morrow evening at eight o'clock. Mr. Holmes plans to reveal who it was that murdered John Ayto, Henry St. John Bosco and Grafton Montague."

Randal Norton glanced nervously at his wife, and fiddled with his neck-tie. "I trust that we are no longer among the suspects, Dr. Watson," said he, licking his dry lips.

"I am sure I cannot say," I replied. "Ah, here is Mr. Clunies-Ross after all."

The old Etonian had just come into the room, having presumably made his way directly from the north wing. "Good morning, Dr. Watson," said he brightly. "Is Mr. Holmes any closer to solving the mystery of Montague's death? I have not seen him this morning."

"He has gone to London, Mr. Clunies-Ross," said I. "But he will be back to-morrow, and desires your presence in the Front Hall at 8 p.m., when he proposes to lay an explanation of the case before everybody in due order. Perhaps you will have the goodness to tell your wife?"

"Certainly, Dr. Watson. Are you going out? I see you are wearing your hat and coat."

"I have already been outdoors, and I must confess I found the experience refreshing, if brief. As Holmes wishes Inspector Lestrade to be present at to-morrow evening's meeting, I think

I will venture forth again, this time as far as the police-station in Windsor."

It was a bitterly cold morning, but the sun was peeping behind the clouds, and there was a vestige of colour in the sky, as I stepped out of the gate-house, and started to make my way along the tree-lined drive which curled around the house towards Pocock's Lane. However, I had not progressed more than a few paces, when I observed the figure of a man cutting off across the snowy lawn and disappearing behind the west wing in the direction of the sunken garden where Sam Parkin had his shed. I decided to follow him, and, making sure that I kept my distance, I was soon nestling behind the conveniently snow-draped bushes which fringed the formal garden. From my place of refuge, I could see that the fellow was a common loafer: in fact, with his collar turned up, his shiny, seedy coat, his red cravat, and his worn boots, he was a perfect sample of the class. The object of his attention appeared to be Sam Parkin's garden shed, and, having first knocked tentatively at the door and received no response, he placed his hand on the latch, and attempted to open it. When this action too met with no success, the man clearly decided that his best option was to use force, and he was on the point of causing some lasting damage to Major Yates's woodwork, when Sam Parkin appeared around the corner, his coarse face crimson with fury. "What you doing there?" he barked, casting a malignant glance at the intruder.

"Just looking for a place of refuge from the storm," replied the stranger meekly.

"Storm? What storm? Ain't no storm as I can see!"

"Bad weather, then. Snow. I'm frozen 'alf to death, an' I thought I could get bit of warmth in this 'ere shed. I was'n' doin' no 'arm, guv. Honest."

"No harm! You're trespassing, that's what you are! Well, I'll teach you!"

The gardener's lips curled in a sneer, and as he sprang forward, there was a sudden gleam, and I saw a long and evil-looking blade protruding from his clenched fist. "I'll slit yer throat for you, you devil!" he yelled, lunging with his weapon, and causing a streak of crimson to appear on the stranger's hand.

"Don't hurt me, for Gawd's sake," cried the intruder, his face now as white as a fish's belly.

But Parkin's own visage was set hard, and there was a baleful light in his terrible, grey eyes. "I'll slice out your innards, and butter them all over the lawn," he hissed, moving menacingly towards his prey.

But I had had enough. It seemed to me that the intruder had meant no real harm, and that Parkin had grossly over-reacted to his attempt to seek refuge in the potting-shed. "Leave him alone, Parkin," said I, emerging from behind the bushes. "Your employer would not thank you for committing a fourth murder on his property."

"Fourth murder!" ejaculated the intruder. "What is this place? 'ave I wandered into an insane asylum?"

"Your hand is injured," said I. "Come with me to the house, and I will dress it for you. I am a doctor."

"Not likely!" replied the stranger. "I'm not stayin' 'ere a moment longer. Get away from me! Bloomin' madhouse!"

Holding his bleeding hand, he turned and ran across the snow-clad garden towards the drive, disappearing around the corner into Pocock's Lane. I felt sure that, after his nasty experience, he would be unlikely ever to return.

"Well, Parkin," said I sternly. "Don't you think you treated that fellow rather roughly? He seemed fairly innocuous to me."

"He was trespassing, wasn't he? And, for all we know, he was the murderer, come back to do more mischief."

"I don't think so. I believe he was exactly who he said he was: a harmless wayfarer, looking for shelter. But, talking of the killer, Mr. Holmes requests your presence in the Front Hall to-morrow night at eight o'clock, when he promises to reveal that person's identity. I doubt very much if the guilty party will prove to be the innocuous intruder who has just departed. Very well, Parkin. You may go."

The gardener nodded mechanically, and retired to his precious shed. What it was that he kept in it, and guarded so jealously, I had no idea. Putting the matter out of my mind, I rejoined the drive-way which led out of the grounds of Tilstone Court, and resumed my journey into Windsor.

The approach to Eton had become extremely slippery, the steady flow of pedestrians to and from Slough having caused the snow to become impacted, thereby creating a surface which resembled a sheet of glass. Eton High Street was hardly less hazardous, and as I approached the toll-bridge across the Thames, I nearly fell twice on one stretch of pavement which had been turned into an "ice-slide" by some of the more adventurous children of the town. I was quite glad when, as I began to climb the hill past the Curfew Tower with its distinctive candle-snuffer roof, the snow began to fall again, covering the treacherous surface of the path with a steadily deepening layer of boot-gripping powder. By the time I had reached Windsor Police Station, I could scarcely see through the blizzard which swirled about me, and I was glad of the respite as, brushing the cold, wet flakes from my face, I fought my way into the small, red-brick building which Lestrade had made his head-quarters.

I was greeted by Inspector Atkins, the official whose

perfunctory investigation of the murder of Major Yates's secretary, John Ayto, had aroused such exasperation in my friend. "Is Inspector Lestrade in?" I enquired. "I have an important message for him from Mr. Sherlock Holmes."

"You must be Dr. Watson," replied the inspector cordially. "I am a keen reader of your memoirs, and a great admirer of your colleague. You will find Inspector Lestrade in the office."

Lestrade was warming his hands at the fire, and seemed pleased to see me. "Come in, Doctor," said he hospitably. "Have you any news from Mr. Sherlock Holmes?"

"Only that he wishes you to come up to the Court at eight o'clock to-morrow night. Bring at least two constables with you, as you can expect to make an arrest. Oh, and Holmes wants you to place additional officers at all exits."

"Good Lord! Whoever it is that Mr. Holmes has in mind must be a dangerous fellow. But with two big men to restrain him, and me to fix the derbies, I hardly think he is going to evade our clutches. Why, if we are to carry out Mr. Holmes's instructions to the letter, we will need to call on every constable in the area! Still, I suppose if he thinks it is necessary, we will have to humour him. Experience has taught me that it is prudent to trust Mr. Holmes's instincts in these matters. Do you know whom it is that he suspects, Doctor?"

"I have no idea. He keeps his cards very close to his chest."

"I have myself been giving the affair considerable thought, and personally I believe Professor Moriarty is our man. I talked it over with Mr. Holmes after the Montague murder, and I know he thinks Moriarty is only the brains behind the business. But I am not so sure. If only I knew how he got into that locked room!"

"So you think Professor Moriarty killed all three men?"

"I concede he may have had an accomplice – or even

accomplices. From what Mr. Holmes told me, Major Yates has been communicating with Moriarty in secret, and Porson has also been seen in the vicinity of the entrance to the priest-hole. Moreover, I still have my suspicions about Mr. and Mrs. Norton, the paying-guests. At first, I thought they were being framed, but who is to say they were not simply very careless or very stupid? It is significant too that their alibi for the Montague killing is Porson, who, as I say, is almost certainly a confederate of Moriarty."

I left Lestrade agonizing over how any of these suspects could actually have committed what appeared to be an impossible murder, and started to make my way back to Tilstone Court through the steadily worsening snow-storm. By the time I had reached Castle Hill, the fresh fall lay about four inches deep, and the prospect of a cup of tea – or, better still, a glass of something more warming – began to look distinctly attractive. Therefore, instead of continuing on down the hill towards the river, I turned right, and made my way through the King Henry VIII Gate, which leads into the grounds of Windsor Castle. It had occurred to me that Major Yates, who spent so much of his time at his apartment in the Horseshoe Cloister, might be at home this afternoon. The atrocious weather meant that the parade-ground which stretched before me was deserted. Indeed, as I walked across it, I noticed that there was only a single set of footprints in the newly fallen snow, from which I was able to deduce that somebody had recently left the Cloister in the direction of the gate-way through which I had just passed. Tracing these footprints back to their point of origin, I crossed under the archway that led into the red-brick and timber crescent, and saw that the person who had made them had started his lone journey from the very apartment I had come to visit: No. 21, the Castle residence of Major R.M.I. Yates. The covered passage-way which skirted the crescent was only completely covered from above. Consequently, a great deal of snow had blown through from the open courtyard that was encircled by the terrace, and drifted against the doors and walls of the buildings. The footprints were thus visible right up to the front door of Major Yates's apartment. No tell-tale sound of musical activity came from within, but I raised the heavy knocker none the less, and let it fall with a clatter against the brass plate on the door. However, there was no response, and I concluded that Major Yates was either at choir practice in St. George's Chapel or still at Tilstone Court. Disappointed, I turned to leave, but, as I did so, I glanced down at the pile of snow which had formed against the base of the door, and in which the deep impression of a boot was clearly visible. Sticking out of the snow which surrounded this footprint were a number of feathers similar to those which had fallen from one of the spoilt pillows which Holmes and I had discovered in the priest-hole at Tilstone Court. Knowing my friend's fondness for the *outré*, I bent down, and picked up three of these feathers, which I then placed in another of the envelopes which my long association with Sherlock Holmes had accustomed me to carry with me at all times. Finally, I made my way back across the parade-ground and out of the castle into the blizzard-swept streets of Windsor.

By the time I had arrived back at Tilstone Court, I was chilled to the bone, and the snow was so deep that there was no longer any distinction between the drive-way and the lawns which bordered it. Indeed, I was beginning to worry that, if the weather did not let up soon, we should be cut off altogether, and Holmes would not be able to reach us in time for his appointment the following evening. Imagine my surprise, then, when, as I battled my way towards the gate-house, I perceived two heavily clad figures struggling through the snow towards me with a large suit-case. As they drew nearer, I was able to see who they were. "Dr. Watson!" exclaimed one of the two. "I did not see you there. I imagine you are wondering what we are doing out here in the snow."

"Not at all, Mr. Norton. You are trying to escape. But I fear you will not get far in these conditions. Besides which, if you leave now, you will only throw suspicion upon yourselves. You would do better to remain at Tilstone Court, and face the music. The outcome may not be so bad as you think."

"Perhaps you are right, Dr. Watson. But when we considered the weight of evidence against us, it was difficult not to panic."

"I understand your concerns, of course. Now, come back to the house with me, and warm yourselves before the yule log."

The three of us were soon in the Front Hall, stamping our feet, and shedding our stiff, snow-caked over-coats. As I had predicted, a mighty fire was blazing hotly and odorously in the hearth, and the sensation soon began to return to icy fingers and frozen toes. Major Yates was seated in an arm-chair close to the fire, and I decided to waste no time in passing on Holmes's message to him. "Mr. Holmes has gone to London," said I. "But, weather permitting, he is to return on the morrow, and requests that you will join him in this very room at 8 p.m. for his report. Perhaps you would be good enough to inform Porson?"

"I chanced to overhear something of what Mr. Holmes said in the Drawing Room this morning," replied Major Yates. "Of course, my butler and I will be there. But I fear even Mr. Holmes will not be able to explain how Montague died alone in a locked room. Unless it was some bizarre form of suicide: extreme self-mutilation, followed by cutting of the throat."

It only remained now for me to speak to Mrs. Montague, and I should have fulfilled the whole of Holmes's commission. When I eventually tracked down the grieving woman in the Little Drawing Room, she received the news of my colleague's imminent disclosure without excitement, but promised nevertheless to attend the gathering in the Front Hall the following evening. I retired to bed shortly after supper, satisfied that I had contacted all the persons whom Holmes had nominated, but still worried lest the continuing heavy snow should prevent his return.

However, when I looked out of my bedroom window on the morning of the 29th of December, the sun was shining, and Parkin had already begun to clear the snow from the drive. I felt sure that, if there were no further falls before the evening, there was a good chance that Sherlock Holmes would get through.

Such indeed proved to be the case, and my friend arrived back at Tilstone Court around four o'clock in the afternoon. He seemed in high spirits, and asked me straight away if I had managed to put all his arrangements in place.

"Of course, Holmes," I replied. "But I have some other news for you. It seems that Moriarty has returned to the priest-hole after all. He avoided our ash-trap, but the empty pillows had been moved, and I found these on the floor."

I produced the envelopes in which I had placed the cigarette-ash and stub and the bread-crumbs.

"Bravo, Watson!" exclaimed Holmes. "I always thought Professor Moriarty was a cool hand. To return to his hiding-place when he must have known I had discovered it shows nerve indeed."

"Perhaps more importantly," I added, "I saw William Clunies-Ross dropping a gun down the well in the courtyard."

"I confess the news does not surprise me. Anything else?"

"Parkin discovered an intruder in the grounds, and would have done him grievous harm if I had not intervened."

"Tell me, what was this trespasser's object in invading Major Yates's premises?"

"He was trying to get into Parkin's shed."

"And Parkin quite naturally objected?"

"With a knife."

"Dear me. The gardener has a vicious streak, it seems."

"Also, I paid a visit to Major Yates's apartment in Windsor Castle, and found these on the doorstep."

I showed Sherlock Holmes the feathers which I had discovered sticking out of the snow.

"I applaud your powers of observation, Doctor," said Holmes warmly, "but I do not believe these possess any great relevance to the case. Is that all?"

"When I returned to the Court, I came across Mr. and Mrs. Norton on the point of departure. I convinced them that it was in their best interests to stay."

"You have done well, Watson. I, meanwhile, have been extremely busy in London, and have succeeded, after much research, in tying up all the loose ends. To-night you will finally learn who it was that killed John Ayto, Henry St. John Bosco and Grafton Montague."

"Not to mention, *how* Grafton Montague came to meet his death in a room that was locked and bolted from the inside."

"Oh that," said Sherlock Holmes disdainfully. "That was the easy part."

12: The Camden Ripper

By eight o'clock in the evening, everybody had congregated in the Front Hall as Holmes had requested. Sherlock Holmes himself stood in front of the fire, flanked by Lestrade and a couple of strapping police constables. Further officers had been placed at every exit, in accordance with Holmes's instructions. The rest of us were seated in a semi-circle around the hearth. In the centre of the group was Major Yates, in a large arm-chair, with his faithful butler, Porson, standing behind him. Next to the servant was the thick-set figure of Sam Parkin, the gardener, whilst, seated alongside Major Yates, on a settee, were the still nervous-looking paying-guests, Mr. and Mrs. Norton. To their right was Mrs. Montague, red-eyed and bolt upright in her chair, her hand held protectively by Mrs. Clunies-Ross, who was sitting close by with her husband.

"Thank you all for being so prompt," said Sherlock Holmes cordially, lighting his black clay pipe. "I propose to address the three murders which have taken place at Tilstone Court, not in the order in which they occurred, but in a manner which corresponds to my train of reasoning, and which began with the peculiar circumstances in which Grafton Montague met with his death.

"On the face of it," (continued Sherlock Holmes) "that third murder was the most problematical of them all, since it appeared to have been impossible. Alerted by the noise of a gunshot, we arrived at a door which, it transpired, was both locked and bolted from the inside, a fact which I was able to verify the moment it had been forced open. Yet that moment also proved to be the turning-point in the whole case. For, from an examination of the door, I was able to deduce not only who had murdered Grafton Montague, but how they had gone about it.

"I directed Dr. Watson's attention to the evidence in question at the time, but, whilst he observed what it was that patently provided the key to the solution of the whole affair, he failed to infer from what he had seen. Perhaps you would be good enough to share with us the fruits of your appraisal, my dear fellow?"

"You mean from my scrutiny of the door? Certainly. I observed that there were splinters of wood upon the carpet in front of it, and that the section of the door-frame to which the socket containing the bolt had been fixed was also splintered, indicating both that the door had been forced open, and that it had been bolted shut when that forcing took place. I also noticed that the key was on the inside of the door, and that the door was locked."

"Was that all?"

"I think so, Holmes."

"Did you not also observe that the cracked woodwork on the door-frame where the socket had been affixed was flush with the wood all around it?"

"I did. But I fail to see…"

"Why should that be? As you pointed out, there were several splinters of wood on the carpet, and one would have expected further splinters to be sticking out of the frame at the point where the socket had been forcibly wrenched from its mooring. Yet these latter splinters were flush with the surrounding woodwork. This would imply that, while the door had undoubtedly been forced – and at a time when it had been both locked and bolted from the inside – it had since been pulled shut again, causing the socket, with the bolt still inside it, to press against the door-frame from which it had been removed, and to flatten the splinters in the process. This placed a whole new complexion on the sequence of events which had preceded our arrival at the Library. For one thing, it explained how Grafton Montague could have been murdered in a room that was locked from the inside. But equally, it pointed to the identity of the murderer. For whoever had broken down the door to let us into the room must have known, from the lack of resistance, that the door had already been forced; and failure to comment on that fact implied that that person was himself the guilty party.

"Now the door to the Library is a sturdy one. I do not believe that one person could have forced it open, when it was locked and bolted, by *pulling* it from inside. It must have been pushed open, and this implied that two people were involved: one who had remained in the room to lock and bolt the door shut; and one who had forced it open by pushing it from without. I am, of course, referring to Sam Parkin and Major Reculver Yates.

"I believe the sequence of events was as follows. Major Yates had succeeded in luring Grafton Montague to the Library by referring him to a book which contained information about Tilstone Court's priest-hole. All the other guests, meanwhile, had either retired to their rooms or were otherwise engaged, and the coast was clear for Major Yates and Parkin to carry out their pre-conceived plan. Together, they entered the Library, where Grafton Montague was reading. From the fact that we heard no cry from the victim, I imagine that one of the two conspirators must have covered his mouth with his hand and held him still, while the other slit his throat, before indulging in an orgy of further violence, repeatedly stabbing the unfortunate historian in the chest. For reasons that will become clear in due course, I believe the murderer was Sam Parkin, the gardener, while Major Yates acted as his accomplice.

"Major Yates then left the room, and his gardener locked and bolted the door after him. Then the major put his shoulder to it, forcing it open, and letting Parkin out, after which the two of them pulled the door shut from the outside. It was now necessary to alert the household to the fact that a murder had taken place. Major Yates went back downstairs to the Front Hall, and Sam Parkin fired a gun on the landing, before hiding it in the cupboard which stands outside the Library. Because the weapon was discharged *outside* the room, the report was louder than the one which had been heard in the Drawing Room when Henry St. John Bosco was killed. This seemed curious at the time, since the door to the Drawing Room had been open, while it was thought that Montague had been shot in the Library, behind a locked door. When interviewed, only Parkin claimed the sound of the latter shot had been no louder than the former, but then he was trying to conceal the truth about where it had been fired."

"Pardon me for interrupting, Holmes," said I. "But why exactly was the shot fired at all?"

"Because Major Yates and Sam Parkin could not afford Montague's body to be discovered by chance. For the illusion of the locked door to work, they had to be the ones who appeared to force it open, and the others merely witnesses to that act. Of course, Major Yates knew that his guests would be unlikely to damage his property without his permission, and Parkin and he were quick to do the deed before anyone had a chance to join them and notice the curious lack of resistance from the door. The gunshot was merely the cue for a staged conjuring trick.

"As soon as the door had been opened, I carried out my examination, and realized how the deception had been accomplished. Although I was convinced that the gun had been fired outside the room, and that it had probably been hidden in the cupboard on the landing, I said nothing, as I did not wish to alert the murderers to the fact that I had discovered their secret. There was still much that I did not understand – and two more murders to be solved. Moreover, I had yet to discover the motive for the killing of Grafton Montague, and why it had been carried out in such a sadistic fashion. One thing, however, was clear to me. Whoever had murdered Henry St. John Bosco, it could not have been Major Yates or Sam Parkin: both had been with me in the Front Hall when the shot which killed him had been fired.

"It was not until the morning after Grafton Montague's death that I began to understand. Together with Watson, I examined the landing outside the Library, and discovered the bullet which had been fired to alert us to the fact that the historian had been killed. The gun, however, had been removed from the cupboard, presumably by one of the two conspirators. However, I was still in the dark about both the motive for the crime and the identity of the murderer of Henry St. John Bosco and John Ayto.

"It was when I was sitting in the Drawing Room after

breakfast that inspiration came to me. If you remember, Watson, Major Yates was seated at the desk in the window, writing a letter. At some stage in my reverie, I chanced to glance up at that window, and suddenly I saw the key to the whole mystery. I believe Dr. Watson thought that it was something *outside the window* which had excited my interest. But, on the contrary, it was what I could see that was *reflected in it*. I refer to the *face of Major Reculver Yates*.

"Of course, I had looked at that face many times before. But now it was as though I was viewing it for the first time. It was a florid face, with deep-sunk, fat-encircled eyes, which oscillated from side to side. But remove the corpulence and the ruddiness, and what did you have? Nothing less than the face of Professor Moriarty himself: the same eyes, the same reptilian oscillation. Major Yates was Moriarty's brother, James.

"Suddenly I felt the hairs stand out on the back of my neck. 'Major R.M.I. Yates' was an exact anagram of 'James Moriarty'! My mind was racing. For, if Major Yates was not who he said he was, might not the same thing apply to his house-guests? Here, then, could be the key to the motive for the murder of Grafton Montague, and for those of Henry St. John Bosco and John Ayto. I resolved at once to go to London, in order to consult my case-notes on all those unsolved crimes which I had suspected were the work of Professor Moriarty's minions – as well as the relevant records held by Scotland Yard. I was determined to root out the true identities of Major Yates's Tilstone Court cronies.

"I turned first to Sam Parkin, Major Yates's so-called gardener, and quickly found evidence that he is, in fact, Israel Sless, otherwise known as 'Porky Sless' or 'the Camden Ripper', a vicious killer hired by Professor Moriarty to 'remove' anyone who stands in his path. The sobriquet

'Camden Ripper' dates from the time when, at Moriarty's behest, he brutally murdered and robbed an entire family, including three young children, a crime which, for years, has remained unsolved, but which bore all the hallmarks of Professor Moriarty's evil genius. The Camden killings were characterized by a level of sadism which was extreme even by Sless's standards. In particular, the body of the youngest child had been horribly mutilated, its throat cut, and its chest hacked to ribbons with a knife. This was the work of someone who revelled in the act of killing for its own sake, and explains why Grafton Montague met such a gory end, and why 'Sam Parkin' reacted so violently when a harmless wayfarer tried to break into his garden shed.

"But, if Porky Sless had killed Grafton Montague on behalf of Professor Moriarty or his brother, what had been their motive? And who had murdered Henry St. John Bosco and John Ayto?

"I needed to find out more about the historian, and about how James Moriarty had gone about the task of assuming the identity of Major Reculver Yates."

13: The Master Blackmailer

During the foregoing discourse, Inspector Lestrade's assistants had moved in quickly to cuff the two men Sherlock Holmes had accused. Major Yates had offered no resistance, but Sam Parkin – or Porky Sless, as we now knew him – had shown signs of making a bolt for it, a move forestalled by the zealous police constable who barred his way. Meanwhile, my friend had resumed his narrative.

"After Major Yates had left 221B Baker Street on the 20th of December," (said Sherlock Holmes) "I looked him up in my index of biographies. I discovered that he was the son of Sir Frederick Yates, the ex-Cabinet Minister, that he had been educated at Eton and Oxford, and that he was a former member of the First Bengalore Pioneers. As such, he had served with Colonel Sebastian Moran, the one-time Chief of Staff to Professor Moriarty.

"Following my discovery of the true identity of the man who was passing himself off as Major Reculver Yates, I resolved to carry out some further research. It became clear that

Colonel Sebstian Moran, Professor Moriarty and his brother, James, had all been educated at Eton and Oxford at the same time as Reculver Yates, although James Moriarty – and Yates himself, who, like James, was born in 1842 – did not become students at the University until two years after James's brother and Sebastian Moran. If not at Eton, then certainly at Oxford, the two Moriartys and Moran, together with a number of other prominent intellectuals, both older and younger than themselves, formed the nucleus of an association – with the elder Moriarty brother at its head – which was to become a mighty criminal organization. Reculver Yates, while not part of this group, was acquainted with its members, and later joined the same regiment as Sebastian Moran.

"The entry for Major Yates in my index of biographies was based on that which appeared in a recent edition of *Who's Who*. When I returned to London yesterday, I took the opportunity of consulting a number of earlier editions of that work of reference, and discovered some important discrepancies. Here, for instance, is an entry for Reculver Yates which appeared in *Who's Who* several years ago. '*Yates, Reculver Merevale Jonathan, Major.* Formerly First Bengalore Pioneers. Born London 1842. Son of Sir Frederick Yates, the Conservative politician and Cabinet Minister. Educated Eton and Oxford. Served in Afghan Campaign, Sherpur (dispatches) and Cabul. Address: Conduit Street. Clubs: The Anglo-Indian, the Tankerville.' Does anything strike you as significant?"

"Why, the Christian names!" I exclaimed excitedly. "According to the entry in your index – and to the legend which appears above his front door in the Horseshoe Cloister – Major Yates's initials are R.M.I., standing for Reculver Merevale Iain, not Reculver Merevale *Jonathan*."

"Anything else?"

"There is no mention of his living at Tilstone Court or Windsor Castle, or of his being a lay clerk at St. George's Chapel."

"That is because at the time he was still living in his rooms in Conduit Street, next to Colonel Sebastian Moran, his former commanding officer.

"I believe what happened was this. Major Yates – the real one, that is, not James Moriarty – was a reclusive man, with few friends apart from his former military acquaintances – and many of those had been killed on active service. His father, Sir Frederick Yates, likewise, lived a solitary life, in the home of his recent forefathers, Tilstone Court, with only an old housekeeper for company. When Sir Frederick died, this servant inherited enough money to be able to retire to a small cottage in Cornwall, and Tilstone Court passed to Sir Frederick's son, Reculver.

"It was at this juncture that Professor Moriarty intervened. His criminal ventures had yet to realize any significant revenue, and he was on the look-out for any opportunity to acquire wealth and influence. Through his colleague, Colonel Sebastian Moran, he knew that Major Yates was virtually unknown outside his immediate circle. At the same time, Moriarty's brother, James, was also a military man, albeit of higher rank – a Colonel – and from a different regiment. Together, the two brothers travelled down to Tilstone Court with Major Reculver Yates, to help install him in his new home. They made sure, I have no doubt, that his arrival at the house was conducted in secrecy, and that there was nobody on hand who was acquainted with the real owner of the property.

"Professor Moriarty then arranged for Major Yates to be murdered – it is doubtful that he committed the crime himself, for that is not the Professor's way. Colonel James Moriarty became Major Reculver Yates, a role for which his own military background fitted him well, but insisted that the real Major Yates be given a decent Christian burial. As there was no chapel in the grounds of Tilstone Court, and circumstances prevented a proper service in a local church, James arranged for a tomb to be constructed by a local mason, ostensibly for eventual use by himself, and had it installed in the old priest-hole, which was the nearest thing Tilstone Court had to a private chapel. The tomb bore an inscription to 'R.M.J. Yates', which was, of course, the major's real name."

"But why did James Moriarty change the initials when he took on Major Yates's identity?" said I.

"If the burial of Major Yates with all due ceremony was at the insistence of Colonel James Moriarty, I am sure that it was Professor Moriarty who persuaded his brother to make the alteration to the name. He is, above all, a man of supreme arrogance, and when he realized that by changing just one initial, he could make Major Yates's name a prefect anagram of 'Colonel James Moriarty', it was just too much for him to resist. It appealed to his sense of humour, and demonstrated his contempt for the police and all who opposed his criminal ambitions. James Moriarty was in thrall to his brother, and abided by his wishes. Moreover, the entries in *Who's Who* are based on information supplied annually by the subjects themselves. The alteration of one initial was unlikely to be spotted by the compilers, let alone the readership."

"One moment, Holmes," I interjected. "When we opened the tomb, it was empty. What had become of Major Yates's remains?"

"I am sure that they were removed by members of Professor Moriarty's gang the moment they realized I had discovered his hiding-place.

"At the time of the imposture, however, what the Professor and his brother had not realized was that Sir Frederick Yates had not been as wealthy as they supposed. The cost of maintaining such a lavish property in an area prone to flooding had proved to be a severe drain on his finances, and, as I say, Professor Moriarty's criminal activities had yet to net him any sizeable monetary gains of his own. Furthermore, in order to maintain the authenticity of the role he had assumed, it was necessary for James Moriarty to keep a low profile, even when the money did start to roll in. He took to wearing items from the former owner's wardrobe, clothing whose dilapidated condition provided evidence of former wealth but recent penury. As he and his brother grew richer, James none the less forbore to indulge himself in any lavishness which might attract suspicion: he engaged only a modest staff, and maintained his threadbare appearance. Only recently have there been signs that he is wealthier than he has led people to believe. The decorations on his Christmas tree, for example, would be worthy of a royal household.

"During the course of my investigations at Tilstone Court, I discovered two clues which, in the light of what I had now learned, provided evidence of 'Major Yates's' true identity. First, there was the *apologia* for Professor Moriarty which was found in Major Yates's bureau. At the time, this document struck Dr. Watson as being familiar. This was because it resembled the letters which Colonel James Moriarty wrote in his own name in defence of the memory of his brother, following his apparent death at the Reichenbach Falls, and which prompted my friend to pen his own account of that incident in a report which he subsequently entitled 'The Final Problem'.

"The second clue was the missing picture in the Library. Major Yates had claimed it was a view of the south front of

Windsor Castle from the Long Walk. But the picture had clearly been a *portrait*, rather than a landscape. As all the other pictures in the room were portraits of Sir Frederick Yates and other family members past and present, I was now in a position to infer that the missing portrait had been a youthful impression of James Moriarty, placed there to lend authenticity to the imposture. However, the Colonel had clearly had second thoughts. If, as it eventually transpired, I was able to discern the likeness to his brother from a mere reflection in the window, how much more likely that I would have been able to recognize the youthful features of an early portrait, ere age and corpulence had effected their disguise.

"As to Major Yates's position as a lay clerk at St. George's Chapel, this was a chapter in his biography that was added by James Moriarty after he became the owner of Tilstone Court. He had a a fine singing voice, enjoyed the work and – at least in the beginning – found the income useful. The secondary lodging at Windsor Castle was a bonus.

"Having successfully researched the history of James Moriarty's imposture, I now turned to that of his most recent victim, Grafton Montague. Major Yates claimed to have met Montague and his wife for the first time last summer in the Lake District. They had struck up a friendship, and Yates had invited them back to Tilstone Court for Christmas. I am sure that, so far as *Mrs*. Montague was concerned, this was indeed the first time she had met Colonel James Moriarty – or Major Yates, as she knew him. But her husband was already acquainted with him: in fact, he had been a member of his brother's criminal organization for years.

"Grafton Montague had read history at Oxford, although this was long after Moriarty had departed. However, the Professor's evil legacy lived on. Henry St. John Bosco, an older man, whose services had been enlisted by Moriarty – and at that time still a tutor at the University, before he left to become a writer and editor – was himself a leading light in the organization which Moriarty had created, and continued to recruit on the Professor's behalf from each new intake of students. Amongst those he introduced to the syndicate was the young Grafton Montague, who quickly established himself as a master blackmailer for the Moriarty gang.

"When Colonel James Moriarty, posing as Major Reculver Yates, resumed his acquaintance with Grafton Montague in the Lake District last summer, he immediately charged the historian with a new task, which would involve his travelling to Tilstone Court, although, as I say, Mr. Montague kept his wife in ignorance of the real reason for the invitation. Was this task perhaps to do away with the tiresome Henry St. John Bosco, once a useful recruiter for the Moriarty network, but now a writer who was intent on publishing his memoirs – memoirs which might, either by accident or design, reveal damaging truths about the criminal organization of which he had once been a leading member?

"But James Moriarty – 'Major Yates' – had not reckoned with Grafton Montague's treachery. Many times in the past, the historian, acting for the syndicate, had proceeded under threats of exposure to levy blackmail upon his hapless victims. Now he turned his attention to the very people on whose behalf he had operated: in short, he attempted to blackmail his own colleagues.

"Dr. Watson and I saw Grafton Montague extracting money from Sam Parkin – the man whom we now know as Porky Sless, the Camden Ripper, and another paid employé of the Moriarty gang. The fact that a humble gardener possessed so much cash was testament to his criminal *alter ego*, and no doubt

Grafton Montague had threatened to reveal the truth unless he paid up. The elaborate explanation which Sam Parkin gave for being in possession of the money which, in reality, he had been paid for his 'services' – namely that he had worked as a gardener for Montague's father, and had robbed that gentleman after incurring gambling debts – was a work of fiction which Grafton Montague was himself only too happy to corroborate, in order to conceal his own guilty history. I don't suppose Sam Parkin ever was a gardener, and only undertook nominal tasks in the grounds of Tilstone Court for the sake of appearances.

"Grafton Montague's blackmailing activities extended beyond the Camden Ripper, however. The money which Dr. Watson and I discovered in his bedroom was more than four times the amount we had seen him extract from the gardener. When quizzed about this, Mr. Montague attempted to fob us off with a story about Major Yates having borrowed money from him in the Lake District, a sum which the owner of Tilstone Court had since repaid. I believe that, in reality, Montague was blackmailing Major Yates – about his true identity and his role in a major criminal organization.

"*Blackmail*, then, appeared to have been the reason why Grafton Montague was murdered by Sam Parkin and Colonel James Moriarty. But was Grafton Montague himself guilty of the murder of Henry St. John Bosco? Let us look at the evidence. When St. John Bosco was killed in the Drawing Room, Grafton Montague was nowhere to be seen. Earlier he had been in the Library with his wife and with William and Rosalind Clunies-Ross, but the latter couple had retired to their bedroom, while Montague himself, so he claimed, had 'heard the sound of the waits in the Front Hall and resolved to join the party downstairs'. However, again according to the historian, he had been deflected from this purpose by the noise of a door being opened in the north-west angle-turret, and had gone to investigate. Are we to believe that he knew nothing of the presence of Professor Moriarty in the house and of his hiding-place in the priest-hole? As a keen historian, he must surely have at least known of the existence of the latter. In short, was this story of a stranger in the tower a mere fabriacation? Did Grafton Montague, acting on behalf of the Moriarty brothers and Porky Sless – all worried, as indeed was Montague himself, about the possibility of exposure in Henry St. John Bosco's forthcoming memoirs – enter the Drawing Room and shoot the writer dead with his revolver?

"But here we hit a snag. If Montague had killed St. John Bosco, he must then have gone to his own bedroom, placed the gun on his bed, and returned to the south wing, before climbing the tower to lend credibility to his cover story about a mystery intruder. But why had he bothered to take the revolver back to his room at all? Even if he had intended to hide it in his suitcase, but was prevented from so doing by circumstances beyond his control, that action simply made no sense. Why not just leave the weapon at the scene of the crime, and then deny any connection with it? And even if his wife were to recognize it and give the game away, that would be equally damning wherever the gun was discovered.

"Perhaps, then, it was *Mrs.* Montague who had committed the crime, and tried to frame her husband. We know that, for a time at least, she suspected him of conducting a liaison with Mrs. Clunies-Ross, so it is quite possible that she bore him a grudge. Could it be that Grafton Montague was telling the truth when he said that he went straight to the Tower Room? Could it be that, while he was there, Celia Montague, using her husband's gun, slipped into the Drawing Room and shot Henry St. John Bosco, before taking the weapon back to her bedroom and placing it on her husband's bed? True, the action would have been fraught with risk, but it would have been possible. And did she then return to the Library, where she was discovered later, apparently too frightened to leave the room?"

Celia Montague rose to her feet, her face all drawn and grey, with restless, frightened eyes, like those of some haunted animal. "It's a lie, Mr. Holmes!" she cried passionately. "I am innocent. I was in the Library all the time, just as I said."

"Do not trouble yourself, my dear," said Holmes soothingly. "I do not believe that you did anything untoward. The objection that I raised to the case against your husband applies equally to you. Why go to the trouble of placing the gun on his bed when a simple statement as to its ownership would have equal force?

"I was strongly inclined to believe both your story and that of your husband. This would imply that Grafton Montague did not know that Professor Moriarty was still alive until that gentleman appeared at the window late on Christmas Eve. Montague's story about a mysterious stranger in the tower and his decision to investigate was true, and, given the historian's propensity for blackmail, it was perhaps understandable that the secret of Professor Moriarty's survival was kept from him.

"It was the shock of seeing Professor Moriarty alive at the window of the Front Hall, I believe, that led to the row which Grafton Montague had with Major Yates at his apartment in the Horseshoe Cloister after the service at St. George's Chapel on Christmas morning. Major Yates claimed that the argument had centred on Montague's failure to tell him about Sam Parkin's shady past, but, as we know the whole story about gambling debts and the assault and robbery of Grafton Montague's father was a complete fabrication, I do not believe that was the case. I think Montague was angry that he had been kept in the dark about Professor Moriarty's survival, and attempted to levy further blackmail on the strength of it. With his knowledge of the history of Tilstone Court, he would have realized by now, as I did eventually myself, that Moriarty was using the old priest-hole as a hiding-place, and he now threatened to tell the police unless he was paid more money. This provoked the angry reaction from Major Yates which Dr. Watson and I overheard.

"It was not just..." began Major Yates falteringly.

"Yes, Colonel Moriarty?"

"Nothing. It was nothing."

Major Yates lapsed into silence, and Sherlock Holmes resumed his address.

"We may fairly conclude, then," said he, "that neither Grafton Montague nor his wife was responsible for the murder of Henry St. John Bosco. And since both Major Yates and Sam Parkin were in the Front Hall with Dr. Watson and me at the time of the killing, they could not have done it either. So who did murder the editor? My thoughts now turned to the singular matter of William Clunies-Ross's aptitude for billiards."

"But he did not pot a single ball," said I with a touch of bewilderment.

"That was the singular matter."

14: The Gosling Street Bank Robber

"From the moment I saw William Clunies-Ross in action at the table," (continued Sherlock Holmes) "I knew that he had never handled a billiard cue before in his life. So why was he so keen to challenge Dr. Watson to a game? Even before I carried out my research in London yesterday, I suspected that William Clunies-Ross was involved with Major Yates (or James Moriarty) and Sam Parkin (or Israel Sless) in the plot to murder Grafton Montague. For, apart from his eagerness to keep Dr Watson and me occupied while the killing took place – Watson by playing him at a game of which he himself clearly had no practical experience, and me by enlisting my services as a scorer – Clunies-Ross had twice before aroused my suspicions by hob-nobbing with the gardener. The first occasion was after my return from Windsor on the 22nd of December, when Dr. Watson and I surprised the pair of them in the Library. Why should a well-bred and educated man like Clunies-Ross bother to engage a common gardener in conversation inside his master's house? After some initial embarrassment, Clunies-Ross tried to fob us off by claiming that they had been discussing the arrangements for the Christmas decorations. But both men seemed ill at ease, and I was convinced that, in reality, they had been discussing matters of greater moment. The second time was at the Crown and Cushion on Christmas Day, when Dr. Watson and I were returning from St. George's Chapel with Mrs. Clunies-Ross. The old Etonian insisted that it had been a chance meeting, but when I espied them through the window, they were deep in conversation, and seemed the best of friends.

"I went to London, then, convinced in my own mind that William Clunies-Ross had been involved in the plot to kill Grafton Montague, and further evidence was waiting for me when I returned, and heard Dr. Watson's account of the old Etonian's movements while I had been away. It became clear that it had been Clunies-Ross who had retrieved the gun from the cupboard outside the Library, before disposing of it by dropping it down the well in the courtyard which lies at the heart of Tilstone Court.

"But, as I say, even before receiving this confirmation, I was convinced of Clunies-Ross's involvement in Montague's death, and this knowledge influenced the direction of my researches, both among my own archives and those held by Scotland Yard. I soon found enough evidence to show that William Clunies-Ross's real name was Fraser Digby, and that he was a member of the organization which the future Professor Moriarty started at Oxford University. We already knew that William Clunies-Ross – or Fraser Digby, to give him his real name – had been a school-friend of James Moriarty (later to become Major Yates) at Eton. But the two men also studied together at Oxford University, where Digby, who achieved first-class honours in his chosen subject of geology, was widely recognized as the cleverest student of his generation. After leaving Oxford, Fraser Digby worked for Professor Moriarty, and became a notorious thief, whose speciality was running tunnels to bank-vaults from adjacent buildings. He later took the young John Clay under his wing, who himself had been to Eton and Oxford, and who was recruited to the Moriarty gang by Henry St. John Bosco. Digby taught John Clay everything he knew about constructing tunnels, knowledge which the latter was to use when he attempted to steal French gold from the Coburg branch of the City and Suburban Bank. That crime – which Dr. Watson has chronicled under the title 'The Red-Headed League' – was never traced to Professor Moriarty, but he was undoubtedly the mastermind behind it, as he was behind all of John Clay's criminal enterprises. For his own part, Fraser Digby's most famous crime – although it is only now that we have finally been able to lay it at his door – was the Gosling Street Bank Robbery. In that case, the thieves made away with eight thousand pounds by tunnelling into the premises from a nearby shop, which had been closed on the spurious grounds that it was structurally unsafe.

"Here, perhaps, I should mention Rosalind Clunies-Ross – or Mrs. Fraser Digby. Unlike Celia Montague, who knew nothing of her husband's criminal connections, Rosalind Digby was herself a member of the Moriarty gang, albeit a minor one. An accomplished pick-pocket, she befriended, and fell in love with, Fraser Digby, and went on to act as his accomplice in a number of bank robberies and other major crimes.

"Fraser and Mrs. Digby (William and Rosalind Clunies-Ross), together with James Moriarty (Major Yates) and Israel Sless (Sam Parkin), conspired to kill Grafton Montague because he was blackmailing them, and threatening to expose their criminal history. Whether he would have risked going to the police when he was himself a member of the gang and guilty of a number of crimes, not least blackmail, is a moot point. But the conspirators were not prepared to take the chance. And prior to this, there had been another threat to their organization: Henry St. John Bosco, the man who, for years, had recruited on behalf of Professor Moriarty at Oxford University, was intent on publishing his memoirs. Would he, unwittingly or on purpose, give away some of the gang's secrets?

"If Major Yates and Sam Parkin were the men responsible for the murder of Grafton Montague, then it was William Clunies-Ross who killed Henry St. John Bosco. Moreover, when John Ayto had died, suspicion had fallen, rightly or wrongly, on Randal Norton, whose stick had been used in the crime. William Clunies-Ross therefore deemed it wise to implicate the paying-guest in the death of Henry St. John Bosco as well.

"Fraser Digby's (William Clunies-Ross's) first priority, however, was to destroy St. John Bosco's manuscript. When Clunies-Ross was discovered outside the editor's room in the east wing shortly after he had burned the memoirs and left a threatening message in their place, his rather feeble explanation for being there was that he had been looking for Grafton Montague because he wanted to lend him a book about the history of Windsor and Eton. But why should he mistake St. John Bosco's room for Montague's, when the latter's was in fact only two doors away from his own in the west wing? The story was an obvious falsehood, and in reality William Clunies-Ross had not only vandalized St. John Bosco's room, he had also planted, in Randal Norton's room, the copy of *The Times* from which he had manufactured the threatening message.

"Incidentally, while Henry St. John Bosco denied knowing William Clunies-Ross (or Fraser Digby) when he was at Oxford, he must have done so, as both were members of the Moriarty gang. The fact that St. John Bosco was not prepared to admit this may have been an indication that the criminal organization had nothing to fear from the publcation of his memoirs after all. However, there was a good chance that the editor would re-write his autobiography following the destruction of the original manuscript, and Fraser Digby and his colleagues were not prepared to risk the potential consequences. St. John Bosco had to be killed, and the blame thrown upon Randal Norton, who would become the chief suspect once the mutilated copy of *The Times* was found in his chest of drawers.

"However, at this juncture, something occurred which caused James Moriarty (Major Yates), Israel Sless (Sam Parkin) and Fraser Digby (William Clunies-Ross) to modify the scheme which they had devised. During my initial interview with William Clunies-Ross after the eradication of St. John Bosco's memoirs, I gave no hint as to the direction of my thinking. But when I interrogated him again, I showed him from my questions that it was really *Grafton Montague* and not Randal Norton who was under suspicion. I asked Clunies-Ross if Grafton Montague had had a scratch on his face when the old Etonian had finally caught up with him, indicating that I suspected the historian of being my nocturnal assailant. And my question concerning Montague's movements after the alarm had been raised on the night of Ayto's death suggested that I suspected him of that crime as well.

"By now, the three conspirators had already decided to do away with Grafton Montague because they were tired of being blackmailed by him. So, if I already suspected the historian of killing John Ayto, why not implicate him in the murder of Henry St. John Bosco too? He would make a far more convincing red herring than Randal Norton, who had already been practically discounted as the murderer of John Ayto, and if Montague were himself to be murdered, he would not be able to retaliate by spilling the beans on his former colleagues. Clunies-Ross thus abandoned his attempts to incriminate Randal Norton, and targeted Grafton Montague in his place.

"When we heard the shot that killed Henry St. John Bosco on Christmas Eve, Dr. Watson, Major Yates, Sam Parkin, Porson and I immediately rushed up the ornamental stair, and found William Clunies-Ross on the landing, about to enter the Drawing Room. Clunies-Ross claimed that he had been returning from his bedroom in the west wing, when he had heard the shot. He had already looked in the Dining Room, but had found it empty.

"What *actually* happened was this. Earlier, Mr. and Mrs. Clunies-Ross had been with Mr. and Mrs. Montague in the Library, the next room along from the Drawing Room. After a while they had left, saying that they were going to return to their room in the west wing, but in fact they both joined Henry St. John Bosco in the Drawing Room next door, where he was working at the desk.

"Shortly after this, Grafton Montague left the Library too, saying he was going to listen to the waits in the Front Hall. But, hearing a noise in the tower, he went off to investigate that instead.

"William Clunies-Ross then shot Henry St. John Bosco, using a gun that he had found in Grafton Montague's suit-case. Standing just two feet away from his victim, he pointed the weapon at St. John Bosco's head; the editor lunged forward, grasping Clunies-Ross's waist-coat, and wrenching off a button, which fell to the floor and rolled under the arm-chair; and then the old Etonian fired, causing the blood to spurt from St. John Bosco's head into his face. Clunies-Ross used a handkerchief to wipe the blood away, before replacing it in his pocket, and later burning it in his bedroom, where I found the charred remains. He then passed the murder weapon to his wife, who had been charged with the task of returning it to Montague's suit-case, in the belief that its discovery there would incriminate him. Both Mr. and Mrs. Clunies-Ross had by now left the Drawing Room through the connecting door to the Dining Room. They did not know how quickly people would get to the scene of the crime once they had heard the shot, and could not risk either being found with the body or being seen coming out of the murder room. The fact that the door to the Drawing Room was open, and the interior illuminated, would be bound to make that room the first port of call for any newcomers, and once they had entered, it would be safe for Clunies-Ross to slip out of the Dining Room and join them, and for Mrs. Clunies-Ross to make her way to the west wing. In the event, Clunies-Ross had time to get out on to the landing before anyone came up the ornamental stair, and Mrs. Montague was too frightened to leave the Library. Mrs. Clunies-Ross, I imagine, left the Dining Room, and set off for Montague's room in the west wing, while we were examining the body in the Drawing Room.

"Rosalind Clunies-Ross knew that Montague's bedroom was somewhere near her own, but it had been her husband who had stolen the gun in the first place. Now, in her hurry and confusion, she made a mistake, and found herself in the wrong room. Although she did eventually locate the right one, the delay would prove extremely problematical. The plan had been to replace the weapon in Montague's suit-case, where it could be discovered by the police or me. Mrs. Clunies-Ross had put the gun down on Montague's bed, and was about to lift the suit-case down from the top of the wardrobe, when she heard Dr. Watson and me approaching with Mrs. Montague. Unable to escape from the room – or even to retrieve the weapon from the bed – before we made our entrance, she hid in the wardrobe, and was there when we came in. Mrs. Montague immediately recognized the gun as belonging to her husband, but its presence on the bed represented an inexplicable act of stupidity on his part if he had indeed been the murderer.

"Dr. Watson, Mrs. Montague and I then went to Mrs. Clunies-Ross's bedroom. According to William Clunies-Ross, he and his wife had retired there after leaving the Montagues in the Library. Mr. Clunies-Ross had 'returned to fetch a book', before being distracted by the gun-shot. But Mrs. Clunies-Ross should have been there – as indeed she *would* have been if the business of placing the gun in Montague's suit-case had gone according to plan. As it was, the delay caused by going to the wrong room, and then having to hide in the wardrobe, meant that the Clunies-Rosses' bedroom was empty when we arrived. When questioned about this later, Mrs. Clunies-Ross invented a story about having gone to Porson's room to procure a night-cap.

"As soon as we had returned to the south wing, Mrs. Clunies-Ross made her escape from the wardrobe – where, incidentally, a brooch had become detached from her costume and fallen to the floor – and made her way to the Drawing Room. However, the discovery of the gun which she had left on Montague's bed, and of the brooch she had lost in the wardrobe, would lead, as we shall see, to a host of complications.

"When Grafton Montague arrived at the scene of the crime after his abortive 'ghost hunt' in the tower, his reaction to the fact that a murder had taken place, and that the weapon used had been his own gun, was very different from that of his wife. Where Mrs. Montague had seen only the theft of her husband's property for use in a crime, Grafton Montague perceived a deliberate attempt to incriminate him in the murder of Henry St. John Bosco.

"But why did he suspect that William Clunies-Ross was the man behind this bid to frame him? Well, he knew that Major Yates, Sam Parkin and Porson all had alibis, having been down in the Front Hall at the time of the murder with Dr. Watson and me. As for the Nortons, while they could not prove that they were in their room, there was a particular reason why Montague did not suspect *them* – which I will come to in due course. Montague knew that his own wife was innocent – she was not even aware of her husband's criminal activities. But William Clunies-Ross had been found outside the murder room: not only *could* he have committed the crime, he was the *only person* who could have done so. Morevoer, he had the motive, being part of the criminal organization whose members Montague was blackmailing.

"At this stage, Grafton Montague did not suspect Mrs. Clunies-Ross of having been involved in the murder at all. So far as he knew, while he had been up in the tower when the crime was being committed, she had been in her bedroom. He did not realize that it would have been impossible for William Clunies-Ross himself to have planted the gun in the historian's room and to have returned to the scene of the crime in time to 'discover' the body. But he was sure that Clunies-Ross had killed St. John Bosco, and convinced that the old Etonian had tried to implicate him in the murder.

"Armed with this knowledge, you might think that Grafton Montague would have publicly accused William Clunies-Ross of the crime, and tried to clear his own name. *But there was a potent reason why he could not afford to do so, and that reason will become clear presently.*

"What Grafton Montague did do, however, was to confront William Clunies-Ross with his suspicions. This was the real cause of the fight between the two men in the Library on Christmas Day. Grafton Montague accused William Clunies-Ross of being the murderer of Henry St. John Bosco, and of trying to incriminate him by using his gun and leaving it on his bed. A brawl ensued, but since neither man could risk revealing the real reason for it, they invented a story about William Clunies-Ross having made advances to Mrs. Montague. The latter, who had left the room before the fight had developed, later denied that there had been any flirtation between the old Etonian and herself; while Mrs. Clunies-Ross flatly refused to believe the story at all, as it simply did not fit with her knowledge of her husband's character.

"However, Montague's resentment of Clunies-Ross's attempt to frame him persisted, and he continued to retaliate by himself flirting with the old Etonian's wife, ignorant as he was, at least at first, of the part she had played in the deception. No doubt Montague hoped to make Clunies-Ross jealous, and this was some small revenge for the wrong which the latter had done him.

"The matter was further complicated, however, by the discovery of Mrs. Clunies-Ross's brooch in Montague's wardrobe. Although Grafton Montague pretended not to understand the reason for its presence, he knew that the brooch did not belong to his wife, as she did not possess any jewellery (his suggestion that it might have been a gift to her from Clunies-Ross was disingenuous, for he was aware that there had been no liaison between them). In fact, he guessed that the brooch must have been dropped there by Mrs. Clunies-Ross while she was in the process of returning the gun to his room, and that she had therefore been involved in a conspiracy against him. However, Mrs. Montague, who suspected her husband of conducting an illicit affair with Mrs. Clunies-Ross, when, in fact, he was only trying to annoy the old Etonian, eventually confronted her rival, and accused her of adultery. Mrs. Clunies-Ross made up a story about having gone to Montague's room to borrow a book, and how – fearful of a scandal – she had hidden in the wardrobe when she heard Mrs. Montague approaching. Of course, if Mr. Montague had himself had a chance to hear this explanation, he would have known it to be a fabrication. But he would probably have kept quiet anyway, having no wish to tell his wife the truth, since that would have involved revealing his own criminality; whilst the story had the additional virtue of establishing his innocence so far as any serious romantic involvement with Mrs. Clunies-Ross was concerned.

"By now, as I said before, William Clunies-Ross, Major Yates and Sam Parkin had decided to do away with Grafton Montague. Whilst they had been at pains to throw suspicion on him for the murder of St. John Bosco, they trusted that purely circumstantial evidence would be insufficient to lead to his arrest. For although, as I said before, there was a reason why Montague could not afford to expose Clunies-Ross as the Editor's killer, this would cease to be the case if he were himself to be apprehended for that crime. It was necessary for the historian to be silenced before he was compelled to spill the beans on Clunies-Ross in particular and Moriarty's gang in general – and while suspicion still rested on him for the murders of both Ayto and St. John Bosco.

"One moment, Holmes," said I. "How do you explain the evidence of Henry St. John Bosco's two diaries?"

"Very simply. While Grafton Montague would only have informed on William Clunies-Ross in the event of his arrest for the murder of Henry St. John Bosco, there was something he could do straight away to throw the police off his scent. He decided to frame Randal Norton, the man on whom suspicion had first fallen following the murder of John Ayto, and whom William Clunies-Ross had himself tried to incriminate before targeting the historian.

"Grafton Montague searched Henry St. John Bosco's room, and found a diary, which he intended to plant in Randal Norton's bedroom, after interpolating a number of incriminating entries. However, unfortunately the diary was full, and it was necessary for Montague to obtain a second, blank, diary, in which he wrote St. John Bosco's name and several spurious references to the paying-guest, painstakingly copying the editor's hand-writing from the original. The genuine diary was then burnt in Montague's fire-place, and the forgery planted in Randal Norton's suit-case.

"Well done, Lestrade. I see you have lost no time in adding Mr. and Mrs. Clunies-Ross – or should I say Mr. and Mrs. Digby? – to your 'bag'. I suggest you also arrest Porson. There is no doubt that he is a member of the gang, and that, by keeping Professor Moriarty's whereabouts secret, and plying him with food and drink, he was aiding and abetting a wanted man."

"There is still one point on which I am not clear," said I, as the handcuffs clattered upon the butler's wrists. "I understand that Clunies-Ross, Yates and Parkin conspired to murder first Henry St. John Bosco and then Grafton Montague. But they could not have killed John Ayto."

"That is quite true, Watson. Clunies-Ross and Major Yates were in St. George's Chapel at the time, and Sam Parkin was in the Crown and Cushion. *So who did murder Colonel Moriarty's secretary?*"

15: The Hackney Forger

"In order to answer that question," (said Sherlock Holmes) "it is necessary to go back to the meeting between Major Yates and Mr. and Mrs. Montague in Cumberland last summer. As I suggested before, this was no chance encounter, although Mrs. Montague believed it to be so. But what was the *real reason* for the meeting?

"We have already established that it was not to arrange for Grafton Montague to kill Henry St. John Bosco. That crime was committed by William Clunies-Ross. I suggested earlier that Grafton Montague began to blackmail his colleagues *after* he arrived at Tilstone Court. But what if he had been blackmailing them all along? What if the meeting in the Lake District had been arranged by Grafton Montague to enable Major Yates to make the latest payment? What if, after all, Major Yates had taken the opportunity of that meeting to invite Grafton Montague to Tilstone Court so that he could perform a task for him? And what if that task had been to murder not Henry St. John Bosco, *but John Ayto*? Grafton Montague was never going to turn down the chance to earn the substantial amount of money which he would be paid for such a mission. And what's more, it was in his own interest to kill the secretary. John Ayto was clearly about to turn informer on the criminal organization for which he worked; and that included Grafton Montague, the master blackmailer.

"Incidentally, I believe the cash which Dr. Watson and I found in Grafton Montague's room represented the payment he received for the crimes he was engaged to commit, and not just the fruits of his blackmailing activities. But, to return to the murder of John Ayto. It seemed obvious that the torn scrap of paper in the victim's hand was part of a larger document which had been wrenched from his grasp at the time of his death. That fragment contained three pairs of initials, one of them somewhat indistinct: 'J.C.', 'F.D.' and 'I.S.(?)'. In the light of what we now know about Professor Moriarty's gang, it is clear that these letters must have referred to 'John Clay', 'Fraser Digby' and 'Israel Sless'. Add to that the fact that John Ayto had arranged to meet Inspector Lestrade at Tilstone Court in order to tell him what he knew about 'several major crimes', including the Gosling Street Bank Robbery, which was masterminded by Fraser Digby (or William Clunies-Ross), and we are left in no doubt about the motive for John Ayto's murder. What's more, when we searched the secretary's room, we found the remains of a common-place book, the rest of which had been either stolen or destroyed. This had no doubt contained many press cuttings relating to felonies carried out by the Moriarty organization, and indeed a few of them had escaped unscathed, including an account of John Clay's ingenious attempt to steal French gold from the Coburg Branch of the City and Suburban Bank.

"With that in mind, I endeavoured to find out more about John Ayto during my visits to Baker Street and Scotland Yard yesterday. I soon discovered that his chief claim to fame was as a forger, and that for years he operated from premises in Hackney, where he set up a counterfeiter's outfit. He eventually came to the attention of Professor Moriarty, and was taken under the latter's wing. Ultimately he became Colonel James Moriarty's secretary, and continued to produce bundles of forged bank-notes for the gang right up until the time of his death. Indeed, if you remember, some hundred such notes were found on his corpse. It is also the case, I believe, that, while Fraser Digby trained John Clay in the art of tunnel construction, then that notorious murderer, thief, smasher *and forger* learned the last of his trades from John Ayto, the greatest counterfeiter and coiner in London.

"So how did Grafton Montague set about killing John Ayto? Well, however desperate he was for the money which he was to be paid for the task, he had no intention of being caught. He therefore decided to try and implicate somebody else in the crime, and he chose as his victim Randal Norton, the paying-guest. Montague knew that Norton kept his Penang lawyer walking-stick in the stand near the front door, and it was thus conveniently to hand when the historian found Ayto seated in the Front Hall, poring over a piece of paper on which he had written the initials of all those members of Moriarty's gang about whom he had information he was ready to divulge to Inspector Lestrade on the morrow. As soon as Montague entered, Ayto must have jumped guiltily to his feet, before being challenged about the contents of the document he had been studying. When the secretary proved evasive, Montague suspected the worst, and, seizing Norton's stick, struck him a heavy blow on the head. Ayto crumpled to the floor, and Montague wrenched the incriminating paper from his grasp, leaving a small fragment behind in his victim's hand. He then returned to his bedroom, having hidden the stick somewhere temporarily *en route* – possibly in that handy cupboard outside the Library. Finally, when the alarm had been raised, and everybody, including his own wife and the Nortons, had descended to the Front Hall, Montague retrieved the stick, and planted it in Randal Norton's wardrobe, before himself coming downstairs. That would explain the delay in his arrival which was noted by Porson, the butler.

"It also becomes clear now why Grafton Montague knew that it was not Randal Norton who had killed Henry St. John Bosco and attempted to implicate *him*. The historian was aware that Norton was innocent of the murder of John Ayto, having himself committed the crime and tried to implicate the paying-guest by using his stick. So there was no reason to suppose that Norton had anything to do with the second murder either.

"Moreover, we can understand why Montague was reluctant to expose William Clunies-Ross as the real murderer of Henry St. John Bosco, in order to clear his own name. He knew that if he informed on Clunies-Ross, he risked himself being exposed as the murderer of John Ayto. For there was no doubt that, as a close friend of James Moriarty, William Clunies-Ross would be aware of Montague's guilt.

"Finally, we come to the question of the part played in the murder of John Ayto by *Mrs*. Montague. It is true that she gave her husband an alibi, by claiming that he was with her in their bedroom at the time when the crime was committed. But she did so in the utter conviction that Montague was innocent. No doubt he asked her to cover for him, and she agreed to do so out of loyalty. The discovery of the stick in Norton's wardrobe added to her conviction that her husband was guiltless and that her mendacity was justified. And when Montague's gun was found to be the weapon that killed Henry St. John Bosco, it never occurred to her to deny that it belonged to her husband, so convinced was she that he was not the murderer. She may have been less incautious, had she taken time to consider the consequences.

"The mastermind behind all three murders was, of course, Professor Moriarty. Following the capture and arrest of most of the members of his organization, he had been hiding out at the home of his brother with those few of his colleagues who still remained at large: James Moriarty himself (masquerading as Major Yates); Fraser Digby, the Gosling Street Bank Robber (William Clunies-Ross); Israel 'Porky' Sless, the Camden Ripper (Sam Parkin); Henry St. John Bosco, the recruiter-turned-writer and editor; John Ayto, the Hackney Forger; and, latterly, Grafton Montague, the master blackmailer. But the blows suffered by Moriarty's gang had been grievous indeed. Most recently, the Professor's Chief of Staff, Colonel Sebastian Moran, had been foiled in his attempt to kill the person who had inflicted these injuries – namely Mr. Sherlock Holmes – and he too was now out of circulation. And there were those amongst his own organizaton who threatened to destroy what little remained of it: for some years, Grafton Montague had been blackmailing several of its members, although he believed Professor Moriarty himself to have been killed at the Reichenbach Falls; John Ayto, who had long acted as secretary to his brother, was threatening to turn informer; and Henry St. John Bosco was planning to write memoirs which might very well, either by accident or design, expose some of the secrets which the Professor wished to be kept hidden. As well as these internal enemies, I remained a thorn in his flesh, and he lusted for revenge, following his failure to defeat me at Reichenbach and Colonel Moran's *débâcle* with the airgun at Baker Street.

"Professor Moriarty, together with those members of his

gang who remained indisputably loyal to him – namely his brother, James (Major Yates), Fraser Digby (William Clunies-Ross) and Porky Sless (Sam Parkin) – devised a cunning plan, whereby he would rid himself of all those who threatened him and his criminal enterprises. The plan was based on his knowledge of Grafton Montague's avarice. Montague would be paid a substantial sum to kill John Ayto, before the latter could grass to the police. The historian would gain financially, rid himself of a threat to his own liberty (he stood to lose as much as anybody from Ayto's proposed revelations), and, at the same time, provide an alibi for Moriarty's co-conspirators.

"However, the murder of John Ayto was only the first part of a four-legged programme. Part Two would be the removal of Sherlock Holmes, the meddlesome criminal agent who had brought about the destruction of most of Professor Moriarty's empire and nearly that of its leader as well.

"At the time of Major Yates's visit to Baker Street, I could not understand why he was so worried that Randal Norton, his paying-guest, would be arrested. Since the alternative was that one of his own friends was guilty of murder, this seemed inexplicable. Or, at least, it was until one realized that Yates's fears for Norton were merely a pretext to get me to come to Tilstone Court. And once I was there, Grafton Montague would be able to carry out Part Two of Professor Moriarty's plan: the murder of Sherlock Holmes.

"Grafton Montague attempted to smother me in my bed, but I resisted, and managed to scratch his face in the process. I was never convinced by his explanation that the wound had been caused by an accident in the bedroom.

"I have no doubt that Part Three of Moriarty's scheme was for Grafton Montague to murder Henry St. John Bosco as well.

Bear in mind that, apart from the consideration of the money he was to receive, all three potential victims – Ayto, St. John Bosco and I – were as much a threat to him as they were to his colleagues. However, I believe that, at this stage, Grafton Montague lost his nerve. In murdering John Ayto, he had attempted to throw suspicion on Randal Norton. But that had not led to the paying-guest's arrest. And after his failed attempt on my life, Montague could see that I was beginning to suspect him of both crimes. He therefore declined to fall in with the proposals presented to him by Professor Moriarty's brother respecting the killing of Henry St. John Bosco.

"William Clunies-Ross and Sam Parkin – who were helping Major Yates put Professor Moriarty's scheme into effect – therefore decided to murder Henry St. John Bosco themselves. Initially, as I have explained, Clunies-Ross, the person nominated to carry out the crime, tried to throw suspicion on Randal Norton, by planting the mutilated copy of *The Times* in his bedroom. But, when it came to the actual killing, Clunies-Ross endeavoured to frame Grafton Montague instead, by using his gun.

"In order to understand the real reason for the change of heart, it is necessary to look at the wider picture. Remember, Grafton Montague was a threat to Professor Moriarty's organization himself, because of his blackmailing activities. If Part One of the plan was to use Grafton Montague to kill John Ayto (the informer), Part Two was to get him to murder Sherlock Holmes (the enemy), and Part Three – at least initially – was to persuade him to do away with Henry St. John Bosco (the potential tell-tale), then Part Four was for the other members of the gang to kill Grafton Montague (the blackmailer), and to make it look like suicide, brought on by remorse for the previous murders. What Clunies-Ross realized, when he learned that I did indeed suspect Montague of killing John Ayto and attacking me, was that framing the historian for the murder of St. John Bosco would be just as effective as getting him to commit the crime himself: in either event, it would appear that Montague was the guilty party; and the 'suicide' would be engineered before an arrest could be made and the truth revealed. Bear in mind that Montague was constrained from informing on William Clunies-Ross by the hold the latter had over him for the murder of John Ayto. Only in the actual event of an arrest would Grafton Montague be compelled to spill the beans.

"So Part Three of the scheme took place, not as originally planned, with Grafton Montague killing Henry St. John Bosco, but with William Clunies-Ross committing the crime, and incriminating the historian in the process. Now it was time for Phase Four of the plan – the murder of Grafton Montague – to be put into effect.

"We have seen how the historian was killed in a room which was apparently locked and bolted from the inside. The idea, as I have explained, was that it would look like suicide, because the victim would be found alone with his throat cut. Unfortunately for the conspirators, there were two things which caused the scheme to fail. The first was that they did not bargain with Porky Sless's (Sam Parkin's) savagery. If he had simply slit Montague's throat as planned, then the illusion of suicide would have been maintained. But so filled was Parkin, the 'Camden Ripper', with the lust for blood, that he could not resist mutilating the body by slashing repeatedly at the chest with his knife, after the victim had been killed. Of course, the police, believing the room to have been locked from the inside, may have been forced to conclude that this mutilation had been self-inflicted, having been brought on, they would assume, by self-loathing resulting from the two murders he had committed earlier. And that brings us to the second reason why the plan did not succeed: *the failure to eliminate me from the investigation*.

"I alone saw how the illusion of the locked and bolted door had been created. I alone *knew for certain* that the chest wounds had not been self-inflicted, and that Montague had been murdered. Yet it is quite likely that the conspirators would have got away with their scheme, if I had been dispatched as intended.

"It is not clear to me who it was that attempted to murder me the second time. Perhaps the person who threw the slate at me from the roof of the north-west angle-turret was Grafton Montague. He knew that I suspected him of having killed John Ayto – and probably Henry St. John Bosco as well. He also knew that I was convinced it had been he who had tried to murder me before by smothering me in my bed. So, even though he had refused to kill Henry St. John Bosco, it may well have been Montague who was again my assailant on this occasion. However, it is equally possible that the attacker was Professor Moriarty himself. At the time, I thought he must have been scared off as a result of his sudden exposure at the window of the Front Hall on Christmas Eve. But Dr. Watson tells me that there are signs that he is still occupying his hiding-place in the priest-hole, so perhaps the Professor has more nerve than I have given him credit for. Whatever the case, I am sure Moriarty was behind the attack. It certainly bears his hall-mark. I have not forgotten the occasion when, as I walked down Vere Street, a brick came down from the roof of one of the houses, and was shattered to fragments at my feet. That was undoubtedly the work of one of Moriarty's agents, preceding as it did, by only a few days, my fateful encounter with the Professor in Switzerland."

At this juncture, there was a sudden clatter of footfalls on the stair, and an extremely tall, thin man came hurtling down into the room. He was carrying a revolver, which he pointed directly at Sherlock Holmes, and he fixed my friend with deep-sunk, puckered eyes which slowly oscillated from side to side. "Well, well, Mr. Sherlock Holmes," said Professor Moriarty (for it was he). "We meet again. I have been eaves-dropping – at first from the priest-hole in the wall, and latterly from the top of the stair. It was I who hurled that slate. I am not so easily frightened off, you see. I have never had the slightest difficulty in eluding your grasp or that of any other man."

"At any rate," replied Sherlock Holmes calmly, "you will not evade it on this occasion. I had anticipated that you might make an appearance, and for that reason arranged with Mr. Lestrade to have policemen stationed at every exit. You will gain nothing by shooting me, for your fate is already sealed."

"You are forgetting what I told you on the occasion of my visit to Baker Street a few days before you succeeded finally in closing your net about my great organization. I said that if you were clever enough to bring destruction upon me, then I should do as much to you."

"And yet your gang was rounded up, and I survived your personal attack at the Reichenbach Fall."

"Certain key members remained at liberty. And, like you, I did not die in Switzerland. No doubt you were surprised to see me when I made my unwitting appearance at the window on Christmas Eve. You believed that I could not have escaped the consequences of that deadly duel above the abyss."

"I saw you fall, hit a rock, and splash into the water. Of course, I believed you dead."

"As I plunged into that boiling chasm, I was myself convinced that my number was up. I felt the creaming spray about my face, and saw the glistening coal-black rocks hurtling towards me. Then my leg struck a boulder, I felt a searing pain, and I was flung free of the rocks into the breaking water below. The next thing I knew, I was entirely submerged. I was conscious that my leg was broken, but that I was otherwise unharmed. My instinct, of course, was to surface as soon as possible, but fortunately the brain acts rapidly at such moments of crisis, and I realized the wisdom of remaining out of sight. I held my breath, accordingly, and swam under water towards the rocks immediately under the fall, before raising my head above the surface and taking in a deep breath of fresh air. As I did so, I noticed with satisfaction that a thick, flickering curtain of spray must conceal me from above, and so I dragged myself on to the rocks, and lay there panting and exhausted.

"By now, so I discovered later, you had started to climb the cliff behind you, and made your way on to the ledge from which you observed Dr. Watson and his following investigating the circumstances of our supposed deaths. I, meanwhile, had realized the true horror of my predicament. It would have been utterly impossible for me to have scaled the sheer wall of the abyss even if my leg had been intact. As it was, I faced certain death from exposure or starvation. I lost consciousness for a while, but I was brought to my senses by a huge rock, which fell from above, and splashed into the water a few feet from where I lay. My heart gave a leap. I had forgotten that Colonel Moran had been keeping guard during the course of our struggle. He would have seen me fall, and was now trying to dispatch you by hurling stones at you from the top of the cliff. When you did not follow the rocks into the chasm, I knew that you must have survived the onslaught, although at this stage I did not realize that you had taken pains to create the illusion that you had yourself fallen into the abyss. However, I saw that my own chances of survival depended upon my making my presence known to my confederate on the cliff-top, who must have believed me dead. I therefore swam out into the boiling waters in front of the fall, and waved frantically, in the hope that Colonel Moran would notice me, before returning to the comparative safety of the rocks.

"I lay there for what seemed like an eternity, drifting in and out of consciousness, until, at last, I saw a long rope being lowered into the shaft, followed by the virile figure of my friend and former chief of staff, Colonel Sebastian Moran. Seeing me in the water still alive, he had gone to the home of the Swiss youth I had employed to entice Dr. Watson back to Meiringen before the fight on the brink, and secured the means of my rescue.

"Some time later, after a period of convalescence, the two of us made our way back to London. So far as I was aware, we alone knew that you had survived the struggle at Reichenbach. But I was convinced that, eventually, you yourself would not be able to resist returning to the capital, and, when you did, I would be ready for you. Although several prominent members of my organization remained at large, including Colonel Moran – considered by many to be the second most dangerous man in London – and me – whom you believed drowned – I had a huge score to settle. I therefore placed a sentinel outside your rooms in Baker Street – one Parker, the garrotter.

"When we received intelligence that you were indeed back in London, I arranged for Colonel Moran to carry out your execution. He had already had notable success with the modified airgun which I had commissioned from Von Herder, the blind German mechanic: it had proved remarkably efficient in dispatching the Honourable Ronald Adair through the open window of his residence in Park Lane. But when we attempted to dispense the same treatment to you, Mr. Holmes, you turned the tables on us. Moran found himself shooting at a wax bust, and then being arrested for his trouble.

"I went into hiding in the home of my faithful brother, who had taken up residence under the assumed name of Yates. Here were gathered the few remaining members of the once mighty organization which I had created and you had contrived to decimate: Colonel James Moriarty, Fraser Digby, Porky Sless, Henry St. John Bosco and John Ayto. My sole remaining ambition was to gain revenge on my enemies. These included several of my own people who, by accident or design, threatened the continued existence of my operations. I devised a plan which involved another long-standing member of my gang – Grafton Montague, the blackmailer, himself also now a hated enemy. He would help me to get rid of Ayto, the traitor, and St. John Bosco, the literary loudmouth, and then we would get rid of *him*. But my chief quarry, Mr. Holmes, was always *you* – you who have ever been a thorn in my flesh; you who have incommoded, inconvenienced, hampered, persecuted and all but destroyed me. You would be enticed to the Court by the dangled carrot of a juicy and intriguing murder; and then you would finally receive the punishment which you so richly deserved.

"You think you have beaten me, Mr. Sherlock Holmes. You are still alive, and you have rounded up all my agents. The game is up. And yet even now you cannot win it. May I remind you again of my promise to you when I confronted you in your rooms: if you are clever enough to bring destruction upon me, rest assured that I shall do as much to you."

"And may I remind *you* of my reply: I said that if I were assured of the former eventuality, I would, in the interests of the public, cheerfully accept the latter."

"To which *I* replied that I could promise you the one but not the other. Well so it shall be."

Professor Moriarty's revolver cracked, and I saw the blood spurt from the front of Sherlock Holmes's waist-coat. His legs buckled, and he fell to the floor, where he rolled upon his back, and lay still.

16: The Final Contest

I rushed over to my friend, and took his wrist in my hand. His eyes were glassy and unseeing, and there was a great crimson stain on his chest, but, to my surprise, his pulse appeared to be normal. "I don't understand..." I began.

"It is quite simple," replied Sherlock Holmes with a smile. "Surely you did not believe I would allow Moriarty to get the last word. Under my waist-coat," he added, patting his breast. "A bullet-proof under-garment."

"But the blood...?"

"Merely a stage prop to aid verisimilitude. Inspector Lestrade, I believe Professor Moriarty has gone back upstairs. Be good enough to send your men after him. And alert the constables outside to the possibility that he may attempt to make his escape by climbing down from the roof, rather than using a more conventional mode of egress. I am sure the three of us are quite capable of guarding the prisoners."

Lestrade instructed one of his officers to go and look for Moriarty, and the other to fetch reinforcements from outside, as well as to warn those who remained to be on the look-out for any unusual activity. Soon two constables had followed their colleagues up the ornamental stair, and the search was under way in earnest.

However, some half an hour later, Professor Moriarty had still not been apprehended. A thorough check of all the rooms on the first floor of the house, as well as both the angle-turrets, had yielded no sign of the fugitive, and the officers in the garden were prepared to swear that he had not left the building. "Have you looked in the priest-hole?" enquired Holmes with a touch of exasperation.

"Not yet," responded Inspector Lestrade. "But if that's where he is, then we will catch him like a rat in a trap!"

"Come, Inspector," said Holmes imperiously. "I believe I know what has happened."

Leaving the prisoners in the care of Lestrade's men, the three of us made our way to the Tower Room, and removed the wooden panel that barred the entrance to the ancient hiding-place. "Proceed with caution!" cried Sherlock Holmes. "Moriarty thinks he has eliminated me, and it is certain that he will not allow himself to be taken alive. For that very reason, I suspect, the danger has already passed, but we cannot be sure."

Having lit a candle to illuminate our passage, we climbed down the rope-ladder into the shaft. But it was soon clear that Professor Moriarty was not waiting for us in the chamber below. "I confess that I am not surprised," said Sherlock Holmes. "The Professor was a desperate man. He was prepared to forfeit his own life in the Reichenbach Fall, so long as he was able to bring destruction upon me. And that was before his organization had been entirely crushed. Now that I have completed the job, he has nothing left to live for. Cornered, and with no prospect of escape, his only thought is to revenge himself on me. So he kills me, and then faces a stark choice: to allow himself to be captured and hanged for his crimes; or to take his own life. I believe he has chosen the latter. Lestrade, Watson, help me to remove the lid from this tomb."

Together, we dragged the heavy stone slab clear of the sepulchre, and lowered it to the floor. Then we leaned forward, and shone our light into the interior.

It was empty.

Sherlock Holmes was visibly taken aback. "I was sure we should find the Professor's body inside," said he with a grunt of annoyance. "But clearly the villain is still at large."

However, a further painstaking search of the whole of the house proved unproductive. At midnight, Inspector Lestrade and the rest of his men, apart from a couple of sentinels who were left to guard the front and back of the Court, returned to Windsor with their captives, and Holmes and I retired discontentedly to our beds.

Nothing of moment occurred during the night, and the following morning neither of the constables who were guarding the house had anything to report. Holmes was moody and restive over breakfast, and afterwards insisted that we return to the priest-hole. On our arrival, he satisfied himself – as I had done on a previous occasion – that no hidden doorway was to be found in the north wall of the chamber, where the speaking-hole was located, and where part of the masonry had been temporarily removed to facilitate access for the tomb. "The kitchen is below us," said he at length. "So even if there was a way down, Moriarty would have been seen by the cook and the maid. According to the police, they were both working down there all evening. And, in any case, there is no exit from the kitchen, save up the flight of stairs leading to the corridor and the door on the north side of the Front Hall. If he had made his escape through the hall, we should have seen him ourselves. Lestrade sounded the walls of the basement, and found them quite solid. None the less, I should like to see for myself."

Moments later, I was following my friend through the Front Hall, and down into the kitchen. "Lestrade was quite right," said I, surveying the gloomy, old-fashioned room with a keen eye, "The only way in and out of here is via the flight of steps we have just descended. Perhaps a child could escape through the fire-place and up the chimney, but not a grown man. And, in any case, as you pointed out, the cook and the maid were down here the whole time. The room is not as spacious as I had anticipated, however. It must only extend about two-thirds of the way under the Front Hall. The western part – and the hidden chamber – lie beyond its compass."

At this point, I looked up. Sherlock Holmes was standing stock-still in the middle of the room, a flush of colour in his pale cheeks, and a look of comprehension in his hitherto lack-lustre eyes. Suddenly his features twisted into a fierce scowl of self-deprecation. "Watson, I have blundered!" he barked. "How could I have been such an imbecile! Of course! The spoilt pillows! Pray heaven we are not too late! And yet I fear we must be. Come, Watson! Back to the priest-hole! There is not a moment to be lost!"

Together, we raced up the winding stair to the top of the north-west angle-turret, and lowered ourselves once more into the shaft. At the bottom, Sherlock Holmes made a bee-line for Major Yates's tomb. "Help me to push it, Doctor," said he. "It probably runs on castors set into grooves in the floor."

Sure enough, the stone sepulchre slid easily away, to reveal another deep shaft in the earth beneath. "You were right, Watson," said Holmes, panting from his exertions. "The kitchen does not extend under the priest-hole. This shaft is undoubtedly the entrance to a tunnel, and that was how Professor Moriarty made his escape."

A rope had been hung from the top of the hole, and, taking his candle in his hand, Sherlock Holmes lowered himself into the abyss. When he had reached the floor of the tunnel, he called up to me, and I followed him down. Once at the bottom, I could see, by the light of the candle, that we were at the start of a long, dark passage which led southwards under the grounds of Tilstone Court, in the direction of the Thames. "I wonder where it goes," said I, taking a step forward. Almost immediately, however, my foot struck a hard object on the ground next to the tunnel wall, and I came to an abrupt halt. "What is it, Holmes?" I cried, a chill of fear passing down my spine.

Sherlock Holmes shone the candle at my feet, and I shrank back in revulsion when I saw what it was that I had struck. For there on the tunnel floor was a human skeleton.

"What in heaven's name does this mean?" I stammered, shivering in the cold, damp atmosphere of the eerie passageway. "These are the remains of the real Major Yates," said he in reply. "When Moriarty realized I had discovered his hiding-place, he knew that he had to remove Major Yates's skeleton from the tomb. But to have brought it through the house would have been too risky. How much easier to dispose of it in this hidden tunnel."

"Look, Holmes," I cried, bending down and picking up some objects which lay on the ground next to the bony remains. "More feathers! Did Moriarty bring the contents of those pillows down here?"

"He did."

"But why?"

"Because of where this tunnel ends up. Follow me."

Holding his candle in front of him, and shielding it from the draught with his hand, Sherlock Holmes set off along the dark passage, with me following closely behind him. It was bitterly cold, and as we passed under the river, the steady drip of moisture from the tunnel roof became increasingly persistent. "This is a masterpiece of construction," said Holmes. "No doubt the work of Fraser Digby – or William Clunies-Ross, as we have come to know him – the geologist and bank-robber who passed on his knowledge of tunnelling to John Clay. Have you worked out where we are going yet, Watson?"

"We appear to be heading in the direction of Windsor Castle. But surely they cannot have tunnelled that far?"

"You are forgetting that the passage had already been started from the other end. Don't you remember what we were told when we visited the Curfew Tower? The guard who took us down to the basement, which once housed the dungeons, said that there were the beginnings of a tunnel there, through which a prisoner had hoped to escape. I imagine that Digby – who, incidentally, I strongly suspect of being a descendant of the Digby who was involved in the Gunpowder Plot – has merely extended the passage, and in more than one direction. Look! See here how it branches off. That is the original line, which leads directly to the dungeons of the Curfew Tower. And here is Digby's branch, which I am sure we will find comes up in the basement of Major Yates's apartment in the Horseshoe Cloister."

At the end of the tunnel, we came to a recess in the wall, the back of which was lined with wooden panelling. Sherlock Holmes gave this a sharp push, and it fell open, enabling us to climb through into the basement dining-room of No. 21, The Horseshoe Cloister. "Now you can understand how Major Yates got back to Tilstone Court so quickly after our visit to the

Castle three days before Christmas. We did not see him pass us on our way back through Eton for the simple reason that he never came over-ground at all, but by the more direct route of the secret passage. We already knew that his claim to have taken a short-cut across the frozen river was a lie.

"You can also appreciate how Moriarty managed to come and go from the priest-hole without disturbing the cigarette-ash trap which we set for him. Once he realized that we had discovered his hiding-place, he never left it save via the secret tunnel. And, knowing he had that escape route, he could afford to stay on in the chamber for as long as he wanted."

"But I still don't understand about the pillows and the feathers."

"After Moriarty had unwittingly revealed himself at the window of the Front Hall, he became a wanted man again. He could not afford to be seen in public, and therefore needed to assume a disguise. I have already drawn attention to the family likeness that exists between the Professor and his brother, James. Both have the same deep-sunk eyes and reptilian oscillation of the face. Both are of approximately the same height. Even though, unlike the Professor, James Moriarty is a man of full habit with a florid complexion, if these dissimilarities could be eliminated, the former had much to gain from assuming his brother's identity: not least, he would be able to come and go from the Horseshoe Cloister without exciting comment. To effect the disguise, he applied rouge to his face, stuffed cotton-wool in his cheeks, and padded out his shirt, coat and trousers with the feathers he obtained from the pillows whose cases we found abandoned in the priest-hole. When you visited Windsor Castle on the 28th of December, and found feathers on the door-step of this apartment, together with a set of footprints leading across the parade-ground, what you were looking at was evidence that Moriarty had come from Tilstone Court along the secret tunnel, and then walked through the castle grounds disguised as his brother. I have no doubt that the Professor made his escape yesterday by the same route and in the same manner.

"Tell me, Doctor. When we came here together on Christmas morning, and were the unintentional auditors of an argument, how many voices did you here?"

"It is funny you should mention that, Holmes. At the time, I was convinced that there were three. But after Mr. Montague had come out, and we found Major Yates at home alone, I assumed I must have been mistaken."

"I came to the same conclusion. However, I now believe that Professor Moriarty was here too, and left via the secret passage before we made our entrance. Major Yates very nearly told us as much yesterday, but stopped himself when he realized that he was in danger of revealing the existence of the tunnel.

"The argument was a three-sided one between Grafton Montague and the two Moriarty brothers. Montague was angry that Professor Moriarty's survival had been kept from him, and, if he had seen the Professor emerging from the tunnel, may have attempted to levy blackmail upon him as a result. No doubt James Moriarty would then have pointed out that the historian was in no position to issue threats, having himself undertaken the murder of John Ayto on the gang's behalf; while Montague would have taken both Moriarty brothers to task about their attempt, through Clunies-Ross, to implicate him in the killing of Henry St. John Bosco as well."

"But should we not be pursuing Professor Moriarty instead of standing here talking, Holmes?" said I impatiently.

"What is the point? He will be long gone by now. I imagine that, once he left the castle grounds, he caught a train to London from one of Windsor's two railway stations, and then escaped to the Continent, or even further afield. I regret to say that ex-Professor Moriarty of atrocious celebrity has won the final contest between us."

"How can you say that, Holmes? You have solved three murders, and rounded up all the remaining members of his gang."

"Perhaps so. But that does not alter the fact that the biggest fish of all has slipped through my net."

We returned to Tilstone Court along the secret passage without exchanging a single word, and, on our arrival, I could tell, from the drawn look upon my friend's ascetic face, and the brooding of his deep-set and inscrutable eyes, that he was suffering from one of those violent swings of mood to which he was prone, and which took him, in an instant, from devouring energy to extreme languor. I had no doubt that, in his mind's eye, he was already reaching for the bottle on the corner of the mantelpiece in the old room in Baker Street, and taking his hypodermic syringe from its neat morocco case. "What will happen to Tilstone Court now?" said I, in an attempt to shake him out of the torpor which held him in its grip.

"Oh, I made some enquiries whilst I was in London, and unearthed a distant relative of the real Major Yates, who, it seems, will now inherit the place. He is married, and lives in Kent, and all the signs are that he will not only move in, but also keep on the existing staff. As for us, Watson, we have outstayed our welcome here. Perhaps you would have the kindness to pack my bag for me, and then look up the trains in Bradshaw."

Some quarter of an hour later, we were ready to depart. "The snow still lies thick," observed Sherlock Holmes. "But I do not anticipate any fresh falls for a while. As you say there are frequent services to Slough from Windsor Central Station, with good connections to Paddington, I suggest that, in the manner of the spurious Major Yates, we forgo the comfort of a four-wheeler, and take one last stroll up Castle Hill."

And so we drew on our ulsters, and, with a backward glance at the old house which had harboured so many dark secrets, passed into the pale sunlight of the winter's day.